FRACTURED HONOR

A CRIMSON POINT NOVEL

KAYLEA CROSS

FRACTURED HONOR

Copyright © 2018
by Kaylea Cross

* * * * *

Cover Art and Print Formatting:
Sweet 'N Spicy Designs
Developmental edits: Deborah Nemeth
Line Edits: Joan Nichols
Digital Formatting: LK Campbell

* * * * *

ISBN: 978-1726297455

Dedication

For Katie, who helped me dream this place and its characters up in the idyllic mountain village of Leavenworth, WA.

Love you bunches.

xo

Author's Note

Welcome to the beautiful town of Crimson Point on the wild Oregon Coast, with all its hidden dangers and drama set against the dramatic, rugged landscape. I hope you'll fall in love with this place, and the new cast of characters I've dreamed up.

Happy reading!

Kaylea Cross

Chapter One

"I've got movement, eighty yards northeast of target. One male, two bodyguards exiting a silver Toyota pickup," Captain Beckett Hollister murmured into his mic.

Lying prone behind some scrub brush on a ridge overlooking the valley below, he watched the target through his high-powered binos in the cold, November dawn. A mud-colored brick compound Beckett's twelve-man Special Forces A-Team had been sent out last night to

provide recon on, now slowly beginning to lighten on its eastern side as the first weak rays of sunlight peeked over the Anti-Lebanon Mountains.

They'd been waiting up here since oh-dark-hundred, providing intel to command back at headquarters outside of Damascus. The mission was fluid, could change at any time from a simple recon job into a direct assault on the position, or providing backup for the Delta unit currently on standby to perform the captures and hostage extraction.

"Copy that," headquarters responded. "Can you get a

visual ID on any of them?"

Without lowering the binos, Beckett spoke in a low voice to Jase Weaver, his assistant operations and intel sergeant, stretched out beside him. "Recognize him?"

Jase Weaver was quiet a few moments while he did his own assessment. "Negative."

Whoever the newcomer was, he wasn't their high value target, or even on the list of suspects they'd been given at the mission briefing. Which meant the three American security contractors being held hostage down there by the wanted militant leader were going to have to wait a while longer for rescue. Command wanted Delta to perform the assault and rescue, not Beckett's team, and only when the militant leader was present. Because that would allow them to do a one-and-done op.

Beckett had been through and seen a lot over his twenty years of service to his country, but this kind of situation never got any less infuriating. Fucked up as it might be, at the end of the day, capturing this HVT was worth more to the American government than saving its imprisoned citizens—who had been sent here on its dime in the first place to guard some of its officials.

Beckett and his team didn't give a shit about the politics behind it; they were here to do their job. But no matter what command said, it was impossible to disregard their three countrymen being held down there. He and his team had read the files on the captives. Knew their names and faces, where they came from. Two of them were Army vets, men who had served their country faithfully before turning to contracting. Beckett wanted to help get them out.

Except all he could do right now was wait and watch.

He remained silent with the rest of the twelve-man team spread around him in two groups as the minutes ticked slowly by, until more than an hour had passed. Lowering the binos, he cupped his gloved hands and blew on his frozen fingers to thaw them. At this elevation and time of year, this part of Syria was damn cold. His nose and lips had gone numb hours ago, and he could barely feel his toes even with the thick winter socks and heavy boots.

"Damn, it's as cold here as it was back in Afghanistan," Weaver said in a low voice.

"I hadn't noticed."

"That's because you're freaking *old*. Most of your nerve endings are probably already dead."

Beckett cracked a smile. "I wish." At thirty-nine, he was the oldest on the team and his body definitely felt all the aches and pains that came with two decades of punishing military service. A little less feeling in some areas would be welcome right now, especially in his bothersome lower back that felt like it belonged to an old man most days.

"Well, give it another couple hours and it'll be just above freezing again. We can pretend we're in the mountains in California instead of here."

"By all means, pretend away." Special Forces life wasn't easy. Now that he only had a few more months left in his contract, Beckett was seriously considering getting out this time when his time was up. The Army had given him a lot but his service had already cost him several nagging injuries, more dead friends than any man should ever lose, and his marriage. It was time to do something different, and he wanted the chance to enjoy what was left of his life.

Or at least try to.

He shifted to reach into his front pocket for the last of his MRE, now a frozen lump in its package. Tasted bland as hell but it was protein and calories that would keep his core temp steady and his belly full, so he couldn't complain. And as soon as they completed this mission, there was a hot shower and a pot of coffee waiting for him back at base. He didn't even care if it was stale, as long as it was hot and black.

"I'm guessing you don't feel like sharing that."

Beckett glanced at Weaver. "Not really."

"Jerkface."

"That's Captain Jerkface, to you." He made a low grumbling sound of appreciation as he chewed the next bite, earning a grudging chuckle from his teammate that cut off sharply a split-second later, his face growing serious as he watched through the rangefinder.

"They're moving the prisoners," Weaver said.

Beckett snatched up his binos and took a look. Sure enough, armed guards were herding the prisoners from the building into an open courtyard in the center of the compound. One guard for each of them.

He informed command, his mind already racing ahead. Moving the prisoners out into an exposed position where they could be seen only made sense if the captors intended to put on a show and make a statement to anyone watching. Even if they couldn't see Beckett and his team, they had to know the American government had people watching. Right now Beckett's A-team was the only unit close enough to offer some kind of response and make a rescue attempt if things went south.

"Hey, Cap. Seven o'clock off the courtyard," one of his men said.

Beckett focused there, his heart jolting when he saw a new man emerge from the shadows to stand at the edge of the courtyard, dressed in a dark suit instead of traditional garb. "You guys all seeing this?" Spread out as they were at various points along the ridge, everyone had a different vantage point and angle.

"Affirm," Weaver and another one of his guys said at the same time.

"Snipers, what's your status?" Beckett asked.

"Alpha and Bravo teams both green at this time."

Beckett informed command. "Be advised, a secondary HVT is on scene." He gave the man's name. A guy affiliated to the HVT the government was desperate to capture in this op. "Looks like he's inspecting the hostages. Both sniper teams are green."

"Copy that, team leader. Hold your positions."

"Roger. Is the assault force en route?" Command had been annoyingly silent about the Delta team's positioning. If they were going to do the captives any good, they'd better be damn close already.

"We're alerting them now."

Translation: the Delta boys weren't getting here anytime soon, and likely wouldn't even be launched unless the primary HVT showed up.

He shelved the curse in his head. "Understood. Request permission to move in for—"

"Negative. Hold your position."

Beckett clenched his jaw and didn't respond. He was trained to be calm under pressure, in any given situation. To maintain a clear head and make decisions, sometimes hard ones, in bad circumstances.

Even in a firefight his heart rate didn't elevate much. But being this close with that asshole right out in the open and in their sights, and not being able to act while three American lives were on the line tested his resolve.

Beckett watched the newcomer position himself in the middle of the courtyard to study the prisoners. All blindfolded, hands bound behind them. All of them had taken beatings recently.

Beckett wanted to get in there, capture the secondary HVT and save the hostages while they had the chance. Not wait to see if the primary HVT would magically appear in time so command would let them act.

"Oh, shit, Cap…"

He tensed at Weaver's low voice and shifted his gaze right. Down in the courtyard, a struggle had broken out.

One of the hostages must have reached his limit because he was now fighting back against his captor.

Cole Goodman. An Army vet-turned-contractor from Ohio.

Shit.

The two men rolled on the ground for a moment before the captor came up on top, straddling his bound and blindfolded prisoner. He landed several brutal punches to the helpless man's face while the militants swarmed around the remaining prisoners like angry bees.

Beckett and his team were too far away to hear what was being said, even with the parabolic listening dish, but it was clear that things had just taken a deadly turn.

He informed command of what was happening, then spoke to his sniper teams again. Both responded that they were green. One command from him, and they could help even the odds down there.

Things were out of control. They had maybe seconds to do something to prevent the worst. Take out the armed men and the bodyguards, maybe stop what he knew was coming next. "Sir, request permission to—"

"Negative."

He took a breath, tried again. "Sir. We need to act *now* if we're going to save those men."

"Captain, you will maintain your position and await further orders," the man said in a clipped voice.

It took everything Beckett had to keep his tone professional. "Understood." He shared a loaded look with Weaver, the frustration eating him alive as he went back to watching what was going on in the courtyard.

Only the self-control drilled into him from almost two decades in the military and the desire to avoid seeing his guys wind up facing court-martials and dishonorable discharges for disobeying orders kept him from giving the command to open fire on the tangos.

"They're gonna kill them," Weaver said, his voice flat.

Beckett didn't answer. With orders and rules of engagement preventing his team from doing a goddamn thing other than watch, they were forced to remain where they were and let the inevitable unfold.

He watched through his binos with a sinking heart as Goodman was seized by the hair and dragged to his knees. Blood covered his face. He struggled weakly but the beating had depleted his strength and even without that he had no chance against so many armed men.

The other two captives were lined up and forced to their knees beside him. One of them bowed his head. His mouth twisted, shoulders jerking as he faced the certainty of his death.

Beckett's heart drummed in his ears. "They're about to execute the hostages," he told command, his entire body rebelling at what was happening. *For fuck sake, let us do something. It's not too late to stop this.* But it would be in another few seconds.

It took a moment for the response to come back. "Understood. My original order still holds."

Cold spread through him. He forced himself to lie still, called on all his discipline and his ability to emotionally detach as he watched the armed militants gather into a line in front of the hostages, but it didn't ease the sickness inside him. Three militants stepped forward in front of the doomed men, raising their weapons.

Around him, Beckett's entire team was silent. All of them having front row seats to watch the executions. It took everything he had not to close his eyes or look away.

The militants opened fire.

The AKs' reports echoed sharp across the valley floor and up the side of the ridge to Beckett and his team. Down in the courtyard, all three hostages lay sprawled dead or dying in the dust, their hands still bound behind them.

He took a deep breath. "All three hostages down," he reported quietly even as anger seethed inside him.

"Copy that."

A wave of resentment pulsed through him. This. *This* was the kind of shit that ate through a man's soul and haunted him the rest of his life.

He drew another quiet breath. *I'm done.* The thought was loud and clear in his head.

"Snipers, what's your status now?" he asked, though he already knew the answer because the HVT had just stepped back inside the building.

"Alpha and Bravo both red at this time."

They'd not only sat back doing nothing while the hostages were executed, they'd also missed the window to take out the secondary HVT. Now that asshole was safely barricaded back inside the compound, laughing at them while American contractors lay dead in the courtyard.

Those men hadn't had to die. God*damn* it.

"Captain, return to base with your team. New intel suggests the primary HVT is headed to a different location."

"Roger that." It was a relief to finally lower the binos. But even though he no longer had to look at the dead men his team could have saved, he would still see their faces for a long time whenever he closed his eyes.

He couldn't wait to get out of here. "Come on, boys. Let's go." He eased backward down the rear side of the ridge before standing and shouldering his ruck, welcoming the stab of pain in his lower back that shot down the rear of both legs. The shadows were deeper here, the cold penetrating bone deep.

It didn't match the ball of ice sitting in the center of his chest.

Next to him, Weaver didn't say a word, his jaw set, anger and frustration burning in his aqua gaze. Beckett understood. He was done with this shit.

The heavy, sick feeling that condensed in the pit of his

belly as they humped back down the ridge for extraction solidified his decision. He was so damn tired of the wasted lives, of the weight he carried on his conscience.

It was time for him to get out and go home. And not simply stateside to North Carolina, where he'd been stationed since earning his green beret.

Home.

To Crimson Point, Oregon. The only place outside of the Army where he'd ever truly felt like he belonged.

Chapter Two

The lamplight glowing in the front windows made the gray-shingled craftsman house look so warm and inviting against the late November gloom. Beckett could practically smell the Thanksgiving feast from here, could almost hear the chatter and laughter of the people inside.

But how the hell could he make himself go in there when he felt half-dead inside?

He turned off the engine and sat there in the driveway for a few minutes, feeling anything but festive. A cold, relentless rain pounded on the roof of his truck as he worked up the nerve to go ring the doorbell.

Three weeks had passed since the failed op in Syria, and it still haunted him no matter how hard he tried to shake it. That day had somehow broken the lock on the vault where he kept everything he wanted to compartmentalize, and he couldn't shut the lid anymore.

Nights were the worst, when his subconscious ravaged him with dreams that were a combination of nightmare and flashback. So many times he woke in a cold sweat with his heart in his throat, his conscience accusing him that he was the reason those men had died.

Two of the hostages killed had been single, but Cole Goodman had been engaged and planning to be married just after Christmas. His family and fiancée would never know the truth about how he died.

The incident was classified. The government would either have told them nothing, or made up some bullshit story about his death to cover up the truth when they released his body to the family. Today, eleven days after burying Goodman, they had spent Thanksgiving knowing he was gone forever, without any answers to help give them any sense of comfort or closure.

Not that the truth would have given them any comfort, but rather the opposite.

Beckett knew what had happened out there, and his conscience was still grappling with it. With the guilt.

It told him he didn't deserve to be back here in his beloved Oregon Coast today. Didn't deserve to enjoy the holiday when helpless men had been murdered on his watch.

Then there was the news he had received this afternoon, the entire reason he'd come home for a short leave in the first place. Right now it felt like he was one more kick away from crumbling, and for a man who prided himself on his inner strength, that shook him to his core.

Beckett consciously relaxed his taut muscles and exhaled. He wasn't good company right now, and looking at that cozy front entry before him, part of him didn't want to intrude on their celebration. Hard enough to see the idyllic Buchanan family portrait he was sure he would find inside. A hundred times harder to see it today with everything going on inside him and come face-to-face with the forbidden woman he'd wanted for too damn long now and could never have.

Get moving, soldier.

He made himself pick up the gift on the passenger seat

anyway, his lower back protesting with a sharp twinge as he slid out of the truck. Years of carrying heavy rucks up and down mountains and other punishment had taken its toll, leaving his body with a daily physical reminder that his service had changed him forever.

A gust of sharp, salt-scented wind hit him as he hunched against the driving rain and strode up the walkway to the front door painted a cheery red and decorated with a dark evergreen wreath for the holidays. Mixing with the wind, the muted roar of the ocean came from behind the house, positioned on the bank just a few hundred yards up from the beach.

On the front porch, sheltered from the rain, he listened to the murmur of voices and muted laughter coming from inside. He could picture the scene so easily. Everyone would be eating and talking around the large table, enjoying each other's company. And Sierra would have her beloved camera with her to document it all for posterity.

On the other side of that door, warmth and life beckoned to him, while he stood outside cold all the way to his soul.

Steeling himself, he rang the bell.

Footsteps sounded in the entryway, then the door swung open. The happy Thanksgiving greeting he had ready died on his tongue as he stared at the vision before him. He'd thought he was prepared for what the sight of her would do to him, but he'd been wrong. A hard pressure hit him in the center of his chest, like he'd just taken a round to the heart.

Sierra wore a raspberry-red dress that hugged every delectable curve, her long, chestnut-brown hair falling in loose waves around her shoulder. Her face lit up at the sight of him, her deep blue eyes widening in surprise. "Beckett!" She stepped forward and threw her arms around his neck in a warm hug, pressing that luscious body against him. "Oh, it's *so* good to see you."

He returned the hug, a little stiff and awkward. She was only eight years younger than him but most of the time he felt ancient compared to her. She was warm and open; he was closed and cynical.

And so empty inside that right now he forgot what happy felt like.

"You too." He released her immediately and leaned back, putting some distance between them.

Every damn time he saw her, the attraction got stronger. He didn't like it. Wasn't even sure when he'd first seen her as a desirable woman instead of his best friend's little sister, but somewhere over the past three years since his divorce had gone through, he could no longer see her in the platonic way he had before.

Now Sierra Buchanan was the most beautiful thing he'd ever laid eyes on and his body and mind didn't care that she was practically his family. Good thing his heart—or what was left of it—did.

She stepped back, gave him another high-wattage smile that in spite of everything going on began to thaw the icy void inside him. She'd always done that for him, warmed him from the inside out even on the days when the wind blew the coldest. "Come in."

He thought about simply handing over his gift, saying a quick hello to Noah and the other guests before leaving, but his feet were already taking him onto the rug in the entryway.

Sierra shut the door against the cold wind and faced him, the top of her deep red dress dipping down to reveal the sexy cleavage he shouldn't be noticing and was trying his damndest not to stare at. "Are your parents here too?" he made himself ask.

"Yes, they flew in a couple days ago. Guys, Beckett's here," she called out over her shoulder, then faced him again. "I wish you'd let us know you were coming home, we would have invited you. Come on, take off your coat and stay awhile. I'll get you a plate," she said, heading for the kitchen. "We were just putting all the leftovers away."

"I can't stay," he said, stopping her in her tracks. It was too hard to be here now.

Not that his argument had any effect on her, because she shot him a frown and shook her head. "You can stay for a plate." She grabbed his hand and towed him behind her.

His lifelong best friend Noah appeared in the kitchen doorway dressed in casual clothes instead of his sheriff's uniform, a towel over one shoulder, his parents behind him. "Hey, man," he said with a big smile, and pulled Beckett into a quick, back-slapping hug. "Didn't know you were back."

"Just got in the other night." Only his father had known he was coming back.

"Beckett, hi. It's wonderful to see you again," Mrs. Buchanan exclaimed, an older version of her daughter as she drew him into a Chanel-scented hug. The top of her head barely reached his collarbones and her familiar smell triggered a cascade of nostalgic memories, of family dinners and summer vacations the Buchanans had included him in. Since it had been just Beckett and his dad for most of his life, the Buchanans had been the extended family he'd never had.

"You too." He let her go and shook Mr. Buchanan's hand. "Sir."

"Great to see you, son."

Noah wiped his hands on the dishtowel. "You here on leave, or…?"

"Yeah. Just for a few days," Beckett answered.

"So short?" Mrs. Buchanan said, sounding disappointed.

Beckett nodded. "I had some things to take care of here at home, but they want me back asap."

She studied him a moment, but when he didn't say more, took her husband's arm. "Let's get this boy a plate before he fades away." They retreated into the kitchen, leaving him alone with Sierra and Noah.

Sierra tilted her head to study him, a slight frown creasing her forehead. "Everything okay?"

She still read him well. Too well. "I came to tell you both I'm getting out. It's time."

"Out of the Army?" Noah asked, clearly surprised. "Will you be moving back for good, then?"

He nodded. "I've got a little over three months left to serve, but yeah, that's the plan."

"Oh, that's great," Sierra said with a smile. "Bet your dad is excited about that. Did you guys have Thanksgiving dinner?"

"No." Not even close.

"You should call him, invite him over here for something to eat. We've got plenty. You guys can help us put up the Christmas tree after."

She had no way of knowing how her words twisted him up inside. "Thanks, but he's not up for company right now." *Neither am I.*

She and Noah both looked at him sharply. "Why, what's wrong?" Noah asked.

There was no point in hiding it. They would find out soon enough, and they were like family to him. "Terminal cancer." The words still shook him, made the ice come creeping back.

Sierra gasped, one hand going to her mouth. "No."

He nodded, still stunned by the news. "He's got six months left, they think. Maybe more. Could be less."

Her eyes filled with sympathy and understanding and she lowered her hand. "I'm so sorry."

"Yeah. Jesus, I had no clue," Noah said with a shake of his head.

Beckett shrugged. "He didn't want anyone to know he

was sick."

"Is that why you came back?" Sierra asked.

"Yes. He got the initial diagnosis last week. I wanted to be with him at the appointment yesterday when they gave us the prognosis."

"What about treatment options?" Noah asked, frowning in concern.

He shook his head. "He doesn't want to go through any of that if it would only buy him another few months at most. Not after seeing what my mom went through." Cold spread through his gut at the memory. He was about to face all that again, and he dreaded it more than anything.

"I'm so sorry," Sierra said.

"Me too," said Noah.

"Thanks." Tough as it had been to get that news and a hard timeline on the remainder of his father's life, at least Beckett would never have to regret not being there with him when it was handed down.

"Is there anything we can do?" Noah asked.

"I would sure appreciate it if somebody would check in on him over the next few months while I'm gone."

"Of course, we'll take care of it." No hesitation, and Sierra nodded her assurance too.

"Thank you." It meant a lot to him.

"It's the least we can do, man." Noah clapped him on the shoulder, squeezed. "You guys are like family to us."

"I know." God, he needed to go.

"Beckett, better get in here and start on this mountain of food my wife's piled on this plate," Mr. Buchanan called from the kitchen.

He wasn't really in the mood to eat, even if he was hungry, and being around his second family tonight was bittersweet. He would stay for a little while, maybe see if he could take his dad home a slice of pumpkin pie to cheer him up a bit. "Okay."

"Come on." Sierra gave him a little smile and took his

hand, leading him into the kitchen, her citrusy scent trailing in her wake. Her camera sat on the island, no doubt full of pictures of their family holiday.

He did his best to be sociable and visit while he ate, even if his heart wasn't in it. He'd missed them all, especially Noah and Sierra. Well, he'd missed Sierra *too* much, and couldn't seem to stop his thoughts from going where they shouldn't where she was concerned. Her in that dress was forever etched into his mind now. As well as the fantasy of peeling it off her.

"You're gonna stay and help us with the tree, right?" Mrs. Buchanan asked. "It's tradition."

He put on a smile. A tiny part of him was tempted to stay. To escape his reality for a little while longer and spend time in this cozy, loving place with people who cared about him. "Wish I could, but I have other plans. Do you think I could steal a piece of pie for my dad?"

"Of course you can. In fact, you can have a whole pie. We made one too many. And I'll pack you up a container of whipped cream for it, too."

"You're the best."

She rose and patted his cheek. "I love you, and I'm so glad you came."

His whole chest tightened, all the emotion he kept carefully suppressed pounding against the sides of the vault with the busted lid. "Love you too." She'd been like a second mother to him after his own had passed away when he was eleven.

As if she sensed his distress, Sierra stepped in. "I'll walk you to the door."

Thank you.

He said goodbye to Noah and Mr. Buchanan then followed Sierra, trying and failing to keep his eyes off the sweet curve of her ass outlined by the dress. Damn, perving over her made him feel like shit. He'd known her since she was born, for Chrissake. She had always been like a little sister to him.

But something had changed all that, and he didn't know how to shut off these new feelings.

In the foyer while he slipped his boots on Sierra paused in front of him and glanced at the gift he'd brought. "What's in the box?"

He'd wrapped it before heading over. "Oh. It's for you."

"For me?" Grinning, she picked it up, gave it a little shake, her eyes sparkling with curiosity. "It's heavy. Can I open it?"

He prayed she had no clue he wanted to bury his hands in her thick, shiny hair and kiss her, stroke his tongue into her mouth to taste all that warmth and sweetness. Lose himself in her, take that memory with him when he went back overseas. "Sure."

She undid the paper and opened the box, a little gasp leaving her throat. "Oh, it's beautiful," she said, pulling out the hand-woven blue-and-white blanket.

"I saw it at a market during my last deployment in Afghanistan and thought you'd like it." He'd bought it because the deep blue reminded him of her eyes. Not that he was telling her that.

She hugged it to her, and he wished it was him instead of the blanket. God knew he would love to be wrapped around her like one. "I love it. Thank you."

He fisted his hands against the urge to reach for her. "You're welcome." He had to go. Right the hell now.

But Sierra set the blanket aside to search his eyes for a moment, and he had the eerie feeling she saw through his gruff exterior, all the way to the wall of ice around his heart.

Then she reached her arms up to encircle his neck, pressing her sweet curves to him in a tender hug that made his entire body react. "Happy Thanksgiving, Beckett," she said softly.

Because she couldn't see his face, he allowed himself a moment's weakness and squeezed his eyes shut as he hugged her in return. Savoring the contact, her platonic love and affection. Knowing he could never have more than that. "Thanks," he said gruffly. "You too."

"Here's some leftovers to take with you," Mrs. Buchanan announced, hurrying from the kitchen with a bulging bag in her hands.

Becket quickly stepped back from Sierra. "One pie?" he asked, the side of his mouth kicking up. There was way more than pie in there.

Mrs. Buchanan shrugged and waved a dismissive hand. "And a few other things." She held out the bag to him. "You say hello to your dad for us."

He didn't have the heart to tell her about the diagnosis. Noah and Sierra could tell their parents once he left. "I will. Goodnight." He bent to kiss her on the cheek, then stole one last look at Sierra, planting the sight of her into his memory so he could take it with him, and walked out into the cold, driving rain.

He climbed back into his truck with the feel and scent of her burned into his brain, and the certainty that he'd made the right decision in leaving when he had. The pull she had on him was too strong. And it was time for him to face the stark reality awaiting him.

Except he now had another problem looming on the horizon.

Crimson Point was a small town. He couldn't avoid her forever. When he moved back here for good in another few months, for both their sakes he had to somehow figure out a way to stay the hell away from her.

Chapter Three

Four months later

Sierra eyed her friend from across the hospital cafeteria table in concern. A low buzz of conversation filled the room, the place busy enough that she didn't have to worry about anyone overhearing them if she kept her voice low. "Is everything okay, Moll? No offense, but you look like you haven't slept in days."

"Yeah, that's kinda part of being an ER nurse," Molly Boyd teased in her light North Carolina drawl with a wry smile that didn't quite reach her gold-green eyes.

Sierra put down her fork. Molly wasn't fooling her. There was way more to it than just being tired, and it bothered her that her friend was trying to hide whatever it was.

They'd been friends ever since Molly and her former Green Beret husband moved to Crimson Point from North Carolina, so Carter could work with Beckett's father at his custom renovation business. He'd needed a job and had been struggling to fit back in to civilian life after being medically discharged for a traumatic brain injury that had left him permanently disabled.

"No. Tell me what's wrong," Sierra insisted. Molly and Carter had been having problems for a while now, and she suspected things were getting worse.

Molly sighed. "I meet you for lunch so we can spend time together and have a nice visit. Not to bitch about my problems and ruin your day."

Ruin her day? Insulted, she sat up straighter. "Sorry, but as your best friend that offends the hell out of me. Start talking. Is it Carter?"

Molly leaned back in her chair and crossed her arms, staring at Sierra for a long moment before speaking. "Yes. He's getting worse."

Dread curled in the pit of Sierra's stomach at Molly's grave tone. "How much worse?"

"You sure you want to talk about this?"

Sierra frowned. "Of course."

"Okay, then, it's kinda like living with Jekyll and Hyde. On any given day I never know which Carter I'm getting."

That didn't sound good. She pushed aside the spike of annoyance that Molly hadn't told her before now, because this wasn't about her or her feelings. "How long has it been like this?"

"Going on two months now."

Jesus, that was half of their friendship. Sierra shook her head. "Moll. I can't believe you never said anything. You know I'm here for you no matter what, right?" It was important that she know that. Important that Molly trusted Sierra to have her back.

Looking flustered, Molly glanced away. "I know. But it's not something we want people to know about. This is a small town. Word spreads fast."

Sierra leaned in, cocked her head a bit. "You don't even want me to know?"

Those gold-green eyes came back to hers, full of sadness and embarrassment. "Even you. Sorry. And not because I don't trust you."

"No, don't apologize. I get it." Sierra's heart ached for her friend. Molly had noticeably changed over the past few weeks. Normally outgoing and fun-loving, now she rarely wanted to socialize, and her trademark smiles and infectious laughter that made her the life of any party were almost nonexistent.

"So what's happening now?" she asked. The last Molly had told her, Carter had started to become forgetful and lose his temper more easily over little things.

"The worst are his erratic mood swings that just come out of nowhere. One minute he's fine, the next he's losing his shit over something. It's started happening at work, too."

"So then Beckett knows? And Jase?" Beckett was out of the military now and back home for good to run his father's specialized renovation business. He'd brought Jase on as well. The three of them had served together for a long time in Special Forces until Carter had been medically discharged last year.

"They know he's getting harder to deal with."

She hadn't heard anything around town, and since it wasn't a big place, the incidents were either isolated, or Carter and Beckett had managed to keep them under wraps. "Anything else?"

"He's forgetting things more and more, even people's names sometimes. He's not sleeping much. And now a lot of the time it seems like he's itching for a fight everywhere he looks."

Sierra shook her head. Carter was huge, even bigger than Beckett or Jase, and that was saying something. With his size and training he could do some serious damage with one blow from a fist. Molly was half his size. Unease crawled up her spine. "Has he threatened you or anything like that?" She hated to ask, but she needed to know.

"No, nothing like that. It's just I'm on a never-ending

roller coaster these days. I tiptoe around on eggshells most of the time, trying my damndest not to set him off. And so…" She lowered her gaze. "Lately that means I've been avoiding him as much as I can."

Sierra hid a wince. That had to be awful, basically hiding from your own husband.

According to Molly, before the brain injury their marriage had been wonderful. "I'm sorry."

Molly nodded, her springy, espresso-colored curls bouncing around her face. "Thanks."

"So I'm guessing whatever meds he's taking aren't working anymore?"

"No. He's already been misdiagnosed three times. They've ruled out schizophrenia or bipolar disorder. There are no visible lesions in his brain anymore, and his last CT looked completely normal. But he still gets terrible headaches, and the tinnitus hasn't gone away. They know it's all from the TBI, but not how to treat it, and they've got him on so many different things, trying to stabilize his moods."

Molly exhaled and continued. "It's such a mess. Almost all of them have side effects, then they want to put him on more meds for those. At least with my background I have the education to understand the interactions. We've been trying to wean him off as many pills as we can, but it's a matter of finding out what works for him. And lately, what used to work isn't working anymore, no matter what dosage we give him." She shook her head, her frustration clear.

"Is he depressed?" Sierra would be.

"Depends on the day. Sometimes he's up and down a few times within twelve hours. Some days he's almost manic, on top of the world, and others he can barely drag himself out of bed."

Sounded a lot like bipolar disorder to her, so what else could it be? "That's awful." She loved Carter and hated that he was suffering.

"Yes. He refuses to go to any more counseling sessions and he fired his VA psychiatrist last week when he was having a really bad day."

Sierra frowned, her concern growing. "Moll, are you safe with him?" she asked quietly.

Molly tensed and looked away. A moment later her shoulders sagged and she ran a hand through her curls. "Honestly? Sometimes I'm not sure."

Shit. That scared her. Sierra swallowed, forced herself not to say anything, give Molly a chance to talk, even though she wanted to urge her friend to get out now, protect herself.

Molly gave a rueful laugh. "I know what you're thinking. Believe me, I've thought about leaving so many times, even though it's the last thing I want to do. But the truth is, I'm not sure I can keep going on like this anymore. It's not a marriage and hasn't been for a long time." Her gaze lifted to Sierra's, full of secret pain. "What kind of person does that make me, Si? What kind of wife walks out on her husband when he's going through something like this?"

"One who's afraid for her safety." Alarmed, she reached across the table for Molly's hand, squeezed it. Carter was a big, burly and bearded teddy bear of a man. Him in a rage wasn't something she could picture, but the thought was scary as hell, and she was worried for Molly. "Promise me you'll listen to that little voice in the back of your mind. If you feel threatened or endangered at all, you get the hell out of there, just to play it safe. You can come stay with me. Or Noah, if you need protection. Beckett or Jase too." Any of the guys would protect Molly if it came down to that.

Molly gripped her fingers tight, her light brown complexion paling as a desperate light entered her eyes. "You can't tell them. Swear to me you won't." Her voice was tense, urgent.

Sierra wanted to argue, but if she did Molly wouldn't tell her anything more. "Only if you swear to protect yourself and leave if you need to."

"I promise."

"All right." She pulled her hand back, let out a breath. She hurt for both Molly and Carter. Things had to get better for them. She hated seeing her friend sad, and didn't want Carter to wind up spiraling out of control. "I'm here for you, okay? Never forget that."

Molly gave her a brave smile. "I won't. Now can we talk about something else, please?"

Even though she wanted to ask more questions, she had to let this drop. "Sure."

"And this is why I love you more than cake."

Sierra grinned. "More than cake? That's saying something, right there. And speaking of, I think I saw a couple slices of frosted chocolate cake in the pastry case over there when I came in. If anyone deserves them, it's us. Am I right?"

"Girl, you know you are."

"Okay. You stay put." She rose and started for the counter, stopping when the exterior door to the cafeteria opened and Beckett strode through in his standard jeans and open plaid flannel shirt with a white T underneath it. She wished she had her camera to snap a picture of him, the image of rugged male perfection.

Her heart fluttered when that dark-chocolate gaze landed on her, his light-bronze face going blank with surprise at seeing her there. "Hey," he said, his deep voice stirring a wave of warmth inside her.

His posture was stiff as he stood there, his stance almost impatient. As though he was irritated at bumping into her and having to spend a few moments being polite. Why did he always seem so aloof around her now? They'd been friends all of her life but something had shifted between them over the past few years, almost as though he'd put an invisible wall between them. It hurt.

She put on a smile anyway, trying to smooth it over. "Hi. How's your dad doing today?" He'd declined more quickly than anyone had imagined, ending up in hospice care three weeks ago. Beckett came in every day to see him. No matter how busy he was with work, he always made time to visit. She admired that a lot.

"Nurses said he's having a pretty good day, so I picked him up some donuts." He held up the paper bag in his fist, stalled for a second before continuing. "What are you doing here?"

She gestured over her shoulder. "I just popped by to have lunch with Molly."

"Ah." He looked past her, lifted a hand. "Hey, Moll. How's it going?"

"Fine," Molly said with her usual bright smile in place. "Say hi to your dad for me."

He nodded and switched his attention back to Sierra, his expression closed, maybe even a little bit wary. What was up with that? "You not working today?"

She co-owned and operated the only vet clinic in town. "I've got three surgeries scheduled after lunch. All castrations."

He grimaced. "Poor buggers."

Sierra laughed softly. "Don't worry, it's all done as humanely as possible. They don't even know what happened until they wake up."

He nodded, glanced away again before meeting her eyes once more. Impatient to get going.

It made her feel nine years old again, back to being Noah's annoying little sister, a nuisance they didn't want tagging after them.

The thought was deflating as hell. She'd come a long way from being the awkward tomboy he'd known all those years ago. Not that he'd seemed to notice.

He cleared his throat gruffly. "Well. I'd better get up there and check on the old man."

She squelched a surge of self-consciousness, berating herself for it. "Of course. Tell him I send a hug."

"Will do. See you."

"Bye." She stood there for a moment as he walked away, taking the opportunity to admire the back of him since he couldn't see her staring. Those powerful, broad shoulders, his confident stride, his jeans hugging his lean hips and ass. He was all rugged, sexy alpha male, and he'd been the source of most of her secret fantasies for years now.

And he found her annoying.

She allowed herself a deep sigh as he disappeared around the corner. This sucked. Why did he always seem so uncomfortable around her? As if he'd rather talk to anyone else but her? Growing up, he'd gone out of his way to tease and annoy her every chance he got, but he had never ignored her.

The divorce, she realized. Ever since he'd come home on leave a few years ago, after his divorce, he'd treated her differently.

With the exception of Thanksgiving, when he'd let his guard down a little by talking about his dad, and hugging her before he left Noah's place. Beckett was an intensely private man and didn't let many people in. Now he was about to lose his father. Then he would have no one.

That's his choice.

Maybe. But she didn't have to like it.

"You need to get over him," she muttered under her breath, turning back toward the cafeteria. She could feel sorry about what he was going through all she wanted, but that didn't change anything. He remained as unattainable as ever, and she already had two failed serious relationships with emotionally-closed off men. Beckett took that to next level.

When she arrived back at the table, Molly leaned back in her chair and raised a dark eyebrow, one side of her mouth lifting.

"What?" Sierra asked, reaching for her tea.

"Yeah, right, what." Her expression was far too knowing. "You were so busy gawking at him, you forgot our cake."

Cake. Damn. "Be back in a sec."

Molly's soft chuckle followed her to the counter but Sierra shrugged it off. It didn't matter how conflicted her feelings about Beckett Hollister were.

They were never going to happen.

****

The entire way up to the palliative floor and down the hall to his father's room, Beckett couldn't get the image of Sierra out of his head. Seeing her here had thrown him, and now the vision of her in those hip-hugging jeans and formfitting pink sweater that showed off her figure was burned onto the backs of his eyelids.

Damn. Keeping his distance from her wasn't working, and trying to ignore her when they did see each other was impossible—not to mention it made him feel like an asshole.

His dad was propped up in bed reading when Beckett walked in.

Their faces were different but no one would mistake them for being anything but father and son. Their partially-Chinook heritage had given them the same bronze tone to their skin, the same deep brown eyes and hair, though his dad's was now almost solid gray. They were both broad-shouldered with solid builds, though Beckett was a few inches taller and his dad was a shrunken version of his former self due to the cancer ravaging his body.

28

His dad welcomed him with a big smile, his gaze dropping to the paper bag. "Ooh, what did you bring me?"

That bright smile of welcome sent a wave of relief through Beckett. It meant his dad was having in increasingly rare good day today. "Picked you up some donuts. Well, us. You up for some?" Some days he was too nauseated to eat anything, even his favorites.

"You think I'll share?" his dad asked, taking the bag from him and opening it. He looked up, his expression like a kid's who'd just been given a coveted toy. "Raspberry filled?"

"Course." He took the chair beside the bed and waited for his father to hand him a donut. "You look good today," he said, taking a bite. It wouldn't last, no matter how much he wished it would.

Watching his lifelong idol waste away before his eyes without being able to stop it was by far the hardest thing Beckett had ever endured. Even worse than watching his mom succumb to the disease, because he'd been so young back then and hadn't really understood what was happening, or what to expect. He wasn't ready to lose his father too.

"Feel pretty good. I'm getting my second wind, I guess." His dad paused after a couple of bites and lowered the donut, probably waiting to see how his stomach handled it. "Anything interesting going on at the office?"

"Yeah, as of right now we're booked solid through the New Year." He couldn't believe how fast business had picked up once he'd implemented a few changes in marketing.

Crimson Point was a quaint tourist town nestled against the wild Pacific Ocean, and getting more popular every year because of its seaside charm, rugged coastline and beaches. Their company specialized in renovating old West Coast heritage homes and cottages, updating them to all the modern building codes and conveniences without killing the original charm. At the moment they had more work than he knew what to do with, and word was spreading up and down the coast.

"That's what I like to hear. How's the new crew working out?"

They had three full time crews working for them now, Beckett having added one a few weeks ago. "Good." Actually, parts of the new crew weren't doing so hot, but he wasn't going to tell his dad that.

Transitioning back into civilian life had turned out to be harder than Beckett had thought it would be. After spending so many years in the military he was used to routine and a specific chain of command, to having his orders followed immediately and to the letter when he gave them.

Things didn't work like that in the civilian world.

When he'd first come home and taken over the business, all of the guys working for his dad's company were non-military. Beckett didn't like how a lot of them operated. He'd already let a few of them go since taking over, including the project manager, due to what he considered plain-ass laziness.

His dad raised an eyebrow. "Yeah?"

"Yeah, it's all good," he lied. He wasn't going to add any more stress to his father's plate by telling him about every little thing that went wrong at work. Beckett could handle all that himself. And the whole reason he'd taken over things was to keep things running smoothly and take as much stress off his dad as possible.

Taking on the job gave him something productive to do with his time, kept his dad's business going, and gave him a much-needed mental and physical break from a life of rigorous training and combat. Right now he couldn't see himself running the business and staying at a desk job forever. He wasn't sure what he was going to do long term, but this got him up in the morning and gave him something to fill his days, so it was good enough for now.

His father eyed him skeptically. "That's not what I heard yesterday."

Beckett frowned. "Why, what did you hear?"

"That there're a lot of hard feelings going on between the crew and a certain someone in management."

Ah, shit. Still, he tried playing dumb. "Really? Who'd you hear that from?"

"Mrs. Olsen. She stopped by at suppertime yesterday to give me those." He nodded at the stack of books lined up on the shelf beside the bed. "Her son-in-law Rick hired us to reno a cottage down on Honeysuckle Lane."

Beckett suppressed a groan. Rick had probably gone by the place to check on the progress and happened to witness Carter and one of the guys getting into it. Fantastic. God, Beckett disliked dealing with people more and more. "Nah, it's all good, don't worry."

"It's Carter, isn't it?"

Damn. "Dad. It's fine. I'll handle it." To be honest, his former teammate was a giant pain in his ass these days.

As soon as he'd come home and let the former project manager go, Beckett had slid Carter over to fill the position, but lately that wasn't working too well. His friend had changed drastically over the last few months, becoming short-tempered and unpredictable. At least hiring Jase as CFO had been a good idea; the guy was as rock solid in business as he had been on the battlefield and had an accounting degree under his belt.

Bringing guys on board who Beckett had served with not only gave him peace of mind, but also helped them out, giving them a permanent job with steady pay and benefits while they found their feet outside the military. He would hire more veterans as things progressed, try to pay it forward. God knew he needed to do something to ease the guilt piled up on his conscience.

Maybe with enough time he could balance the karmic

scale that at present seemed to be heavily slanted toward bad.

"I'm worried about him," his dad continued. "He's slipping."

Beckett exhaled, wanting to change the subject. Seriously, his dad didn't need any more shit to worry about, least of all this. "I know. I'll talk to him."

Again. For like the ninth time over the past few weeks.

He'd thought about moving Carter out of the project manager position and just making him part of the crew, but that would mean a pay cut and the demotion might make things worse. Carter's behavior was putting him in an impossible position.

His dad shook his salt-and-pepper head. "You're gonna have to make a tough call soon, son. Everybody in this town knows us. Loyalty or not, you can't let him jeopardize the business and your reputation."

He grunted. "Just eat your donut, will you? I'm on it."

His father lifted the donut to his mouth, took a tiny bite to appease him. Beckett's heart sank. Before he got sick, his old man would have polished off most of the bag by now. Now those sunken, deep brown eyes were filled with regret. "I'm sorry I've dumped all this on you. I know it's a lot to ask of you when you're trying to get your life together."

"What are you talking about," Beckett grumbled, stuffing more donut into his mouth. Conversations like this made him itchy as hell. "You haven't dumped anything on me, and you know I was gonna get out of the Army anyhow. I needed something to keep me busy once I got home, and I'm happy to help you out."

He wiped his hands on a napkin, handed one to his dad, and changed the subject. "Anyway, have you been thinking any more about your list?" A bucket list of sorts. Items that his dad wanted wrapped up before he got too ill to be able to tackle them.

His expression turned thoughtful. "I guess backpacking through Europe's definitely out, huh?"

Beckett forced a grin even though it hurt his face to do it. "I think for now, yeah."

"Then just business and estate stuff, and we've got almost all of that buttoned up now." His gaze strayed past Beckett to the window that overlooked a small park. The sky was pure blue today, a few fluffy clouds drifting by on the breeze, the sun glinting off the waves rolling onto the beach off in the distance. "I sure do miss being out there. I miss the water most of all. The smell of it. The way it sounds."

A hundred bittersweet memories hit Beckett at those words. Countless hours spent out fishing with his dad in their aluminum boat. Walking for miles and miles up the beach, picking up shells or driftwood or bits of sea glass to add to the garden his mother had made. Bonfires on the beach in the evenings throughout the summer and fall, when they'd roast marshmallows and hotdogs or steam a pot of mussels and clams they'd gathered and share them with friends or neighbors.

The sea, the coast, were part of them and their heritage. It wasn't right that his father should have to spend his last days cooped up in here, away from the ocean that gave him such peace.

His dad paused. "I miss home. There's no place on earth like Crimson Point."

Beckett didn't answer. They had talked about keeping his dad at home and bringing in a private nurse to look after him, but that would have run through their savings and lines of credit before they knew it. This was the best they could do.

He ran through some ideas in his head. He'd have to talk to the medical staff, but if his dad was up to it in the next little while, Beckett wanted to get him out of here for at least a few hours. Do something together that they used to enjoy, just the two of them. Give his dad some fun, something happy to focus on and a new memory to cherish instead of lying in here day after day waiting to die while his body slowly failed him.

His dad remained quiet, his gaunt gaze growing unfocused. He lowered the unfinished donut to his lap, and moments later his eyelids began to droop.

Beckett reached out to take the donut, then wiped his father's fingers clean while a boulder-sized lump formed in his throat. Cancer was a shitty way for a good, kind man like him to die. Every single day Beckett got with his father now was a gift, and he wouldn't forget it.

"Sorry," his dad said with a weary smile that was a shadow of its former self. "Tired."

"Sugar crash," Beckett said, his tone a lot lighter than the weight in his chest. "I'll let you nap and leave the rest of these here for you just in case." He set them on the side table and stood, pain twisting inside him at the sight of his father's now frail form lying in the bed. "Gonna head into the new jobsite to check on everything, but I'll have my cell on me. Call me if you need anything, okay? I can bring dinner by if you don't feel like eating what they give you."

"Will do." Those familiar deep brown eyes met Beckett's, a distressed expression in them. "Love you, son."

The hitch in Beckett's chest was so sharp it was all he could do not to wince, let alone draw in a breath. "Love you too, Dad." The hitch turned into a deep ache as he walked out into the hallway. He couldn't stand the thought of losing him, but it didn't matter because that day was coming up fast whether he liked it or not.

And when it did, he would have no one.

Chapter Four

After a long day spent running back and forth from the office to the three project sites the company currently had on the go and then a meeting with a prospective new client, Beckett finally got to drive home. The sun was just beginning to set, scattering swathes of red and gold over the calm ocean.

Rose-tinted light glistened on the wet sand and cast a warm glow over the restored clapboard and shingled buildings he passed along Front Street. Seagulls circled overhead, their cries reaching him inside the truck. People had started to put more money into the town within the last decade, sprucing up the shops and restaurants to draw in the tourists that flocked here from late spring to fall. It was still the place he'd known as a kid, and he'd missed it while he was gone.

Turning right off Front Street, he drove half a mile down and turned onto Salt Spray Lane. The narrow lane sloped down through a band of forest as it wound back around toward the water. Until five years ago it had been a dirt road, worn by years of traffic. As a kid he'd ridden his bike through here every day, and he still knew every path that branched from it, knew exactly where they led through the thick forest or down the sandy dunes to the beach.

At the top of the rise, his childhood home came into view.

Beckett smiled. The 1890s Queen Anne-style house stood perched atop a cliff overlooking the prettiest piece of the Pacific coastline in the state. The cedar siding sported a fresh coat of blue and green paint, little bits of cream accenting the scalloped shingles in the upper part of the high turret and in the gables.

It had been in Beckett's family since 1906, and over the years its various owners had left their mark on the Victorian beauty. His childhood bedroom was tucked up in the attic that his father had renovated just for him.

The landscaper was just pulling out of the driveway in his van when Beckett reached it. His dad had preferred to cut the grass by himself, but after Beckett's mom passed away, tending the garden beds on the property had gotten to be too much, so he'd hired Paul to tend them once a week.

Beckett waved at him as he passed by. The garden looked amazing thanks to Paul's care. Beckett's mom would have liked that.

He parked out front of the detached garage, grabbed all his stuff and headed for the wraparound porch. As a kid he had raced barefoot across the lush green grass beneath arbors dripping with honeysuckle and clematis, past the white picket fences that bordered the property where climbing roses scrambled in a riot of color all summer long. When it was warm enough he'd slept in a hammock out on the front porch, guarded by mosquito netting.

After he'd moved back here he had intended to rent a place of his own, but his father had insisted he stay here and the truth was Beckett loved this place and all its memories.

Heading for the back steps, he passed a rosebush just coming into bloom and stopped short when he saw the eight-year-old blond girl sitting on the porch swing. She didn't look up at him, focused on writing in the notebook in her lap.

Beckett sighed. He'd been looking forward to a cold beer and some solitude on the back porch, but she was a sweet kid and wasn't any trouble. He was pretty shitty company right now though, and he had no idea why she kept wanting to hang out here.

"Hey, Ella." She and her single mother lived in the house at the far end of the lane and in the past few weeks she had taken to hanging around his place after school from time to time.

She looked up, her face brightening. "Hi, Mr. Beckett."

He kinda liked it that she called him that. His boots thudded lightly on the wooden porch steps as he climbed them. "Your mom at work?" Ella was so young. Didn't the law say she couldn't be left alone until she was around ten or something?

"Yes, until six."

Who was supposed to be watching her? The mom's new boyfriend? "Do you have a babysitter, or someone who watches you after school until she gets home?"

Ella gave him a sidelong look. "Sometimes."

He let it go for now. "Whatcha working on? Homework?"

"No. I'm making a list of all the reasons why Mom should let me have a dog."

He hid a smile. "Yeah? She hasn't backed down yet?"

"No, but we found one at the dump last week and took him to the shelter, so I'm starting a campaign to get him."

A campaign? Now he was intrigued. "Really. What's involved in this campaign?"

"This list is the first part. My friends and I are going to

37

come up with more ideas tomorrow."

He angled his head to read it. Apart from a few spelling mistakes, he was surprised by the points she had listed. *I'm responsible. I will give you my allowance for a year. I will walk him before and after school. I will feed him and give him water. I will pick up his poop.*

Beckett eyed her. Her mom was tougher than he'd thought, to keep holding out against this much adorable determination. "It's a really good list, Ella."

"Thank you." She frowned in concentration. "How do you spell empathy?"

He spelled it out for her, watched as she wrote it down under the other points. *Having a pet teaches kids empathy.*

Christ. Her mom was in for a whole page of emotional manipulation when she got home tonight. Beckett almost felt sorry for her. "Dogs are a lot of work, you know. You have to be around a lot for them, you can't just take off and do what you want, and you have to exercise them too. What about a goldfish or a hamster or something instead? Maybe your mom would be okay with one of those instead."

Ella wrinkled her nose. "You can't cuddle a fish, and when they die you have to flush them down the toilet. Plus my friend had a hamster, and he bit us all the time. I want Walter."

"That's the name of the dog you took to the shelter?"

"Yes. It was on his collar. Someone took him to the dump and left him there. It's horrible."

Yeah, that was a shitty-ass thing to do to any animal. "Well he's lucky you found him, and now he'll get adopted out into a good home." Theoretically.

"But if a family doesn't adopt him in time, the shelter will put him to sleep."

Wow, no pulling the wool over this one's eyes. "I'm sure someone will take him home."

"But I want to take him to *my* home." Her big blue eyes

were so earnest, it tugged at his few remaining heartstrings. "I promised him he would be mine and that I would take care of him. He's counting on me to change my mom's mind."

Beckett didn't know what the hell to say to that, and thankfully was saved from having to make up something by his phone ringing. Weaver. "Hey, man." *Good timing.* "What's up?"

"Got a situation happening at the new house," Jase said.

Beckett bit back a groan of frustration. *Lemme guess...* "Carter there?"

"Yep. Got a call from the homeowner. He's pretty upset, threatening to dump us and find another builder."

God dammit. Beckett had already sunk a hundred grand into ordering supplies for the custom job. "I'll handle it."

"Want me to go talk to Carter?"

"No. I'll do it." He was the boss, and Carter's former commanding officer. He didn't dodge his responsibilities, no matter how shitty they were.

Damn. There was no way around it; he was going to have to let Carter go. And if it had been any other employee but him, Beckett would have fired his ass a long time ago.

"I'm heading over there to see him now, then I'll call the homeowner," he said to Jase, then hung up, watching Ella, who was still working on her list and seemed in no hurry to go home. It felt weird to just leave her sitting out here on the porch all by herself. Crimson Point was about the safest place he could imagine, but it still felt wrong to leave her. "I have to go take care of some work things. You want me to drive you home?"

She looked up at him. "I'd rather stay here for a while and work on my list, as long as it's okay with you."

What was he gonna say, no? To that face, when she

wasn't doing anything wrong? Nuh-uh. "As long as it's all right with your mom, then it's okay."

"It is."

He raised an eyebrow. "Did she say that?"

"Yes."

Beckett wasn't sure if he believed her, but he didn't have time to argue about it right now. She was safe here and he would talk to Tiana about it later. "You wanna stay out on the porch, or would you rather watch TV inside?"

"Out here's fine. It's pretty."

All right then. He turned toward the stairs, hesitated. "There's a key under the stone that's painted to look like a raccoon in the garden bed beside the back porch if you change your mind. I've got some bottled lemonade in the fridge and you can help yourself to some snacks." What did he even have in there right now?

"Thanks, but I'll just wait here until my mom comes home."

"All right. See you. And good luck with the campaign."

"Thank you. Bye, Mr. Beckett."

"Bye."

As he drove up the driveway toward the lane, he glanced in his rearview at the little blonde sitting on his porch swing and found himself wishing he could sit out there with her instead of dealing with the bullshit he was about to face.

Sometimes adulting sucked ass.

Ten minutes later he parked out front of the two-story shingled house they were renovating, geared for battle. This part of town was a half-mile north of the main strip, a quiet, residential spot. Traffic was light, the sidewalk empty except for Mrs. Olsen, whom he waved at, and a woman walking her dog.

"Is this your house?" the unfamiliar woman called out from down the sidewalk.

He turned toward her, suppressing his irritation. With the improving weather and warming temperatures, the tourists were already starting to trickle in. Not that he had anything against tourists—they were the lifeblood of this community.

He might not be in the mood for small talk right now, but he also couldn't afford to be an asshole to people, residents *or* tourists. "No, I'm the contractor doing the renos on it."

"Oh." She gazed up at the roofline, a hat and sunglasses shading her face, her dog poised beside her. "It's beautiful. Will it be for sale, or does someone already own it?"

"It's owned."

"Darn."

Be polite. You're a businessman now. Fake it if you have to. "You looking to buy in the area?"

"I'm thinking about it. Do ocean-view properties come up for sale here very often?"

Despite his best efforts at making small talk like a normal human being, his mind was already on the coming confrontation once he saw Carter. "From time to time. You might have better luck with a cottage you could remodel. You can ask for more real estate info at the tourist center on Front Street." *And I really couldn't give a shit about any of this right now, so…*

She seemed to take the hint, gave him a polite smile. "All right. Thanks."

While she carried on down the sidewalk with her dog in tow Beckett strode up the newly-bricked walkway leading to the project house's front door to find Carter. Wasn't hard. His project manager was stalking around upstairs, his heavy, angry treads thudding against the newly-laid wood floor planks.

Bracing himself, Beckett jogged up the stairs. He wasn't looking forward to this, but he simply couldn't put it off any longer. Not when the reputation and wellbeing of the business his father had built over the past thirty years was at stake.

Carter stopped when he saw him, a pile of flooring in his arms. "Hey," he muttered, his bearded face dark as a thundercloud.

"Hey." Beckett stayed where he was, folded his arms and waited as Carter set the reclaimed heart of pine planks on top of the others stacked against the far wall. "Heard there was an issue today."

Carter dusted his hands off and turned to face him. "Guy's a fucking asshole."

"Who's paying our salaries at the moment."

"So?"

He fought for patience. "So you can't get into a fight with the guy who's funding this whole project. He's our customer, and like it or not, in the civilian world the customer is always right."

"Not in this case."

"Care to elaborate?"

Carter threw him an annoyed look and set his hands on his hips. He had a rugged face and was built like a bear, but whatever was happening to his mind was starting to show on the outside.

His dark brown hair was too long and from the length of his beard he hadn't shaved in weeks. Dark purple smudges lay beneath his eyes like bruises. Vertical creases marked the center of his forehead to the bridge of his nose, giving him a permanent scowl. He'd lost more weight, his jeans hanging low on his hips. "Not really. If I thought it was important enough to bother you with it, I would've called."

Talking to his former engineering sergeant now was like handling a live grenade with no idea of how many seconds he had left on the fuse. Beckett never knew what was going to set him off these days, or what Carter would do when he lost it. "Well it's important enough that I got a call from Weaver about it."

Carter snorted. "I just knocked the arrogant asshole down a few pegs, that's all." He said it like it was no big deal.

"Yeah, and that's your problem right there. You think it's all right when it's anything but. I warned you about that shit before."

Carter's almost black eyes widened in disbelief for a split-second, then hardened like bits of obsidian. A cynical sneer twisted his mouth. "So it's like that? Over a decade of service together, and you're going to take his side over mine without even knowing how it went down? Where's your loyalty?"

Beckett flexed his jaw. "You really wanna stand there and talk to me about loyalty, Boyd?"

Carter's chin came up. "What's that supposed to mean?"

He knew exactly what it meant, but if Carter really wanted to get into this, fine with him. "We gave you a second chance by hiring you." When no one else would. "You were in a bad place, and you needed steady work to give you an income and a sense of meaning and purpose. That's why we offered you the job in the first place, because we wanted to see you back on your feet again." Technically his dad had offered Carter the job, but he'd done it at Beckett's request.

"Yeah, after you sold me out and had me booted out of the Army with that report you wrote when I tried to come back after the TBI." Bitterness and accusation dripped from every word.

Beckett sucked in a sharp breath. Was he serious? "You weren't fit to serve anymore, and you know it. There was no other option but medical discharge."

"Bullshit. You'd already made up your mind before I set foot back on U.S. soil. And this pity job you offered me meant my wife and I packed up, left everything and everyone else behind in North Carolina to come here to help your dad out."

Becket let out a humorless laugh. "I see. So you did *me* the favor, is that it?"

Carter stuck his jaw out, his pose and body language screaming belligerence. "Yeah, that's right."

This was such. *Bull*shit. Beckett shook his head. "What the hell's going on with you, man? This isn't you." The man standing in front of him now was practically a stranger. The Carter he knew was fun-loving, hard-working and solid in any situation, including combat. The kind of guy you wanted beside you during a firefight, and someone who would give the shirt off his back to anyone who needed it.

"This is the new me since my head got fucked up." He spread his arms apart, a bitter smile on his face. "Embrace it, baby."

"Screw that. Where's the guy I was proud to have under my command?"

Carter gave him a look that sent a chill up his spine. "He's gone, Beck. He died in the IED blast. Don't you *get* it?"

"Then you need to get more help—"

"I've been getting help! What the fuck do you think I've been doing all this time? Huh?" His face twisted with a heartbreaking combination of fury and pain. "You think I *like* being this way? Losing my mind to the point that my own wife is scared of me? That she cringes whenever I get too close now?"

Wait, what? Molly was afraid of him? "What do you mean?" This was the first he'd heard of it.

"It doesn't matter."

"Yes, it fucking does," Beckett said, glaring at him. "If you were anyone else, I would've fired your ass weeks ago because of your behavior. But I've been holding on, trying to smooth things over every time you cause a problem, giving you chance after chance to get a grip on yourself because I know you're going through a hard time. But I won't do that anymore, not even for you. Do you know how many guys I've lost because of you? I can't afford to start losing paying customers too. This town's too small, and the company's reputation is everything." *It's all I've got left.* He bit the words back.

A humorless laugh. "So it's my fault. Automatically it's all my fault, right? Because I'm the crazy, brain-damaged fuck up."

Beckett fought the urge to roll his eyes. He hated when people played the pity card. Couldn't respect it from one of his own, a fellow warrior, no matter how shitty Carter's current situation was. "Nobody said you're a fuck up."

"You just did." Carter shook his head, anger or maybe frustration building in his gaze again. "The guys who quit because I wouldn't put up with their shitty work ethic, and this customer who thinks he can walk all over me and say whatever the hell he wants just because he's paying us. That's on me, huh? I'm in the wrong?"

"Yes. Because I need those guys to get the job done, and we need the customer to be happy so he pays us. You know this. Christ, we've been over it so many damn times over the past few months. What the hell is your problem? Do you *want* me to fire you? Because I'm right there."

Carter took a menacing step toward him, his fists clenched at his sides, face set. Beckett tensed and lowered his arms, ready to defend himself if they came to blows.

Unbelievable. Was the stupid bastard actually going to attack him? Because if he did it wouldn't be pretty. And Beckett really didn't want to make Carter hurt any more than he already was.

Thankfully Carter stopped a few paces away and shook his head slowly, the disgust on his face a punch to the gut. "You know what? You're not worth it. I'm dealing with enough shit, I don't need any more. I don't need this. I don't need you. I'm done." He undid his tool belt, dropped it with a thud on the new floor and stalked past Beckett, heading for the stairs.

Stunned, it took Beckett a moment to recover. "*Boyd*," he snapped out, using his commanding officer voice.

Carter stopped automatically in response, the muscles in his back taut under the fabric of his sweat-dampened T-shirt, but didn't look back at him.

"You walk away right now, like this, and you and I are done." Not a threat. A promise. And he didn't mean just the job. Carter had crossed too many lines with him already. If he crossed this one, Beckett was finished with him, period.

Carter didn't turn around. "Fuck you, Beck." He walked away without looking back.

Left there to stew with impotent rage boiling in his veins, Beckett sucked in a long, steadying breath and battled back the sharp edge of his temper. Fuck this whole thing.

Carter's truck engine roared to life out front, then the sustained squeal of tires came as he peeled away down the street.

"*Shit*," Beckett snarled, wanting to punch something. Ten years of friendship and trust had just imploded in front of him, and there was no fixing it now.

It felt like he'd swallowed a belly full of concrete, the mantle of guilt settling across his shoulders making the ache in his lower back sharper. Now Carter had no job, which meant that soon he would have only his disability coming in. Molly would struggle to cover all their expenses on her own. And that comment about her being afraid of Carter didn't sit well in Beckett's gut.

He whipped out his phone and dialed Jase as he jogged down the stairs. Jase had always been tightest with Carter. If anyone could neutralize this situation, he could. "Hey, shit hit the fan with Boyd and he just peeled out of here like a bat outta hell." He needed to make sure Carter didn't go off the deep end. To have any chance at that, he needed to talk to Molly.

"Ah, shit. He going home, you think?" Jase's tone was worried.

"Dunno, but I want to be there for Molly just in case. Can you meet me over there in ten?"

****

I'll kill him. I'll kill him for what he did to me.

Yeah, Beckett Hollister was living on borrowed time, and he had no freaking clue.

In the rearview mirror Hollister appeared on the sidewalk, locking himself out of the damn project house before climbing into his own truck and driving away in the opposite direction.

Coward. Fucking coward, turning his back on the people who counted on him.

The cold, hard rage had been building for months. Now it had solidified into a core of steel. Unbreakable. Unforgiving.

Hollister had destroyed so many lives, yet here he was, alive and well. He somehow got to carry on living his own life back here in his hometown, where everybody hero-worshipped him because of his service to his country. His sacrifice.

Rage boiled to the surface, hot and out of control. What the fuck did he know about sacrifice? He didn't know the true meaning of the word, or what real pain felt like.

It had taken a long time to find out what really happened that day in Syria. The answer hadn't come as a surprise. Now Hollister had quit the Army and moved back home, as lost as the rest of them.

Crimson Point was claustrophobic. Everyone knew everyone, except for the flood of tourists that were already beginning to trickle in with the warmer weather. There was nowhere to hide here, nowhere to breathe.

With his background, Hollister was a formidable target, even for someone with training. But every man had his weakness. *Now I know his.*

Syria.

More rage stoked the flames, the burning need for revenge. Hollister would die for what he'd done. Shooting him would be easy, but it also wasn't enough. He had to suffer first. Had to know *why* he was dying. For *whom* he was dying.

His life for the lives he'd so carelessly ruined. It was the only way.

Calm down. Breathe. Breathe, like your shrink taught you.

It was so hard to think through the anger. Damn near impossible to find the patience to wait, think this through and plan it properly.

Hollister was best friends with the town sheriff. That made this a lot trickier.

Even though it was hard to wait, there was no other way. So many long, agonizing months had already passed since everything had fallen apart. What was a few days more?

Chapter Five

Sierra let out her last patient of the day—a gorgeous Golden Retriever—and his visiting female owner onto Front Street, and sighed. She'd been in surgery all afternoon and had stayed late to accommodate the pup's owner. Now she was starving and craving a night home on her couch with some takeout while she edited her latest set of photos she'd taken on the beach, but maybe that wasn't a good idea since it gave her all kinds of time to be alone and think about Beckett.

He'd been on her mind all day. What was his problem with her?

Maybe he still thinks you're too young for him to be bothered with.

The thought was disheartening to say the least. She was eight years younger than him, less than a decade. Not that big a gap in her mind, but maybe it was in his, even though they were both adults.

The logical part of her said it was for the best. She'd crushed on him for so long, had built him up in her head to the point of ridiculous. The reality was bound to be a dismal disappointment.

Beckett had about as much romance in him as a rock.

And he was also closed-off emotionally. She would never enter another relationship with a man who kept his feelings to himself all the time. It would make her insane, and eventually make her miserable. So in truth it was safer and healthier for her to just keep Beckett as fantasy material and nothing more.

Her assistant Macy was still at the reception desk out front, breaking her out of her thoughts. "You can go on home," Sierra told her. "I'll lock up when I leave."

After finishing up her files for the day she shut everything down and had the key in the rear door of the clinic when the sound of squealing tires caught her attention. Startled, she glanced toward Front Street in time to see Carter's dark blue pickup peel around the corner and race past her building, tires smoking.

Frozen there on the sidewalk, Sierra caught a glimpse of his face in the instant before he whipped past. The rage in his expression made her stomach cramp, and brought with it a feeling of foreboding. Clearly something bad had happened. And if he was heading home...

Worry for Molly kicked her into high gear. Given their recent conversation and since Carter had been acting unpredictable lately, Sierra wasn't taking any chances. She had to warn her friend.

She locked the door as fast as she could and ran around the side of the building to hop in her car. She headed straight for Molly and Carter's place, calling her friend's cell on the way, but Molly didn't answer.

Molly's car was parked out front when she arrived at the rental house, and there was no sign of Carter's truck. Breathing a little easier, Sierra went around back and rapped on the door, the evening air heavy and strangely muggy for this time of year.

"Come on in," Molly called out.

The scent of something spicy and delicious hit her along with the mellow notes of old jazz the moment she pushed the door open. "It's me. Something smells good."

"Chicken enchiladas." Molly appeared around the kitchen doorway at the end of the hall with a warm smile, her curls pulled up into a ponytail, wiping her hands on a kitchen towel. "You hungry?"

"I'm famished."

"Well get in here and I'll fix that." She disappeared back into the kitchen.

Sierra took off her shoes and started down the hallway. The two-bedroom rental bungalow had been all bland neutrals when Molly and Carter moved in, and her friend had since transformed it with bright pops of color.

Now Molly's bold and vivid personality was evident in every room, from the art to the rich paint colors on the walls. The kitchen and great room were painted a deep, jewel-toned teal, set off by crisp white moldings and cabinetry. Molly had managed to breathe new life into the neglected mid-century property, and now the entire place felt cozy and homey.

"Long day?" Molly asked, glancing up as she pulled a casserole dish from the oven.

"Pretty long." She wanted to ease into this, rather than just blurt out what she'd seen. It might mean nothing. Then again, it probably *did*. "You heard from Carter tonight?"

"No, why?" Molly placed the casserole dish on the counter in front of her, the cheese all melted and golden on top, the rich red sauce bubbling up around the edges of the enchiladas.

"I saw him peel past the clinic as I was leaving. He looked pissed."

"So what else is new?" Molly muttered, cutting them servings.

A little startled by the buried anger in her voice, Sierra let the subject drop. "Did you make this from scratch?" she asked instead.

"Mostly. Except I used roasted chicken from the store instead of cooking my own."

Yeah, she'd made it from scratch. No surprise. "Close enough."

"Exactly. Wine?"

"God, yes."

Molly pulled a chilled bottle of white from the fridge, poured them both a glass, and sat at the kitchen table with a smile. "Ten minutes, then we can eat. Carter was supposed to be here by six, but as you can see he's not here again, so I'm not waiting for him." She took a sip. "What brings you by?"

She could lie. Make up some excuse like she'd just felt like dropping by and hanging out. Except she'd never done that on a work night before, not unless they already had plans. And Molly wouldn't thank her for not being straight with her.

"I was worried about you."

Molly's expression softened. "I'm okay, Si."

"Yeah. I just wanted to make sure you were okay. In case he came here and..." She mentally winced at the last bit, unsure if she'd overstepped or interfered.

"Took it out on me," Molly finished.

She nodded. "Right."

Molly lowered her gaze, her expression falling along with her shoulders. "I appreciate your concern, but if he was that mad he probably went straight to the bar." She picked up her wine, took a big swallow, again not meeting Sierra's eyes.

"Maybe it's nothing. God, maybe I overreacted." She reached for Molly's free hand. "I'm sorry, now I feel stupid. Do you want me to go?"

Molly looked at her, put on a smile. "No, I'm glad for the company. And for knowing you care so much. After what I told you earlier, I can understand why you came over."

"Okay, good. I was ready to get up and slink out the back door," she said with a light laugh.

"No." Molly blew out a breath. "Now let's eat."

"Let's."

Molly was at the kitchen counter serving up helpings of the enchiladas when someone rapped on the front door. Both of them looked toward it as Molly called out her standard, "It's open."

Sierra sat up straighter, her heart rate quickening when Beckett appeared in the doorway a moment later, Jase right behind wearing his trademark charcoal gray tweed newsboy flat cap.

Beckett's rugged face tightened for a moment when he saw her sitting there at Molly's kitchen table. "Hi."

She gave him a bright smile. "Hi. I just dropped by to visit and Molly took pity on me and decided to feed me." Oh, man, it couldn't be good that both he and Jase were here together, but she loved seeing him again.

Beckett nodded, shifted his gaze to Molly as the men entered the kitchen.

Before he could get another word out, Molly faced him and folded her arms, spatula still in hand, a hard look on her face. "What did he do now?"

FOR A MOMENT Beckett wasn't sure how to answer. He was secretly relieved that Sierra was here and Carter wasn't. Things were bad enough between him and his former teammate without adding more friction and hard feelings. At least now he had both Jase and Sierra here to help calm the situation if Carter showed up.

Beckett glanced at Sierra, aware of her gaze on him and the way it made his skin tingle like low voltage electricity, then back at Molly. He didn't want to do this with an audience. "Maybe we should talk alone."

Molly didn't budge. "Nope. Whatever you guys came here to say, you can say in front of Sierra. And I'm guessing it has something to do with Carter screaming up Front Street in his truck as he passed her a little while ago. You want some?" she asked, changing subjects as she dug out another helping from the casserole dish.

Hell. "No, I'm good."

"I'll take some," Jase said, shooting him a *take some, dumbass* frown.

"I bet you haven't eaten," Molly said to Beckett, making him a plate anyway.

He'd learned long ago not to get in Molly's way when she set her mind to something, so he took it with a murmur of thanks and waited until she sat at the table. He seated himself between her and Sierra, across from Jase, who had already removed his hat and was digging into his dinner. Under the appetizing aroma of the meal, he could smell Sierra's tempting citrus scent.

He would so much rather eat her than the enchiladas.

Really damn uncomfortable at this point because he couldn't get her out of his head or keep stalling on this, Beckett watched Molly for a moment. "You sure you don't want to talk about this in private?"

She impaled a bite of enchilada with enough force that her fork clanked on the plate. "Yep."

"I can pop outside while you guys talk," Sierra said, picking up her plate.

Molly shot out a hand and grabbed her wrist to stop her. "No. You already know what's been going on, so there's nothing to hide." She thrust a finger at Sierra's chair. "Sit. Eat."

Sierra did, giving him an uncomfortable look Beckett understood all too well. She would rather be anywhere than here right now because she knew he had bad news.

Molly popped the bite into her mouth, chewed and raised her eyebrows at him. "So? Lay it on me, I can take it. What is it this time?"

Beckett glanced at Jase before speaking. "There was

an incident with the homeowner this afternoon. I went over there to talk to Carter about it. Things…didn't go well. He was pretty damn angry when he left."

She stopped chewing, narrowed her eyes slightly. "Did he break something? Put his fist through the wall?"

"No, but…" Hell. There was no easy way to say this. Jase had stopped eating, was watching him and Molly intently. "We had an argument and I wound up letting him go."

She lowered her fork, her gold-green stare burning into Beckett's. "So he's fired."

Shit. "Yes. I'm sorry, Moll. I had no choice. I can't keep—"

"No," she said, holding up a hand to stop him from continuing. She pressed her lips together, her gaze on her plate. "I get it. You've bent over backward trying to help and accommodate him."

Beckett's conscience pricked him. Had he, though? Had he done enough? He'd tried to help the guy, yeah, but could he have done more? Guilt was slowly eating a hole through his insides.

"There'll be severance pay," he said quietly, not knowing how to make this any easier on her. She didn't deserve any of this, the added burden it would bring. "Six weeks' pay, and I'm going to pay for COBRA if you guys sign up for it, to make sure you guys still have extra coverage for whatever he needs." It sounded lame, even to him. He felt Sierra's stare on him, and his heart got even heavier. This wasn't his proudest moment and he hated that she was seeing it.

Molly pressed her lips together. Nodded. "Thank you. But I've got good medical coverage through work. We can handle it."

Jase put a hand on her shoulder. "Beck had no choice, Moll."

"I know."

The way her shoulders slumped, like she carried the weight of the world on them, made Beckett feel like the biggest asshole in the universe. "Moll, I—"

"No, don't apologize. This is on him, not you. You've got a business to run, and people who depend on you for their livelihood. You can't keep someone on staff who's volatile and constantly causing problems for everyone."

The constriction around his chest eased a little. It shouldn't have surprised him that Molly would understand the situation so clearly. But he still felt like hell about it. He shook his head. "I don't know how to help him anymore."

"That makes two of us," she said flatly, then shook her head. "I figured this was coming. He's getting worse every day, doesn't matter what we try. I guess he's gotta hit rock bottom before he finally wakes up and realizes he's lost everything."

Her last words made him pretty sure she was talking about their marriage. Beckett traded a loaded look with Jase before his buddy turned to Molly.

"We're both still here for you if you need us," he told her. "That's never gonna change."

She nodded once, her gaze fixed on her plate.

"And me, too," Sierra said. "Whatever happens, you've got us."

That brought Molly's head up. The strong, proud façade she always wore cracked for just an instant, her eyes turning luminous with a sheen of tears. "I love you guys, you know. I'm so sorry you've all been put in this position."

"No," Jase said instantly, reaching for her hand. "None of this is your fault. And we love you too. Don't be afraid to lean on us when you need to. We're family. A fucked-up and kinda dysfunctional family, but family nonetheless."

She gave a tight smile that didn't reach her eyes.

"Thanks. But I'm not used to leaning on anyone."

Beckett so got that, because he was the same way. Even when it came to the gorgeous, accomplished woman sitting next to him, who he wanted more than his next breath.

Time to go.

His dinner remained untouched in front of him. He didn't feel like sitting here eating Molly's food after what he'd just told her. "Are you going to be okay?" he asked her.

"Yeah. I'll figure everything out."

"No, I meant…" Jesus, there was no easy way to say this either, and it was too delicate a thing to bring up what Carter had told him about their relationship earlier. "Do you want us to stay until Carter comes back?"

She shook her head. "No. If he's still in a mood that'll just make it worse. Better if you're not here."

Beckett shared another look with Jase, and his teammate tilted his head subtly toward Molly. Understanding, Beckett stood and reached for his still-full plate. "Sorry for the shit news. But what Jase said is true. We're here for you no matter what. Always."

"Thank you."

There was nothing left to say, and he needed to let Jase talk with her alone. Beckett steeled himself and glanced at Sierra. "You heading home?"

Surprise lit her eyes for a moment, but she got the hint. "Yes." Picking up her plate, she rounded the table, dropped a kiss on Molly's cheek and took her plate to the sink.

Beckett waited in the heavy silence as she rinsed it, put it in the dishwasher and followed him out the back door.

WHEN THE DOOR clicked shut behind Sierra, Jase leaned back in his chair and rested a forearm across the top of it, his full attention on Molly. "You okay?" he asked softly.

"Sure," she said in a dull voice, poking at her dinner with her fork.

He hated that this was happening to her. Had tried to be supportive of Carter through all of this, but things had gone too far now. "Look, I know things have been tight financially for you guys with all the treatment and meds he's on." He also knew from Carter that they'd used up pretty much everything they'd saved over the years. Things were going to be even harder now, with only Molly's salary to get them by. "If you need some money to—"

Her eyes flashed with a spark of temper. "Jase Weaver, if you're about to offer me money, I swear to God..."

He shut his mouth. Meant to keep it shut, but the frustration was too much. "Dammit Moll, this is no time to be proud. I hate seeing you struggle."

"So don't look."

He stared at her. Don't look? If fucking only.

Where she was concerned, all he could do was look and nothing more, and there was no damn way he could look away when she needed him most. Not even if it drove the knife in his chest a little deeper every time he saw her.

"No matter what happens between Carter and me, I'll never abandon you, Moll." He'd cut out his own heart first.

She pressed her lips together and glanced away, and it took her a moment to regain her control. "I know you mean well. All of you. But you don't know what it's like. The embarrassment. The pity. The dread."

That last one bothered him the most. He wished he could protect her, but it was a sad fucking thing to want to protect the woman he was in love with from her own husband—his former best friend. "You have nothing to be embarrassed about. You've gone above and beyond to help him."

Her gold-green eyes darted to his. "It's called being a *wife*, Jase."

"Maybe, but I know a lot of wives who walked away from guys in our unit without having to deal with a tenth of the shit you've been dealing with." It seemed like every time they got back from a deployment, someone's wife or girlfriend had packed up and left. Even Beckett's.

But not Molly. Molly was loyal to the core. It was one of the things Jase loved most about her.

She picked up her plate and carried it to the sink, her back stiff. "I said vows that included for better or worse, in sickness and in health. I meant them."

Yes. And he respected her for it. For that enduring loyalty, and her big, caring heart that Carter was too fucking selfish and stupid to appreciate. "I know." *I was there. Dying inside while standing up there watching you give yourself to my best friend.* "But now it's time to start thinking about yourself."

She paused at the sink, her head dropping forward. "I...can't abandon him, Jase. He needs me."

But he doesn't deserve you.

He had to bite the words back before they could fly out of his stupid mouth. She had no freaking clue how he'd really felt about her all these years, and he planned on keeping it that way.

Except dammit, she deserved so much more than Carter had given her over the past four turbulent years of their marriage. She deserved someone who loved her enough to put her first, who showed her how amazing and beautiful she was. Someone who truly appreciated her.

"Moll. You can't save him. You know you can't." Jase was worried about her safety, and her emotional state. Molly was strong, wanted the world to think she was fine, that she could handle anything life threw at her all on her own. He knew better. He wanted to help her. Protect her. He wanted...

59

A lot of things he shouldn't.

She nodded, looking so defeated it was all he could do not to walk over there and pull her into his arms. Her smile could light up an entire room. He missed seeing it. Missed hearing her husky, infectious laugh and seeing the mischievous, playful sparkle in her eyes. "I have to try."

He resisted the urge to rake a hand through his hair in frustration. She wasn't ever going to leave Carter, no matter how shitty things got. She was going to play the dutiful wife until the very end, sacrifice her own happiness and wellbeing on a man who was determined to self-destruct.

Jase appreciated that in a way, but shit. He couldn't shake the feeling that something terrible would happen if she stayed with Carter. He wanted her to wake up and get the hell out before it did. Because it sure as hell felt like something bad was looming.

"Will you be okay here tonight?" he asked. "I can stay until he gets back." Part of him wanted to hunt his old buddy down right now and tear into him for putting Molly through this. Except that would only make things worse and he didn't want to alienate her by interfering.

"I'll be okay. Thanks."

He nodded, couldn't think of anything else to say except, "If you need anything, you call me. Understand?"

Her eyes warmed and the hint of a smile tugged at the edge of her mouth. "Yeah. Thanks, Jase."

Dismissed, soldier. "Anytime." He put his flat cap back on and carried his plate to the sink where she took it from him. And because he couldn't help himself and because he'd always hugged her goodbye, he slid his arms around her.

Molly leaned into him with a little sigh, rested her cheek on his chest for a moment. And for those few seconds, the bittersweet pain was almost unbearable.

She fucking needed him. Needed *somebody* so she

wouldn't have to endure the crushing weight of all this alone. God, what he wouldn't give to be able to call her his. Have the right to touch her, kiss her, take her to bed, taste every inch of her, make her cry out his name as she came around him and then hold her in the darkness every night.

Yeah, Carter was a fucking idiot who didn't realize the treasure he had in her.

Breathing in the fruity scent of her shampoo, Jase pressed a kiss to the top of her tight curls and stepped back, aching inside. "I'm here if you need me."

"I know."

He hoped so. He also wouldn't hold his breath waiting for her to ask him for anything.

He walked outside, the ache in the center of his chest so sharp it was hard to draw a full breath. Sierra was on the front steps, waiting while Beckett finished up a call.

"How is she?" she asked.

Jase shrugged. "You know Molly. Tough as they come."

Sierra nodded. "I'm worried about her. Do you think Carter would ever…?" She left the sentence dangling, but the worry in her deep blue eyes said it all.

Jase's muscles bunched in reflex, his body rebelling at the thought. "Naw. No, Carter would never lay a hand on her." The guy was deteriorating, for sure, but Jase didn't think he would dare hurt Molly physically. If he did, Jase would fucking tear him apart.

Beckett finished his call and faced him. "She okay?"

"She says she is." He glanced down the driveway, unease settling heavy in his gut. The rental property was set back a good distance from the road, with woods on all sides. Isolated, the nearest neighbor a five-minute walk away. "I feel like I should stay. Just in case."

"Might not be a bad idea," Beckett said. "But Molly would hate it."

"I'll stay," Sierra offered. "She's my best friend."

"No," he and Beckett said at the same time. Sierra frowned and opened her mouth to argue, but Jase cut her off. "Not by yourself." It cut him deep to say it, admit that he no longer trusted that Carter wouldn't hurt one of them if he lost it.

Jase pushed out a long breath. "What about the job? Who are you going to replace Carter with?" he asked Beckett.

"I was hoping you. You up for it?"

"I was afraid you'd say that." He grimaced. "All right, I'll act as project manager for now—until you can find a replacement. I like my current job." Numbers and spreadsheets and no stress, no dealing with clients or wrangling crewmembers. Order. Precision. Routine. Time spent working on his '32 Ford. Those were the things he needed to give him stability and keep him busy as he battled to navigate his way back into the civilian world and tame the demons he'd brought home from his years at war.

"You can do both."

Jase laughed dryly. Beck was such a hard-ass. "Oh, can I?"

"I'll look into finding someone. Got any suggestions on where I might start?"

One name immediately popped into his head. "What about MacIntyre?"

Beckett's face went slack with surprise. "MacIntyre."

"Yeah. Scottish guy, former Royal Marine. Six-two, reddish-brown hair, beard. We served with his team at Bagram and—"

"I know who he is." Beckett's expression turned thoughtful. "Think he'd be interested?"

Jase shrugged. "You won't know unless you ask him. But yeah, he might be. Last I heard six weeks ago he was between jobs."

Beckett nodded. "I'll think about it."

When he and Sierra made no move to say goodnight and leave, it finally dawned on Jase that they wanted to talk alone. "Okay, see you guys later."

He hopped into his truck, hoping Beckett would call MacIntyre first thing in the morning. Jase could juggle both positions for a while, but not forever, not with the way the company was growing. After the disaster with Carter, Beckett needed someone he could trust.

And so did Molly.

Chapter Six

L eft alone with Beckett, Sierra did her best to push
aside the magnetic pull he exerted on her and
cleared her throat as Jase drove away. "You didn't
eat. Can we go grab a bite together?" she asked him. They
needed to be out of here before Carter got home.

He frowned slightly, the motion pulling at the scar that
bisected his left eyebrow. "Now?"

"Yes. I need to talk to you."

"About what?"

"Carter and Molly."

He hesitated a second, as though he wanted to say no,
then nodded once. "All right. Where?"

"My place? I'll pick us up some pizza on the way
home."

"Okay. Meet you there in twenty."

He was already parked in her driveway when she
arrived with the pizza. He met her at her car, took the
boxes from her and followed her up the walkway to the
front door. A cool breeze carried the salty tang of the sea,
brushing aside the mugginess from earlier.

Annoying butterflies danced in her stomach at the
thought of spending time alone with him in her place.

She'd fallen in love with the little pale gray-painted cottage the first time she'd seen it, right after moving back from San Francisco a little over four years ago now.

Unlike her brother, she hadn't always wanted to stay in Crimson. In fact, for many years she'd been desperate to escape it.

After meeting her ex in vet school, she had followed him to northern California post graduation, where they'd bought a condo with a gorgeous view and worked at a clinic together. When things had slowly unraveled after that, it had taken her coming home for a visit to realize just how miserable she'd been.

She'd spotted the cottage during a drive around town to clear her head, and right then everything had become so obvious. Her unhappiness in her relationship, and with life in general.

There was nothing worse than being lonely when you were with your partner.

She'd put an offer on the cottage the next morning before catching a flight back to San Fran, ended her relationship that same day, packed up and come home to Crimson. It was the best decision she'd ever made.

This was where she was meant to be. The place where she wanted to raise a family someday. Her adorable cottage was a little over a half-mile from her clinic, just three streets over from her brother's place, and she had a partial view of the ocean through the tall cedars and Douglas firs in the backyard.

Sierra was hyperaware of Beckett behind her now as she entered her mudroom and walked through to the kitchen. With over six feet of powerful, authoritative male presence in here with her, it suddenly seemed a lot smaller.

He'd been over for dinner twice since she'd moved in, but always with other people around. Never just the two of them. This felt intimate, even though she told herself she was being ridiculous. "Okay with you if we eat on the couches?" she asked as she set her purse down on a chair at the table.

He was still standing in the doorway, as though uncomfortable. She wanted to change that, make this as relaxed as possible. She wanted him to be at home here. At home with her, the way he used to be.

"Sure," he said, and followed her in, his gaze snagging on the glass fishing floats in the bowl on the coffee table as he sank onto the couch. "Is that the one we found that day?"

"Yes." Glass artists were common along this part of the coast, and floats were cheap and popular. Every year Crimson Point staged a treasure hunt of sorts from Memorial Day to New Years. Townspeople would hide handcrafted glass floats made by local artisans along a five-mile stretch of beach for people to find. The cobalt-and-aqua swirled glass ball was one of her most treasured possessions because it reminded her of him.

"Seems like such a long time ago now."

"Almost four years." Right after she'd moved home. That day was still crystal clear in her memory.

She, Beckett and Noah had found hers while walking down to the beach for a campfire the last time Beckett had come home for leave just prior to his divorce. He had spotted a glimpse of deep blue nestled high up in the sandy bank above the path they were on. She'd never found one before, so he had hoisted her up on his strong shoulders, holding her steady while she dug it out and crowed in triumph, holding it over her head as he grinned up at her.

That was the day she'd gone from crushing on Beckett to something far more painful.

She'd studied him in the flickering light of their bonfire on the beach that evening. It had been so good to have him home again. To see him smile and hear his deep laughter, admire the rugged, masculine beauty that took her breath away.

Beckett's gaze now strayed to her mantel, where some of her photographs were displayed. Surprise flickered across his face when he saw the one she'd taken of them and Noah at the bonfire that night. She'd flipped her camera around and taken a selfie of sorts, all three of them grinning up at the lens with their faces bathed in the warm glow of the fire.

"I forgot you took that one," he said.

It was her favorite picture of all, better than any candid shot or landscape she'd ever captured. "A shutterbug never goes to the beach without her camera."

"What kind of pizza did you get?" he asked, jarring her out of her reverie.

God, had she been staring? "Meat lovers and a supreme. Here," she said, handing him a plate and opening the meat lovers box for him. It was his favorite.

"So what did you want to tell me about Molly and Carter?" he asked as he took his plate from her.

"I'm really worried about her."

"Yeah, she's got a lot to deal with right now."

"No." He'd misunderstood her. "When I met her at the hospital for lunch she started to tell me a bit more about Carter. She's been hiding a lot of it, pretending she's handling everything just fine. He's deteriorating at a far more rapid pace than any of us realized."

Beckett expelled a breath. "I know."

He *thought* he knew. "She's afraid of him, Beckett."

"Yeah. Shit." He set his plate on his lap, a frown creasing his brow. "I feel bad for leaving her alone, but if I'd stayed it would've set Carter off."

"I still don't know him very well. Not compared to you and Jase. Is he a threat to her?"

He thought about it for a second. "I would have said no even as little as a few weeks ago, but the way things are going, I can't be sure about that."

Not the answer she'd been hoping for. Anxiety swirled in her belly. "God. What can we do?"

"Distance ourselves from him, and be there for her. Nobody can help him but himself. Whether Molly sees that yet, I'm not sure."

"I'm not sure either." Back in her twenties Sierra had been intimidated by the age and maturity gap between her and Beckett, as well as his brooding intensity.

Not anymore.

She liked what she'd seen in terms of how he'd handled the situation with Molly today. That he had come over to talk to her face-to-face, and offer his help. It was clear he cared about her and had more layers to him than he wanted anyone to know about. Sierra had loved the glimpse beneath his impenetrable armor.

She withheld a sigh, wanting things to change between them. No matter what her logical side said, the hopeful romantic in her wanted him to be *hers*, and stubbornly refused to believe that he would remain emotionally closed-off forever. It insisted that in time, once he trusted her, he would open up.

That same thought had led to utter misery in her previous relationships.

"Though she hinted at lunch that they might not make it," she added, glad he was oblivious to her thoughts. Being rejected or laughed at by him would crush her.

"Not a surprise." He took a bite of pizza.

He said it so bluntly, almost as if Molly and Carter separating after seven years of marriage was a foregone conclusion. Of course he'd been through his own divorce, so that might explain his jaded outlook. She cocked her head, curious. "Did you know your relationship was over before you guys separated?" He'd never talked about it.

His expression closed up as he swallowed his bite. "Yeah. For the last couple years, I guess."

Wow, that was a long time to stay with someone when things were that rough. Although he had been gone a lot. "What happened? Noah never told me and I always wanted to ask you." She'd only met his ex once, when Beckett had brought her here for a visit after their wedding back in North Carolina. She had seemed nice enough, though Sierra had done her best to avoid them both, her newly budded feelings toward him making her too raw inside.

He shrugged. "We didn't get along. Things were okay when I was gone, but as soon as I got home from a deployment, the problems would start. Should never have gotten married in the first place."

Sierra nodded. The marriage had definitely changed him. Made him jaded. More remote. "Her loss."

He gave her a strange look. "Her family and friends think it's the other way around."

"Well they don't know you like I do. So it's definitely her loss."

Something like surprise flared in his dark eyes.

"Anyway, if things get worse for Molly and Carter and they do split up, I don't see either of them staying here. Molly will probably go home to North Carolina. I'm not sure about Carter."

"He's got family back in Kansas." He frowned again. "Did Molly say anything about his current prognosis?"

"No, just that the brain injury is the root cause of it all, even though there's no proof, and the mix of meds they've got him on leaves him a mess."

He grunted. "And the drinking sure as hell doesn't help."

"The drinking?"

"Molly didn't tell you?"

"No." Why hadn't she? "Just that he's all over the place emotionally, so she never knows what she's going to get from him. It's hard on her, whether she admits it or not."

"I didn't realize how bad things were between them."

"If Molly's even talking about the possibility of leaving him, then it's bad."

"True," he agreed.

The whole situation was terrible. "I wish there was something we could do."

"None of us can help Carter at this point. That's all up to him." He focused on her, the impact of that deep brown gaze setting off a sizzle of heat in her belly. His quiet intensity drew her with a power she wasn't strong enough to resist.

Against her will, her gaze dipped to his mouth. His features were harsh, even foreboding, but his mouth looked so soft. She'd imagined those full lips on hers so many times, wondered if his quiet intensity would translate to the bedroom.

She was willing to bet it did.

The thought made her heart skip and her blood race, imagining what it would feel like to be on the receiving end of that intensity in bed. To feel that hard, powerful build against her, on top of her. His strong, capable hands holding her in place as he caressed and licked every sensitive spot on her body, then driving into her with urgency. Something told her Beckett would be unlike any other lover she'd had.

He wouldn't be emotionally closed-off then.

She forced her gaze back to his, hoped he hadn't noticed the way she'd been staring at his mouth.

He wiped his hands on his napkin. "If she tells you anything else important, let me know. For now I'm gonna back away and give the situation some time to cool off. But if something goes down, I'll step in."

That made her feel a little better. Beckett could and would handle anything that came up. She trusted him implicitly in that, because he was dependable above all else. "Thank you. I'll definitely let you know."

He picked up his plate and stood, taking her by surprise. "Thanks for the pizza, but I gotta go. Got some work to catch up on."

"Oh. Sure." She took the plate from him, followed him to the door, wishing she had a reason to make him stay.

He opened her front door, paused to look back at her. "See ya."

"See ya."

He closed the door after himself. She locked it, frowning. For a man who had spent most of his adult life performing special operations missions as a Green Beret officer, something about his abrupt exit seemed an awful lot like a retreat.

Chapter Seven

Driving home from a jobsite the next afternoon, Beckett couldn't get his mind off Sierra. His original plan upon moving back home had been to avoid her whenever possible, but now he realized how laughably futile that effort was.

This town was way too damn small for that. And not thinking about her was proving just as impossible as avoiding her. Especially when it came to thinking about getting her naked and under him.

He blocked the thought before it could fully form again, because he didn't have time for that kind of distraction. He'd had a productive day playing catch up at work today, at least. He'd even managed to smooth things over with the pissed-off client after assuring him that Carter was no longer working for the company. The job was going ahead as planned.

Taking Jase's suggestion, he had called up Aidan MacIntyre earlier and left a message saying he had a job offer for him. Whether or not the Scot would be interested was anyone's guess, but Beckett hoped he would at least consider it. He needed someone else at the helm who he could trust.

Partway down Front Street, his gaze snagged on a familiar little figure standing on the eastern sidewalk up ahead, across from the waterfront.

"What the hell is she doing?" He slowed as he approached Ella, pulling to the side of the road to check on her.

Crimson Point was a safe place, and it was four-thirty in the afternoon and broad daylight here on the main street, but it bothered him that she was out here all alone. From what he'd seen, Tiana was a responsible, protective and loving mother. Beckett was ninety-nine percent sure she had no idea her daughter was out here alone. He intended to find out what was going on.

Ella appeared to be putting up some kind of flyer. She held a thin stack in her hand, stapling one to the telephone pole in front of her. She glanced up as his truck stopped at the curb beside her, and he was glad to see the wary expression on her face until she recognized him.

He rolled down the passenger window, leaned over the console to talk to her. The cry of gulls grew louder, the sound of the distant surf muted in the background. "Hey, Ella. What are you doing?"

"Putting up flyers," she answered, her face contorting with effort as she pushed another staple into the corner of the paper.

"Does your mom know you're out here?"

She stopped what she was doing, hesitated a moment before answering. "No." Her gaze swung to him, guilt clear on her face.

He bit back a sigh. She was way too young to be roaming around without adult supervision, even here. He would let her finish up, then take her home and talk to her about this on the way. And he was going to make her call her mom, too.

Glancing up the street, he caught the flashes of white on other poles where she had already stapled up more of them. "Is this part of your campaign?"

She put in another staple. "Yes. I called the pound today. Walter's still there, and that means he only has until tomorrow morning. If nobody adopts him by then, they'll put him to sleep." She lowered the stapler and stared at the sidewalk, biting her lip.

"Oh." *Great answer, Hollister. You have such a way with words. And kids.* "Can I see one of those?"

She looked up and stepped over to hand him a sheet through the passenger window.

Aw, man. Beckett was a hardened soldier who had served in his fair share of hellholes and survived many firefights, but even his battle-weary heart squeezed when he saw the flyer she'd made. A photocopy of something she'd drawn in what looked like colored pencil.

SAVE WALTER! it read at the top in bright red block letters. Beneath it was a hand-done drawing of a brown and white dog with short legs, long ears, tongue sticking out of its mouth, and the droopiest, saddest-looking eyes Beckett had ever seen on an animal. Below that, she'd listed Walter's redeeming attributes.

Friendly. Sweet. Good boy. Deserves a chance. She'd underlined that last bit, followed by the number and address of the pound.

Aww, hell. This kid had such a soft heart, he almost felt sorry for her. His had been soft like that once too, a lifetime ago, before reality had brought his childhood to a crashing, jarring halt the day his mother died. In the years since, he'd seen firsthand how ugly and unfair the world could be.

He switched his focus back to Ella, who was watching him anxiously, her little forehead wrinkled with worry. "How many of these have you put up so far?"

"Eleven. The school librarian printed off thirty for me, so I've got..." She screwed up her nose in concentration for a moment. "A lot more to go." She glanced up and down the street, her expression becoming distressed. "I might run out of telephone poles."

Okay, seriously, this kid. "I'll help you," he heard himself say.

Her face brightened. "You will?"

"Yes." Then he was taking her home where she belonged.

He shut off the engine, undid his seatbelt and climbed out of the cab. She put the flyer where she wanted it, and he dutifully stapled it in place for her.

But at their third telephone pole, a gust of cold wind passed through the buildings. Ella hunched into herself and shivered. "Where's your coat?" he asked her.

"I didn't bring one. I came here straight from school because I have to be done and back home for dinner at six. I have to get them all up—I can't let Walter down. I'm his only chance."

Hell. He looked down at the drawing of poor Walter, then back at Ella. "Why does Walter mean so much to you?"

A touch of anger sparked in her blue eyes, surprising him. "Because he's a good dog and the family who owned him are terrible people for dumping him just because he's old." She was quiet a moment, lowered her gaze. "My dad dumped my mom and I when I was little, and it doesn't feel good to not be wanted. It's not right."

Oh, fuck. No eight-year-old should ever feel that way. "No, it's not right." And he hated that Ella felt that her father had abandoned her.

After weighing his options, he glanced at his watch. The pound closed at five-thirty. They had time. "Come on, let's go see Walter."

Her big blue eyes widened in astonishment. "Really?"

"Yeah. But first I need you to call your mom to tell her where you are and ask if it's okay." He was a single guy without any kids, and even though pretty much all the locals here knew him, he wasn't putting her in his truck without Tiana's permission. "Do you know her number?"

"Yes." She took the cell phone he offered, dialed her mom and blurted out everything in a single sentence without any breaks between words. Then she was quiet a second. "I will. Bye." She beamed up at him as she handed the phone over. "She said okay but she wants to talk to you."

Good. "Tiana, it's Beckett."

"Beckett, oh my God, I'm so sorry about this. She's supposed to be at after-school care right now," she said, sounding exasperated.

"That's what I figured." Ella was looking everywhere but at him, her expression full of false innocence. "She's a determined little thing."

"Ugh, I know. She comes by it honestly, but she knows she can't be running around unsupervised, no matter what the reason. I'll give her a stern talking to when I get home tonight, I assure you. And thank you so much for stepping in, I really appreciate it."

Okay, now he felt better. "No problem. I'll drop her off at home as soon as we're done." He ended the call and motioned to Ella, who was now looking at him out of the corner of her eye. No doubt trying to gauge whether she was in trouble or not. "All right. Let's go. But from now on you don't wander around by yourself after school. Deal?"

She grinned. "Deal."

At the shelter she hopped out of his truck before he could come around to help her out, and raced for the front door, pausing at the last moment to hold it for him and avoid it slamming in his face. The smell of animals hit him at once, along with anxious barks and yips coming from the kennels in the back.

Ella was already explaining herself to the lady at the front desk, then turned to Beckett. "He's down this way, come on!" She all but ran down the hallway, and Beckett was starting to think he'd made a really big mistake by bringing her here. If they couldn't find Walter a home, it would be even more devastating for her now.

He found her around the corner crouched in front of a large cage, her little fingers curled around the chain link. "Walter, it's me. Hi, Walter. That's a good boy, come here," she coaxed, sticking her hand through one of the holes to reach for the dog hidden in the shadows beyond the reach of the overhead lights.

Beckett stopped behind her just as the mutt hobbled out of the darkness. Walter appeared to be some kind of basset hound mix. Maybe. And judging by the amount of white on that muzzle, he was freaking ancient.

His short, stubby little legs shuffled along stiffly, his long, fluffy brown ears flopping. His eyes drooped as much as his jowls, his tongue hanging weirdly out the side of his mouth. His back end swayed a little with each step, his slightly-feathered white tail drooping.

"Yes, that's a good boy, come here," Ella crooned, instinctively doing that female singsong thing that women did whenever they talked to animals or babies.

Walter waddled slowly up to her, stretched his neck out to sniff at the outstretched fingers and sat, peering up at them both with red-rimmed eyes. His left upper lip caught on what appeared to be one of the only teeth left in his mouth, distorting his already crooked face.

Also, Walter stank. The shelter staff obviously hadn't bathed him yet. Or maybe they had and he'd rolled in something.

Beckett wrinkled his nose as he caught a whiff of filthy, unwashed dog, overlaid with a sickly-sweet scent of garbage. Or poop.

"Oh, you're such a handsome boy," Ella said, praising the dog.

Beckett eyed her. Seriously, Walter was in the top five

ugliest dogs he had ever seen, easy. And he'd seen some ugly-ass curs overseas.

Walter sat there looking up at them both with those mournful eyes, unmoving.

Ella turned her head to gaze up at him. "Look, Mr. Beckett, he's grumpy, like you."

Beckett's eyebrows shot upward. Grumpy? Hell.

Ella looked back at the dog. "He's just sad because he was abandoned and now he doesn't have anyone to love him."

Well that is *like me.* He shoved the uncomfortable thought aside. It was a good thing that his ex had left him. He had been about to move out anyway. And he didn't miss her anymore. They were both way better off now.

Beckett stared down at the top of Ella's blond head. God, this innocent kid and her heartfelt words. They were far more powerful than she could ever realize.

Shifting his focus back to Walter, he met the dog's woebegone gaze as it stared up at him from the other side of the cage.

He mentally groaned. Great. How the hell was he supposed to walk away now, and let the dog be put down in the morning? Ella would be distraught, and he couldn't stand the thought of her being that upset over a damn dog when she already felt abandoned by her own father.

He sighed. He'd never considered getting a dog before now. Hadn't had one since he was a kid, and his life was so busy now. The whole situation made him think of Sierra and her big, soft heart, especially when it came to animals.

She'd always loved them. During his teen years she'd taken in countless strays she'd come across, a veritable menagerie of injured and orphaned creatures. Once, when she was about Ella's age, which would have made him about sixteen, she had made him climb through a hedge of blackberry brambles to capture an injured baby rabbit she'd spotted an eagle drop from its talons.

He'd come out of there over forty minutes later bleeding almost as badly as the wounded bunny, but he'd gotten it for her. She'd put the motionless, bloodstained thing in a shoebox with holes in the lid, placed it in the handlebar basket of her little pink bike and raced all the way into town as fast as she could to the vet clinic to save it. The clinic she now owned.

He'd always admired her compassion and drive. Didn't surprise him one bit that she'd made a successful career out of one of her passions. He used to be passionate about things too. But the only things he was passionate about anymore was her, and making his dad's business a success.

It took him a second to realize that Walter and Ella were both staring up at him now, watching him with identical sad, hopeful expressions.

Well, fuck. He folded his arms across his chest and muttered, "How much is the adoption fee?"

Forty minutes later he walked out of the shelter carrying a forty-pound bag of dog food, the proud owner of an ancient, filthy and grumpy mutt nobody else wanted.

A hundred-and-fifty bucks to adopt a dog that was practically at death's door. Beckett shook his head at himself as he walked to his truck. He must have lost his damn mind.

"This is the best day *ever*," Ella gushed, all but skipping beside him, Walter trailing behind her on a new leash Beckett had also shelled out for. Purple, because Ella had picked it.

Beckett grunted in response and opened the back door of the truck cab. He tossed the food in first, then turned to look down at Walter. The dog gazed up at him with a *shoot me now* expression, seeming to either not grasp or appreciate that he'd just been saved from the atomic needle at the eleventh hour.

Ignoring the twinge of pain in his lower back, Beckett crouched down to sit on his haunches in front of the dog. Two feet apart, he and Walter eyed each other for a long moment in mutual suspicion. "You bite me, I'm taking you right back inside," he warned the dog, who in truth was already growing on him a little.

"He won't bite you," Ella said in a tone that said she thought the idea was completely ridiculous. "He's grateful that you rescued him. And besides, he barely has any teeth left."

True.

Beckett scooped up the pungent dog, who was surprisingly heavy given how bony he looked, and lifted him onto the back seat. Walter promptly plunked his arthritic back end down and let out a low groan of what sounded like mingled pain and relief.

Yeah, you and me both, buddy.

Beckett shut the door and opened Ella's, helping her up onto the seat. She immediately swung around to look at Walter. "Look how happy he is," she said, beaming as Beckett came around to slide in behind the wheel.

He glanced over his shoulder. Walter gazed back at him with that droopy-eyed stare, tongue sticking out the side of his floppy mouth, looking about as blasé as a dog could get. He was actually kinda cute, in a so-ugly-he's-cute way.

Well, I've gone and done it now. He was officially a dog owner. Too late to change his mind at this point. "Put on your seatbelt," he said to Ella gruffly, and fired up the engine.

"We'd better stop in town and take down all the posters," she said as he steered out of the empty parking lot. "I don't want anyone to get their hopes up and go to the pound to adopt Walter, then find out he's gone."

Yeah, like there was any chance of that happening. Still, Beckett dutifully stopped at every telephone pole along Front Street, waiting while she hopped out and took down each flyer before climbing back into the truck and moving to the next one.

On the way home from town she sat in the back next to Walter, fussing over him, petting him all over. "Where is he going to sleep, Mr. Beckett? On your bed?"

What? No damn way that was happening. "He can sleep downstairs on the rug by the front door."

When he glanced in the rearview mirror Ella's eyes were wide with horror and condemnation. "He won't like that. He's old, and dogs are pack animals. It's mean to make him be alone, especially at night. He already feels abandoned. And he needs a real bed to sleep in so it won't hurt his back. Remember? The lady said he's got a bad back."

Yet another thing they had in common. Both grumpy, both with bad backs. At least Beckett didn't smell. "I'll make sure he's comfy," he muttered. No damn way that flea-bitten, stinky mutt was coming anywhere near his bedroom though. Walter needed a bath, asap.

"You can get him a memory foam bed at the pet store tomorrow," she suggested, back to petting Walter. "I bet that would help his back."

Memory foam? For a dog? Christ. "I'll look into it," was all he said, fighting the scowl trying to crease his forehead. She and most everybody else around here already thought he was grumpy. No need to prove them right.

He passed his dad's place and continued down Salt Spray Lane to the house where she lived with her mother. Tiana's car was parked out front. "Tell your mom I said hi," Beckett told her.

"I will. Can I come by after my after-school care tomorrow to play with Walter? If I check with my mom first? I can walk him for you, and feed him his supper if you're not home yet."

"Sure. You remember where the spare key is?"

"Yes." Beaming, Ella undid her seatbelt and took him by surprise by leaning between the front seats to wrap her arms around his neck. "Thank you, Mr. Beckett, for saving Walter. You're my hero. And his, too." She kissed his scruffy cheek, popped the door open and hopped out.

A flash of pain stabbed beneath his ribcage. Her words were like an arrow to the chest, hitting the one gap in the armor plating around his jaded heart.

A hero.

He'd joined the military with illusions of becoming just that, but he hadn't felt like one in forever. Not given all the men he'd lost, and the lives he'd taken in the name of duty. The ones he'd killed with a weapon as well as the ones he hadn't been able to save.

Faces flashed through his mind. Former teammates. Some of them laughing. Some of them in agony as they died in front of him.

The hostages from the Syria mission. All dead now.

With effort, he pulled out of the black memories and looked for Ella. She was already racing for her front door, blond ponytail streaming behind her.

"Mom! Mom, we saved Walter!" she cried as she reached the top step that led to her porch.

Beckett drew in a deep breath and let it out slowly, the sudden crushing pressure in his chest easing a little. He waited until Ella threw the front door open, spun around to wave, then disappeared inside.

He'd saved a dog's life and made a little girl's month. A better day's work than he'd done in recent memory.

He turned a little in his seat to look back at his new furry roommate, still perched on the back seat. He hadn't done anything that had made a difference in a damn long time. Maybe saving an old dog wasn't much, but it was something, and it had put a smile on Ella's face.

At any rate, for better or worse, Walter was his

responsibility now.

"Well, Walter, guess it's just you and me now. Let's go home and get you cleaned up."

As soon as they got inside, Beckett was putting him in the shower for a serious date with a shampoo bottle. And first thing in the morning—providing old Walter made it through the night—he was making an appointment to take him in to see Sierra.

And just maybe she'd see him as a hero too.

Chapter Eight

In the back room of the clinic Sierra checked the mama dog and pups she'd just delivered via C-section, gave the groggy new mother's head a comforting stroke and closed the cage door. "Macy, when's my next patient?" she asked over her shoulder. She'd been working nonstop since eight and needed to eat.

"He's already here," her assistant answered.

Sierra blinked. "What? I thought I had a break now."

"New patient called in first thing this morning. Said he's a friend of yours. I had to bump him for the emergency C-section, so I squeezed him in now."

Oh. "Who is it?"

"Can't remember. Want me to go look it up?"

"No, just send him in." She turned to grab her stethoscope from the stainless steel table, and stopped in the act of turning toward the door as Beckett walked in. A little blond girl was right on his heels, holding the end of a leash.

He was literally the last person on earth she had expected to see here. Sierra glanced between him and the girl in surprise. What in the...?

"Hi," he said, then glanced back at the girl. "This is

Ella."

Ella gave the leash a tug. "Walter. Come."

"Uh, hi." Sierra watched in fascination as an elderly basset mix waddled stiffly into her exam room. The dog was…ancient. She glanced up at Beckett, trying to put the pieces together. Must be the girl's dog. "Walter?"

"I adopted him last night from the shelter."

Her eyebrows shot up at that. "Really?" That didn't seem like something he would do. And how did the girl come into this then?

He lifted a broad shoulder, his muscles flexing under the fabric of his shirt. God, he was sexy. "Long story. Anyway, they didn't know much about him except that he was abandoned at the dump."

"His family brought him there and just left him," Ella said in disgust. "My mom and I took him to the shelter, but she wouldn't let me keep him." She smiled up at Beckett, gave him an adoring look. "They were going to put him to sleep this morning, but Mr. Beckett saved him."

Beckett cleared his throat, looking uncomfortable, and on a man that strong and tough, it was adorable. "We don't know anything else about his history. He has a microchip. The shelter contacted the family, but they didn't want him back. I thought I'd better bring him in and get him checked out."

The dog stopped next to Beckett and seemed to sag, all of his folds and wrinkles drooping along with his eyes, tongue and ears. He was so adorably ugly she had to suppress a giggle. "Okay. Can you put him up on the table here?" She motioned behind her.

"Sure." He bent, gently scooped up the dog to lift him up onto the exam table for her, and it seemed like he covered a wince as he straightened. "He's pretty old."

From the amount of white on the muzzle and the advanced arthritis she was pretty sure he had, that was an understatement. "Yeah, I'll say." She stroked Walter's head, smoothed her hand down his neck, palpating the prominent spine and ribs. "He's thin." It made her angry. There was a special place in hell for people who mistreated animals, including dumping their pets when they were no longer wanted or became too much trouble.

"The shelter sold me a special food for senior dogs. He ate everything I gave him for dinner and breakfast. And I didn't see any fleas or anything when I gave him a shower last night."

"You put him in the shower?" She couldn't help but grin at the image as she continued her examination, until she pictured Beckett naked in the shower too, and wound up fumbling with her stethoscope.

"He stank. So yeah."

She liked this unexpected hint of softness from Beckett. Liked it a lot. "His skin is in good condition," she said, checking him over. She examined his ears. "Ears are surprisingly clean." The mouth. "Only a few teeth left, and a pretty decent amount of plaque on them. Might have to schedule a cleaning soon."

She palpated his belly, checked the size of his kidneys, listened to his heart and lungs. "A nice, healthy ticker, Walter, and your lungs are clear," she said, giving the dog's floppy ears a scratch. Had to be mixed with a spaniel breed, given the wavy fur on them and the feathery tail. "Not bad for a senior citizen."

The end of his tail moved feebly.

"Did you see that, Mr. Beckett? He likes her," Ella said, watching Walter with a proud expression.

"Yeah, I saw," Beckett said, watching Sierra work.

"Well I like Walter too," she told them. "I'm going to give him some vaccines just to be sure he's protected, and some heartworm and flea medication. Then I'm clipping his nails, because he's in dire need of a pawdicure."

Ella giggled at the pun, and Sierra gave her a wink.

Walter didn't even flinch as she administered the injections and clipped his nails. It was like he was shut down inside. She couldn't blame him after what he'd been through. Poor guy. "I would increase his food for the next week or so, try to put a couple of pounds on him," she said to Beckett.

"All right."

"Okay, Walter, I think we're all done here. And you were such a good boy you earned yourself a cookie out front." She went to reach for him but Beckett picked him up for her and placed him on the ground. When he straightened he did so slowly, his posture stiff. "You hurt yourself?" she asked.

"No, I'm fine."

Well something was hurting him. She smiled at Ella. "Maybe you could give Walter his cookie at the desk and then take him out for a short walk up and down the street while Beckett and I finish up?"

The girl's eyes lit up. "Sure! Come on, Walter." The dog waddled after her, his head bent low, a long-suffering expression on his face.

When the exam room door swung shut, Sierra entered everything into the computer system before turning to face Beckett. "I didn't know you even liked dogs."

He lifted a shoulder. "I like 'em. Just never thought I would get one. At least not for a long while yet, until I'm more settled and things quiet down some."

Until after his dad passed, he meant.

A pang of sympathy speared her. He was dealing with so much, trying to handle everything all on his own, never asking for help and keeping everyone at arms length while he did it.

"What about you, why don't you have a dog? Or a cat? You love animals."

"I do, but I'm still nursing a broken heart after putting Taffy down." Her shepherd cross rescue she'd had for three wonderful years. "It's only been six months. I'm not ready yet."

"Oh. I didn't know. Sorry."

"It's okay. He passed away while you were overseas." She leaned a hip against the exam table. "So. In spite of everything going on in your life, you decided to rescue a centenarian dog from death row at the eleventh hour, huh?"

He shrugged. "Ella's really attached to him. I couldn't let them put him down, and he's so old I figured he won't be that much trouble."

Uh-huh. He wasn't fooling her. *I see you, Beckett Hollister, and your tender, squishy insides.* Oh, man, this side of him made him even more dangerous to her. "No, I don't think he will be."

"How old do you think he is, anyway?"

"I'd say at least thirteen, maybe more. The good news is, he's not going to be very active. In fact, I'd guess he'll be sleeping most of his remaining days away. A walk up and down the lane once a day will be more than enough exercise for him."

Beckett nodded, looking around the room rather than at her.

Sierra crossed her arms, overcome by curiosity. "So who's Ella?"

His deep brown eyes swung back to her. "She and her mom are in the rental house down the lane from me. Moved in about a month before I came home."

"Oh. And you...hang out with her often enough to feel obligated to adopt Walter for her?"

He grimaced, rubbed the back of his neck. "It's weird, right? I knew the two of us together looked weird."

"Well, not in a creepy way." Only because she knew Beckett, and that he was a good guy beneath that rough exterior. But to others, yeah, it probably looked weird that he was hanging out with a young girl he wasn't related to.

She had known a child predator and Beckett was *nothing* like him. "Are you and her mom...?" She let the sentence dangle, got a frown in return.

"No, nothing like that. She's dating someone, I've seen him drive by and his car parked in their driveway the past few weeks. For some reason Ella's taken to hanging out on my porch after school instead of going home. Maybe she's lonely, I dunno, but most school days she's there when I get home, and stays until her mom gets back from work." He shrugged. "Tiana's got her signed up for after-school care now."

"Ah." It annoyed Sierra a little that she was so relieved he wasn't involved with Ella's mom. Jealousy didn't become her. "Yeah, I guess you don't have much time for dating these days, huh?" She couldn't believe she'd said that. What the hell was she doing, fishing like this? That wasn't exactly the hallmark of getting over him, was it?

"No. You?"

He was only asking to be polite. She turned away to shrug out of her lab coat, grabbed a disinfectant wipe to quickly clean the exam table. "I date here and there." Like her upcoming second date on Friday night with a guy she'd been matched with through an online dating site. Though she'd already sent off an excuse by text this morning to cancel. He wasn't her type and she was tired of trying to force something out of nothing. "Not anything serious since Jeff and I broke up last year."

It didn't matter how many guys she went out with. None of them ever seemed to measure up to Beckett in her eyes anyhow, which sucked for her.

"I heard about that."

"We weren't meant to be." In hindsight, she had walked away later than she should have in that instance too. At least she hadn't let him move in to her cottage. All she'd had to pack up when she ended things were a few drawers in the bathroom and one box of clothes from her closet. "We've both moved on."

"I know how that goes."

Too bad I can't seem to move on from the thought of you and me.

She ignored the mental barb, straightened, and caught Beckett staring at her butt when she glanced back.

He looked up so fast that for a moment she wondered whether she'd imagined it. His gaze snapped to hers for an instant then darted away, back to examining the posters about canine and feline dental and heart disease on the walls. Pretending nothing had happened.

No, he had definitely been checking out her ass. What was that about? Had he finally realized she was a grown woman all of a sudden? Because sure as hell she'd never noticed him checking her out before.

You're making too much of it. He's a guy. They check women out. Let it go.

A subtle tension formed between them as he avoided her gaze for a moment longer. Finally, she cleared her throat. "I just have to sign Walter's rabies and bordetella certificate. If you want to go out front, Macy will help you settle the bill and I'll be right out."

"Sounds good."

The moment the door shut behind him she drew in a deep breath, let it out slowly as she thought about his eyes on her ass. "Stop it. You know it wouldn't work out."

An irritated sound came from her throat. Simply putting Beckett out of her mind wasn't working, especially now that she'd caught him checking her out *and* he'd saved Walter. Seriously, how was she supposed to resist a man like that, even though common sense told her to?

When the paperwork was signed she took it out front, allowing herself to drink in every masculine detail about Beckett as he paid the bill. Her heart thumped when his gaze swung to her. "You didn't charge me for the exam and nail clipping."

"Nope. One good deed deserves another, don't you think?"

"I didn't bring him here hoping for a discount. I brought him here because you're the best vet on the coast."

She grinned, flattered that he thought so. "Well not the *whole* coast. But thank you. And no, you're still not paying for the exam or nail clipping."

He seemed annoyed by that, but then nodded and muttered a semi-gracious "Thank you."

"You're welcome. I'm finished here at just before six. When I'm done I'll pop by with some dog supplies we've got laying around here. That sound okay?"

"Only if you let me buy you dinner."

Her heart fluttered for an instant before her common sense squashed it. *He's not asking you out on a date, dummy. He's trying to repay you.*

She'd take it, and maybe even attempt to put a few cracks in his formidable emotional armor while she was at it. It was high time she got to the bottom of why he'd been so distant with her. "Deal."

Chapter Nine

Beckett glanced around the kitchen one last time to make sure everything was tidy, even though he'd just cleaned up ten minutes before. It was quarter after six. Sierra was coming soon and he wanted the place to be presentable. He'd even set the table and put the Chinese takeout into serving bowls rather than leaving it in the tinfoil containers.

Look at you, getting all fancy.

He scowled at the voice in his head. *Shut up.*

She'd totally caught him staring at her ass earlier. Christ. His entire military career, he'd prided himself on his self-discipline. Had earned a reputation for it. What was it about her that reduced him to a damn horny teenager when she was around?

He swung around to face the front screen door as light, quick footsteps sounded on the steps. Ella appeared at the top, Walter following slowly behind her. "We're back," she announced, pushing the decorative screen door open with a creak.

His mom had thought the creak was charming, and had forbidden his father from oiling it. Beckett hadn't touched it. Every time he heard that creak now, he thought of her. "How did it go?"

"Slow, but I think he liked it. He sort of wagged his tail a couple of times. We saw a squirrel and all he did was growl at it."

"That's because he's lazy." Not that Beckett blamed him. Old fella deserved the down time in his golden years.

"Well, he's retired."

Beckett huffed out a laugh and went over to grab a bottle of wine from the pantry.

Ella eyed the table, then looked at him. "You set a place for me?"

Tiana wouldn't be home from work for a couple more hours, and with Ella here, he wouldn't be tempted to do anything stupid with Sierra. "Mm-hmm. I texted to ask your mom if it's okay, but you don't have to stay if you don't want to."

A big smile broke over her face. "I want to. Thank you."

He had a serious soft spot for this kid. And ugly, unwanted dogs, apparently. As well as the gorgeous, successful town veterinarian. "Sure. What do you want to drink with supper? I've got water, milk, and some lemonade."

"Milk, please." She sat herself in one of the chairs while Walter waddled over and settled under the table with a loud groan.

"Knock knock."

They both looked over as Sierra came up the front steps, a big box in her hands.

Beckett rushed over to let her in. "Hey. What's all this?" She was hot as hell in her violet fitted top that hugged her breasts and a pair of snug, dark jeans. Her chestnut-brown hair was loose around her shoulders, the setting sun glowing in it. She looked sexy and edible and...

And maybe this was a really bad idea, even with Ella here to act as a buffer.

"Just some things I thought Walter might use." She breezed past him, her tantalizing scent trailing after her. She bent to set the box down on the floor, giving him another lust-fueling view of her ass, and pulled out a big folded-up dog bed. "I wasn't sure if you had one for him already, but even if you do, you can never have too many dog beds. This one's memory foam. Orthopedic grade."

Ella shot Beckett a smug look from over at the table. He cracked a grin. "That so?"

"And here are some toys and chewies that will help clean his few remaining teeth a bit if he feels like chewing." She got down on her knees beside the table and reached under it to give one to the dog. "Here, Walter. What do you think of this, huh?"

Beckett gladly took the opportunity to stare at her ass some more. Her position made him imagine peeling her jeans and panties down her thighs, his mouth busy on the side of her neck.

He envisioned grasping her hips while she stayed on her hands and knees, entering her from behind while he wound a fistful of her hair around his wrist, controlling every movement. Working her sweet spots with his hands and cock until she was frantic and begging for release.

Christ. Now the crotch of his jeans was strangling him. And he was damn glad they weren't alone together, because Sierra seriously tested his control.

She backed out from under the table, and this time he managed to wrench his eyes off her rear end before she turned her head and caught him red-handed. "I think he likes it."

Oh, he likes it. Too goddamn much. "Good. You hungry?"

"Starving."

Him, too. But what he wanted was forbidden, and he had to remember it.

"Then let's eat." He pulled out a chair for her, and her

little smile of thanks warmed him inside. He pushed her in, brought over a glass of wine for her.

She blinked at him in surprise. "You remembered my favorite wine?"

He remembered pretty much everything about her. "Yeah, of course, it's from the vineyard down at Seaview Farms." There were always a couple bottles of it out whenever he went to her or Noah's place for a family dinner or get together with friends.

"Well that's very sweet of you, and I appreciate it." She held it up in a toast. "I've earned this today. Cheers, Ella." She tapped her glass to Ella's milk glass. "Beckett."

He tapped his beer bottle to her glass.

Sierra mostly chatted with Ella while they ate, asking her about school, the friends she had made since moving to Crimson Point.

"How come it's called that, anyway?" Ella asked.

"What, Crimson Point?" Beckett said.

"Yes."

"Because a long time ago, back in 1886, a big wooden passenger ship got caught in a storm just off the coast of the point out there." He pointed toward the back porch, with the view of the sea beyond, and in the distance, the lighthouse perched atop the end of the cliff. "It happened at night, so it was really dark and there was no lighthouse here at the time yet."

Her eyes were wide, her little face serious as he continued.

"The ship was wrecked on the rocks just offshore, and the sea was so rough that out of forty-one passengers, only three survived. Settlers here renamed the area Crimson Point because the legend says the water turned red because of..." He paused. Pretty gory stuff to tell an eight-year-old, especially over dinner that included a red sweet-and-sour sauce.

"The dead people's blood?" Ella asked, wide-eyed.

"Uh, yes. I doubt it's true, but that's how it got the name. And a year later the lighthouse was put up so no other ships would wreck here." Cheerful ending for the win.

"Oh." She turned in her chair to look toward the back porch and the view beyond it. "Some kids at school said the point is haunted." She looked back at Beckett.

"Do you think that's true?"

"What do *you* think?" she prompted.

Yeah, no fooling this little one. "I think it's possible."

"Did you ever see ghosts out there at night?"

"A few times, yeah." But he'd seen the ones trapped inside his head a lot more often than that.

Ella got quiet.

"They're not mean ghosts, though," Sierra put in, nudging his knee under the table and saving him from making up something ridiculous to put Ella's mind at ease. "They're just out on the beach trying to look for their lost friends and family, I think."

Ella's mouth turned down at the corners. "Oh, that's so sad…"

"It is. But with the lighthouse, nothing like that has ever happened here again," Beckett finished. "And it would be worse for the people who died if everyone forgot about them and their story." Even as he said it, pain lanced his ribcage.

Sierra darted a look at him, understanding clear in her eyes. He'd lost a lot of friends overseas. He'd lost his mom. At least if he remembered them, they weren't completely gone.

From under the table Walter gave a deep woof. He scrambled to his feet and plodded for the front door, floppy ears perked. A moment later, the sound of a car engine cut through the quiet.

"My mom's here," Ella said, hopping down from her chair. She stopped, turned back to grab her plate and glass, shooting him a guilty glance. "Thank you for dinner. And for taking me with you and Walter to see Miss Sierra earlier."

"You're welcome." He got up and stopped at the front door while she rinsed her plate and cup and put them in the dishwasher. Man, she was such a little sweetheart. He'd never considered himself father material, but Ella made him reconsider that. Maybe someday, if he found the right woman.

Like the one sitting at his kitchen table right now.

At the door Ella slipped her shoes on. "Can I come back tomorrow and visit Walter again after school?"

Like he was gonna say no to that face? "Aren't you in after-school care?"

She hesitated. "No. My mom's boyfriend is coming over early to make us dinner."

"Okay. Then sure. As long as it's okay with your mom."

Her expression filled with relief. "Thanks. Good night. Bye, Miss Sierra," she said over her shoulder on the way out the door.

"Bye, Ella."

Tiana was already out of the car. She waved and called out to Beckett. "Thanks for having her over. I hope she wasn't a bother."

"No, not at all. She's welcome here anytime."

"I appreciate that. She's over the moon about Walter." She greeted her daughter with a sunny smile and a big hug. "Brian's coming over later, and he's bringing dessert. Isn't that nice?"

Ella mumbled something and cast a look back at Beckett that he couldn't decipher, then followed her mother to the car without further comment.

Beckett shut the screen door and turned back to Sierra. And just like that, the atmosphere went from relaxed to a subtle tension permeating the room. They'd eaten dinner.

Now what? He should be hoping she would leave, but instead found himself thinking up excuses to get her to stay. Not his smartest move.

"Want to go sit out on the back porch for a bit?" he heard himself ask. "Sun's about to set."

Surprise flashed in her gorgeous blue eyes, but she nodded. "I'd like that."

Him, too. The masochist in him wanted to spend more time with her.

The wary, jaded part was tired of being alone.

Ignoring that last thought, he took their drinks and pushed open the French door that led to the back porch. Four antique rocking chairs graced the deck planks that overlooked the ocean, each painted a different color. His mom's was a soft pink, his dad's a deep blue, and Beckett's a dark teal green. He sat in that one while Sierra took the pale blue one beside his, and handed her the wineglass.

She flashed him a smile that hit him straight in the heart, and stared out at the view. "This is just as incredible as I remember it," she murmured. She was so damn gorgeous, didn't even seem to realize it. And that only made her more beautiful to him. "It's such a stunning, special place. I'm glad you decided to move back in."

"Didn't have much choice," he said with a wry grin. "I was going to rent somewhere but my dad wouldn't hear of it. And the truth is, I've missed this place." No matter where he went or how long he'd been gone, this would always be home. Even with the all the bittersweet memories and reminders here, he didn't want to leave.

"It's a piece of you. Of all of you," she said, motioning to his parents' rockers.

"Yes." He glanced up at the hand-painted gingerbread trim around the porch ceiling, the manicured garden edging the emerald lawn that spilled down toward the cliff's edge. Below them in the distance, the sun cast gold and peach rays across the sparkling ocean, rolling waves tipped with white foam echoing a muted roar as they crashed onto the shimmering beach.

A sense of peace filled him as they sat looking out at the water. He liked having Sierra here, just the two of them. Enjoyed just being with her, because she seemed to be the only one who could make the ghosts disappear.

She was watching him again. "Thank you for inviting me over. I was actually starting to get a complex where you're concerned, but this gesture makes me feel a little better. Even though I'm pretty sure you asked me over as a thank you."

He angled his head toward her. "What do you mean, a complex?"

She studied his eyes for a moment, the setting sun illuminating hers in a kaleidoscope of different shades of blue. He could fall into them until he drowned if he wasn't careful. "Well, it sure seems like you've been going out of your way to avoid me since you got back home."

Beckett glanced away, staring out at the water. *Yeah, because I want to do bad, bad things to you and it would ruin everything between us and our families.* He refused to jeopardize that. For him the consequences were too high.

"Just been busy, that's all." Damn, with her so close it was harder and harder to hold back his feelings. Impossible not to imagine what it would be like to slide his hands into those thick, shiny waves, hold her still while he learned the shape of that sexy mouth. Her taste. Find out what little sounds she would make as he stroked and teased and caressed. Learn every curve and hollow of her fantasy-worthy shape.

Shit. What would it be like to get her naked, find every sensitive place on her body and then sink inside of her? Stay locked there and absorb the warmth she surrounded him with just by walking into the same room?

He mentally shook himself. *Nope. Noah's little sister. She's your* friend, *dickhead. You don't fuck your friends.* Because that would fuck up everything.

She tipped her head to the side, considering him. "You sure?"

"Yeah." His voice sounded rough.

She narrowed her eyes. "Not sure I believe you. You've been...distant and kind of gruff with me. For the past few years, actually."

Since the divorce and finally admitting to himself that he wanted her. But shit, in keeping his distance he hadn't meant to hurt her. He wasn't sure what to say.

"Did I do something wrong?"

Yeah, you suddenly turned from Noah's sister into the one woman I can't stop fantasizing about. He also knew and adored her, and that made it so much worse. "No."

Her expression said she didn't buy it. "I hate feeling like you can't stand to be around me."

That's what she thought?

He shifted in his chair, uncomfortable as hell. While he wanted to put her at ease, he couldn't tell her why he'd tried to keep her at arm's length this whole time. If she was interested in him—and he was pretty sure she was—admitting it would be a disaster.

"You haven't done anything. I've just...got a lot going on right now. Sorry I made you feel that way." He hoped like hell she would let it go, because with every question her hurt cut into him a little deeper and put him one step closer to blurting out his feelings.

"All right, then. So we're still friends?" She gave him a coaxing smile, a teasing light in her eyes.

He wanted to be a hell of a lot more than that. But he also didn't want to lose her or potentially damage his friendship with Noah if things didn't work out. Life experience had taught him there was a good chance they wouldn't.

It stirred up his emotions, his worst fear looming bright in his mind. He wasn't going to do anything that posed a risk to his friendship with her and Noah. They and their parents were his alternate family. With his dad's time running out, Beckett already faced a bleak future alone. Without the Buchanans, his life would be totally empty.

He shoved the agonizing thought aside. "Of course we're still friends."

"Good." Finally she sat back and sipped her wine.

"I'll even go back to calling you squirt, if you want."

Sierra shot him a dark look. "Don't you dare."

His lips quirked, remembering that day. She'd been just a kid, not much older than Ella, but she'd insisted on tagging along with him and Noah to the beach to dig for clams for a clambake they were planning that night. "I thought it was funny."

"Of course you did. That clam squirted me right in the eye when I picked it up." She aimed a gratified smile at him. "I got the last laugh, though, because I ate him later. So don't call me squirt. Makes me feel nine years old all over again."

Would be a hell of a lot better if he could still see her as nine in his mind. "All right. I'll try not to give into the temptation." Of calling her by the old nickname, and this new, powerful temptation she posed simply by being near him.

"You better not."

He exhaled a quiet breath, grateful for the reprieve, but unable to find peace with her so close yet frustratingly out of reach.

Instead he watched the ocean, took a measure of solace in the rhythm of the rolling waves, aware of everything about her. Her scent. The lines of her profile. The way the breeze tousled her hair.

He tightened his grip on his beer bottle, his free hand curling into a fist on his thigh to stem the urge to reach out and touch her. He couldn't have her, didn't dare consider it, and besides, his track record with relationships was shit. Christ, just look at his failed marriage, and him and Carter. A man he'd served on the front lines with for years. Their relationship was now broken beyond repair.

The darkness inside him began to spread, pulling his mood toward the edge of the black pit in his soul.

Sierra was sweet and gentle. Risks to their friendship and family dynamics aside, why the hell would she want to get involved with him?

He might be eight years older chronologically, but his soul was ten times older than hers. He was a combat-hardened soldier with all the issues that brought, and lugging around a ton of baggage on his conscience.

She didn't need that shit. Wouldn't want him if she truly understood how damaged he was inside.

Beckett clung to his resolve, a sense of relief washing over him. Those were damn good reasons to remain firmly in friendship territory. Because if his control around her slipped, he would be in a shitload of trouble. Sierra was everything he had ever wanted in a woman, and he knew himself.

And so he knew that if they ever crossed that invisible line, there was no way he would ever let her go.

****

"Did you hear Hollister has a dog now?" the waitress said to the customer in the next booth.

What?

"No, really?" a lady said. "I didn't know he even liked dogs."

"Oh, it's the cutest story," the waitress gushed. "I saw him as he brought the dog into the vet clinic this afternoon and heard the whole story. It's an old mutt that looked like it was on its last leg. Apparently he rescued it from the shelter at the last moment before closing yesterday because his little neighbor had fallen in love with it."

"Tiana's daughter?"

"*Yes.* Isn't that the sweetest story?"

The woman sighed. "Lord, if I was twenty years younger, I'd go after him myself," she said with a chuckle. "It's so nice to have a hero like him living in Crimson Point."

Hero.

That word triggered the deep, burning rage that was getting harder and harder to contain. The whole fucking town saw Hollister that way. They glorified him without knowing the facts.

The women's conversation faded into the background. It was suddenly hard to draw in air, the unfairness of it all fueling the rage, stealing the ability to breathe.

That damn dog was just another reason for the people of Crimson Point to worship their hero. But they didn't know him. Not the real him. They didn't know all the dark, dirty secrets he hid.

But I do.

It wasn't the original plan, but the dog might actually help make this easier. Might provide an easier way to get to him. Yeah. Rather than a brute assault, make it look like a coincidence. Maybe meet up with him at the park or something while he was out walking the dog, or along the beach near his house.

Trying to surprise Hollister at his parents' house was too risky. He was too well trained and battle hardened, nearly impossible to sneak up on.

But a familiar face could get up close.

A familiar face could get close enough to catch him totally off guard when he was relaxed, in a place he felt safe. Trained as he was, he could still be attacked by a person he felt safe with.

KAYLEA CROSS

The rage receded slightly, replaced by a steely resolve. Time to go home.

Front Street was teeming with people tonight, families and tourists out enjoying dinner and the sunset. Beyond the buildings along the point, brightly-colored kites fluttered in the crimson and peach-tinted sky.

The idyllic scene only made the pain and anger grow hotter. Deadlier. *I'll never have any of this. Not now that Hollister has destroyed my life.*

Did he ever think about what he'd done? What he *hadn't* done? The cost of it, to the people he'd hurt?

No, of course not. Meanwhile everyone here in this stupid fucking town was happy to keep perpetuating the myth of their hometown hero.

Not for long, though. Soon enough Hollister would get a reminder of what he really was—a traitorous failure.

He'd turned his back on a fellow brother-in-arms. That was unforgivable. And for that he would die.

But before that happened, some psychological torment was called for.

Chapter Ten

Molly fought the urge to tap her foot on the floor as she sat in the doctor's waiting room with her husband. A man who was now pretty much a stranger to her in every way. They'd driven to Portland at first light to be here for this emergency appointment with the specialist.

This had to work. If it didn't, she had no idea what to do next.

Carter paced the small room like a caged lion, occasionally raking a hand through his too-long hair. It was impossible for her to gauge or even guess at his true mood. Before his injury he'd had his hair cut short every four weeks religiously. Now he didn't seem to care about how he looked. Didn't seem to care about much at all except how bitter he was about everything, who had wronged him, and what the world owed him for his service and suffering.

He'd never once stopped to think that she might be suffering as well.

She didn't bother telling him to stop pacing and sit, since that would just get her snapped at and she was sick of it. She'd tried so hard to stay optimistic throughout this whole thing, be the sunshine to Carter's constant gloom. That wasn't possible anymore.

Her happy mask was slipping, and the small ray of hope she'd clung to for so long was fading every day. Just when she thought Carter had finally hit rock bottom, he'd reach a new low. Like getting fired from his job by the man who had gotten it for him in the first place.

The doctor finally arrived. A middle-aged man in a lab coat and holding a clipboard. He smiled at them. "Mr. and Mrs. Boyd. Hello."

Carter finally stopped moving and stepped back to lean against the wall, his massive arms folded across his chest, a wary expression on his still-handsome, unshaven face. His eyes looked bruised underneath, a hollowness to them that stirred unease in the pit of her stomach.

The doctor sat in his chair beside the small desk. "I understand you've been having more problems regulating your emotional state."

Carter didn't answer, merely continued to stare a hole through the man, his hostility obvious, so Molly jumped in to defuse the tension. "Yes. The meds you've got him on aren't helping. He's not sleeping and he's not eating. He's losing weight and..." She glanced at Carter, decided to hell with it and told the whole truth. "There was a confrontation at his work the other day. He lost his job."

The doctor frowned. "I'm sorry to hear that." He focused on Carter. "Are you still having nightmares? Flashbacks?"

"What do you think?" Carter snarled.

"I'm asking you."

"Yeah, every damn night."

"What about suicidal thoughts?"

"Every damn day."

Molly swallowed, forced herself to sit still. The tension pouring off Carter alarmed her. He was like a volcano inside, building up to an eruption. She understood the frustration, but the lack of control over his anger was totally out of character and frankly frightening.

"And what about your relationship?" the doctor asked them both. "Are things better between the two of you?"

Molly was uncomfortable going there, it felt like a betrayal to Carter, but he clearly wasn't going to answer, so she had to. "No. Things have been…more and more unstable."

"In what way?"

She drew a breath. "He's angry. Really angry, all the time. Every little thing will set him off."

The doctor appeared alarmed, glanced between the two of them. "Has there been any violent episodes?"

Molly hesitated. "A few times. Not toward me, but…yes. Some broken lamps, thrown dishes. Things like that." She risked a glance at Carter, flinched inside at the look on his face. Rage. Betrayal.

"I see." The doctor scribbled some notes down on the clipboard. "Well, we can increase the dosage of the—"

"I don't want any more of your fucking drugs," Carter snapped, making her and the doctor tense and look at him sharply. Above his untrimmed beard, his cheeks were a dull red, his eyes glittering. "They don't help, and I already can't function as it is. I can't even get it up anymore. Is that any kind of life? Huh? I can't even fuck my wife now."

Blood rushed to her face. "Carter," she whispered, horrified.

He cut her a savage glance. "What? He wanted to know how I'm doing." He turned his searing gaze to the doctor. "I'm fucking losing my mind, all right? I'm dying inside, bit by bit." He thrust an accusatory finger at the man, rage and frustration pulsing off him in palpable waves. "You said you would help me. That all these damn drugs you've got me on would help, but they're not." His face got even redder. "Why won't you fucking *help* me?" He whirled and slammed his fist into the wall so hard it cracked the drywall.

Molly gasped and shot to her feet, lunging for him as the doctor scrambled back against the far wall. She grabbed hold of Carter's wrist, her heart in her throat. "Carter. No. Don't do this. Please." The muscle and tendons under her fingers were like steel cables drawn too tight. Ready to snap. She could feel the rage seething inside him and it brought the sting of tears to the back of her throat and eyes.

Her plea seemed to reach him because he relaxed a fraction and lowered his arm. His knuckles were split and bleeding, his chest rising and falling with rapid breaths.

The doctor was pale as he collected himself. "You need an increased dosage of the mood stabilizers. And we'll do another CT scan to see what's going on in your brain."

Carter's jaw flexed, his nostrils flaring. "I told you, I don't want any more fucking drugs. Unless you've got something else, maybe a magic wand you can wave and cure me with, then I'm outta here."

The doctor stared back at him a moment before shooting Molly a sympathetic glance that made her stomach drop. "I'm sorry. I don't know what else to—"

"We're leaving," Carter snapped, wrenching his arm free of her grip and turning to stalk out the door.

She stood there a moment, fighting tears. Fighting the need to call him back. Beg him to stay, to try what the doctor suggested. "I'm sorry," she blurted to the doctor, and rushed after Carter.

He was already out in the parking lot by the time she reached him, pacing back and forth beside his truck.

"Are you sure you want to leave?" she asked softly.

He stopped, nodded once. "Yeah."

The faint ray of hope she'd brought with her this morning extinguished. She got into the truck with him.

"If you still want to separate, go ahead and file the paperwork."

His words shocked her so much she was sure she'd imagined them at first. When he remained deathly quiet she glanced at him. "Carter..."

"Just do it, Moll." He stared out his window, his posture and tone radiating defeat that broke her heart. "I'm not going to get better. It's time we both admitted that. I don't want you to wind up like that wall one day."

An icy chill spread through her belly. She darted a glance at his bleeding hand, curled into a fist on his thigh. He was the strongest man she'd ever known. And the most protective. Those hands had been a source of safety and pleasure for her since the day she had met him. In stark contrast, now the strength and violence they were capable of scared her.

The rest of the drive home passed in a tense silence. He got out of the truck as she was putting it into park and stalked into the house. Molly sat there for a few minutes, gathering herself. Maybe he just needed to process everything, and then they could talk about this more rationally.

Her marriage was over. She'd known it for a while now, but had stubbornly clung to the hope that things would get better. Now she realized they never would.

She definitely wanted out, and that made the guilt twist inside her like hot blades, carving her up. If she left Carter, he wouldn't have anyone. Beckett had been forced to let him go. Jase was there to help, but only out of obligation. Carter had slowly destroyed everything good in his life.

Wetness on her cheeks startled her. She wiped the tears away impatiently, steeled herself before getting out of the truck and heading inside, unsure of what she would find. Sometimes after an episode Carter would crash in the guest bed and not come out for more than a day. Others he would yell and throw things.

The house was quiet when she walked in. Too quiet.

Her feet were silent on the wide plank floor as she made her way through the kitchen.

She stopped, her heart lurching up into her throat when Carter's big silhouette appeared in the hallway ahead. She stood there, unmoving, like a deer caught in a hunter's sights.

Carter stepped out of the shadows and into the light. The shattered look on his face drew a sharp gasp from her. He had a packed duffel in one hand.

He was leaving. She should be relieved, but all she felt was devastation and grief.

"Where are you going?" she blurted.

His other reached behind him to withdraw a pistol from his waistband.

Every drop of blood in her body froze. She couldn't tear her eyes off the weapon in that far too-capable hand.

He gave the pistol a half turn and held it out to her by the barrel. "Take this."

She shook her head, backed away. She hated guns. Had spent her training to become an ER nurse at one of the busiest hospitals in Chicago, where she saw multiple times a shift the damage firearms did to a human body. Carter knew how much she loathed them.

He dropped the duffel and took a sudden step toward her, grabbing her right wrist. He pressed the pistol into it, forced her fingers closed around the grip. She knew without asking that it was loaded. "You know how to use this."

She swallowed convulsively, her entire body cold. Yes, she knew how to use it, but even the feel of it in her hand made her shudder.

"Moll."

Somehow she forced her gaze up to his, stared up at him while her heart pounded against her ribs.

"I love you, no matter what. No matter how bad things get or how this all ends, remember that I love you. Please promise me. I'm sorry for everything I've put you through. So fucking sorry."

A sheen of tears blurred her eyes. Her heart was breaking into a thousand pieces, her throat too tight to respond.

"And if I ever…" His voice cracked and a small sob escaped her. "If I ever come after you or threaten you in any way, I want you to take this, point it at my head and pull the goddamn trigger," he choked out.

She shook her head, tried to drop the pistol and break free of his grip.

Carter squeezed tight, forcing her to hold it. "No, listen." There was so much torment in his face. So much fear. "You can't hesitate, Moll. Promise me," he begged, his voice full of agony.

Trembling all over, her insides quivering, she shook her head. "No. No."

"Promise me, sunshine. Don't ever let me hurt you like that. I'd rather die. I'd rather kill myself, but if for some reason I don't, you'll have to do it for me." He let go of her hand.

The pistol clattered to the floor. She tried to back away but he grabbed her, dragged her against him and held her in a crushing grip for a long moment, his face buried in her hair.

Molly was too deep in shock to move or say anything as he kissed her forehead. "Love you. Always," he whispered, then let her go, grabbed his bag and walked out.

Her knees wobbled as the back door clicked shut. A moment later his truck started up in the driveway.

She reached out a hand to steady herself on the wall.

Backed into it and slowly slid down it to the floor, shaking so hard she thought she would be sick. The tears came but she didn't even feel them, the pain inside her too much to bear.

That deadly black pistol lay in the middle of the hall where it had fallen. She closed her eyes, unable to look at it.

Carter was gone. And she was terrified he would do something drastic. Like kill himself.

With shaking fingers she pulled her cell phone from her pocket, managed to dial Jase. He and Beckett would help. They had to.

"Hey, Moll," he answered, the sweet sound of his voice wrenching a sob free. "Moll? What's wrong?" he asked, his voice anxious.

"Carter's g-gone," she said through chattering teeth. "You need to f-find him before he does something stupid."

****

It didn't take Jase long to find his old buddy.

"You called it," Beckett said from the passenger seat, having been pulled away from work when Jase called him about Molly.

"Yup." Carter's truck was parked out front of a bar in the next town north up the coast, a couple miles from Crimson Point. Jase had met him here a few times for beers over the past several months.

"Okay, let's do this," Beckett muttered, getting out of the truck.

Carter was at a table in the far corner, shot glass in hand and a bottle of whiskey in front of him. His elbows were resting on the table, his head bent low. The very picture of defeat and it set off a twinge of sympathy in Jase despite how enraged he was about Molly. "Boyd."

Carter looked up at them, scowled, and helped himself to another shot.

Jase and Beckett went over and sat down across from him. "So. I hear the appointment didn't go so well."

"What are you guys doing here?" Carter muttered, downing the shot.

Seriously? "Molly called," Jase said with tried patience.

He nodded once, avoiding looking at either of them. "She tell you I left?"

"Yep. Right after you shoved a pistol in her hand and told her to blow your head off if you ever came after her." It was so fucking unbelievable he wasn't even sure how to process that.

Another nod, this one defiant. "Yup."

All out of patience, Beckett gave an irritated sigh, grabbed the bottle and plunked it on the windowsill, out of reach. "Jesus Christ, Carter."

Carter nailed him with a hostile glare. "Leave me the fuck alone. I didn't ask either of you to come here."

"Too bad, because here we are," Jase fired back. He shook his head. What the hell was going on with Carter? The TBI was one thing, but the drastic, accelerated onset of mental illness he displayed was scary. "So talk to us."

"I got nothin' more to say." He jerked his head toward the door. "Go."

Jase looked at Beckett, resisted the urge to grab the back of Carter's head and ram it into the table. Maybe another knock would fix whatever connection was loose inside that thick skull.

"Look, we've been through a lot of shit together," Beckett said, trying a more diplomatic approach. "We want to help."

"That's nice." Carter set his shot glass down with a thunk. "But you can't. No one can. And that's why I had to leave."

"And go where?" Jase asked, frustrated.

He shrugged. "Dunno. Don't care."

"You need to check yourself into someplace safe, where they can monitor your meds and make sure you're safe," Beckett said.

"Like what, a VA psych ward?" Carter gave a bitter laugh. "No thanks."

Jase was done pussyfooting around. "What the hell are you doing, man?"

Carter's gaze swung to him. "Taking care of the situation."

Jase shook his head. "Molly's the best damn thing that ever has or ever will happen to you, and you're going to lose her."

"Mind your own fucking business." He glared at Beckett. "And hand me back my bottle. I already paid for it."

Jase refused to let this go. "Is that what you want? To lose her forever?"

Anger ignited in those dark eyes as Carter stared at him in taut silence. "Is it what I *want*?" he finally rasped.

"Well? Is it?"

"I left because it's the only option I have to protect her. We're both fucking miserable and I love her too much to do this to her anymore."

"Help us understand what's going on with you," Beckett said.

"What's happening," he snapped, "is that I've lost my mind, okay?"

Beckett frowned. "Like what? Nightmares and flashbacks, depression and whatever else?"

Because we've all got those, Jase thought. A man couldn't do what they did, see what they had for so long without suffering from PTSD. All of them had their own demons to battle. "So what's going on with you?"

"I can't control it," Carter muttered, back to sullen

now, his gaze fixed on the empty shot glass. "I can't control my thoughts or my emotions, or my anger. Meds don't help. It's getting worse. I forget things. Have times where it's almost like a blackout. Can't remember a damn thing about it, what I said or did."

Jesus. "And there's nothing more the doctors can do?"

"Not except for loading me up with more drugs. And I'm not doing that anymore."

"Well you can't just quit them all cold turkey," Beckett argued. "You know what that'll do."

Carter shrugged. "I'm not doing their dance anymore. I need to clean myself up, see if that helps." But his tone said he doubted it.

"And what about Molly?" Jase said.

"What about her? She's better off this way. She'll file for divorce and move on with her life."

Jase laughed in disbelief. "Seriously? You're not even gonna try to fight for her?"

Carter straightened slowly, that unblinking gaze and slow, deliberate movement telling Jase he'd gone too far. "You're still hung up on her, huh?"

Shock blasted through him, temporarily rendering him mute. They'd never talked about it. Not once since Carter and Molly had gotten together, out of respect for one another. A respect that apparently Carter didn't have for him anymore.

"Yeah, you are. That's so fucking sad, man." Carter gave a cynical chuckle that raked down Jase's spine. "You had your chance the night we met her, and she chose me. *Me*." He stabbed a finger into his chest. "Know why? Because I'm more of a man than you'll ever be."

"That's enough," Beckett snapped as Jase paled under the verbal punch. It fucking *hurt*. "Jesus, Carter, happy now? Did lashing out at him make everything better?"

Carter raised an eyebrow. "Kinda, yeah. Because he knows it's the truth. Molly's mine and always will be." He turned on Jase. "You've always had a thing for her but you couldn't have her because she chose me. And you hate that, don't you? You hate that she's *my wife*."

"She won't be if she divorces your ass," Jase shot back, aching inside.

That dark stare zeroed in on him like a laser, full of a sick kind of triumph that turned Jase's stomach. "At least I had my years with her. How many did you get?"

Jase shoved his chair back and stood. He'd come here to try and help, but Carter was dead set on being an asshole. "You're a mean fucking prick when you're drunk, you know that? Always have been."

"Yeah. Only this time, I'm not drunk." He held out his hand, gestured impatiently to Beckett and the bottle just out of reach. "Give it here."

Beckett stood, giving Carter a look so cold the air temperature dropped a few degrees. "Get it yourself, you self-destructive son of a bitch."

Jase shook his head, sick inside, unable to believe it had come to this. "I don't even like you right now, but I still hope you get your shit together. If you decide you want to get better, call us. Otherwise leave us all the hell alone—including Molly." Without another word he turned and walked out, Beckett right behind him.

At the truck, Beckett clapped him on the back once on the way around to the other side. "Forget what he said. He was being an asshole."

"Yeah." But he couldn't forget those angry, cruel words, because Carter had meant every one of them. And worse, he and Jase both knew they were the truth. Way back when, Molly *had* chosen Carter over him the night they'd met. He'd brought his best game, but the moment she met Carter, that was that.

She had no clue how he really felt about her. And

that was the way it needed to stay.

Jase climbed behind the wheel in the bright spring sunshine, the blessed numbness of shock already wearing off and a sense of grief now trying to smother him. Carter was still alive, but for Jase it felt too much like his best friend was already dead.

Chapter Eleven

Beckett walked out of the newest renovation project and strode down the new concrete walkway in the sunshine to his truck with Sierra. Spotting the flyer tucked beneath his windshield wiper, he grabbed it before opening the door for her.

"Thanks," she said, hopping in.

"Welcome." He shut the door, started around the front of the hood and unfolded the paper. He stopped, cold prickling over his skin when he read the hand-printed message.

You have no honor.

What the hell?

He spun around, scanned up and down the street. He'd only been parked out here for a few minutes, just long enough to drop off the paychecks. The only people he saw was Mrs. Olsen and the woman with the Golden Retriever who'd asked him about the house. The sidewalk behind him was empty. Who the hell had put it here?

Crumpling it up, he shoved it into his pocket and got in the truck. He had enough shit to deal with. He wasn't going to add anything to it. For the past three hours he'd been trying to get past the ugly confrontation with Carter.

The things Carter had said to Jase were unforgivable. He had no idea if there was any truth to them or not, and didn't really care. Carter should never have said them.

What a goddamn mess. Beckett didn't understand why Carter was acting this way. None of them did.

"Did the nurses say your dad's having a good day?" Sierra asked him as he pulled away from the curb. She'd come by the jobsite to surprise him and the crew with cupcakes from Sweet Spot bakery and had asked to come visit his dad with him.

He'd thought about saying no, for maybe two seconds before giving in.

Something had shifted between them last night and he wasn't sorry, even if it put him one step closer to crossing the line with her. Last night was also the first night in weeks that he hadn't woken up gasping and covered in sweat from a nightmare.

Instead he'd lain in bed in the middle of the night tormented with thoughts about her rather than his ghosts. Finally, to ease the unbearable ache in his cock he'd stroked himself off while imagining undressing her and burying his face between her spread thighs, fantasizing about her cries of pleasure as he'd made himself come all over his chest and belly.

Wasn't the first time he'd jacked off thinking about her, and it surely wouldn't be the last. He was so screwed. What he felt for her wasn't casual, and it wasn't going away. If anything, it was getting stronger. And harder to resist by the moment.

Having her with him now improved his mood, even if it was impossible not to think about backing her against the nearest wall and kissing the hell out of her. "He's having an okay day," he answered. "I've been making plans for a surprise for him, but he needs to have a really good day before I can make them happen."

"Well I hope he gets one soon."

"Me too."

Her scent and nearness teased him throughout the drive, and on the way up to his father's room. It was hard for Beckett to have others see his dad declining like this, but he liked having her here, and that she cared enough to come visit his dad on her own when she stopped by to see Molly.

His dad was propped up reading when they walked into his room. He gave them a big smile and set his book down. "Well, now. About time I had someone good looking come and visit me. Sierra, how are you, sweetheart?"

"I'm great, Mr. H. How are you feeling today?"

"Oh, it could be worse."

"I brought you something. Had to hide it from your son, otherwise it wouldn't have made it here," she said, opening a paper bag and taking out a cupcake. "It's double chocolate. That's your favorite, as I recall."

"You remembered right." He took it from her, gave her a fond smile that made Beckett's lips twitch. His father had always had a soft spot for Sierra. "I'll just save this for later." He set it on the tray next to his bed, where his lunch remained untouched.

"Of course." Though Sierra had to have noticed the full plate and the weight he'd lost, she didn't say anything, just kept her sunny disposition firmly in place as she took the seat beside his father's bed and reached for his hand.

The sight of their joined hands sent a bittersweet pang through Beckett. He loved her easy affection, secretly yearned to experience more of it himself. As well as the passion he sensed inside her. The next time he got her alone, he wasn't sure he'd be able to keep his hands off her. With her he was holding onto his control by a thread, and that worried him.

It was in his nature to take charge, in and out of bed. That was who he was. She was small and soft and sweet.

Could she handle what he would demand of her sexually? Her complete surrender, on his terms.

"Anything interesting happen here today?" she asked his father.

"Not a damn thing."

"Well, your son has something to tell you," she said, laughter in her eyes as she looked up at Beckett.

His dad turned his head toward him. "Yeah? What's that?"

Beckett slid his hands into his pockets. "I got a dog yesterday."

His father gave him a startled frown. "What?"

He nodded, pulled out his phone to show him some pictures. "It's a long story."

"Good. You know I love stories. Start at the beginning," his dad said, his face cracking into a grin as he scrolled through the photos. "He's old."

"Yep. His name's Walter." He filled his dad in on the details, then his dad handed back the phone, amusement twinkling in his dark eyes.

"Never thought I'd see the day. Where's Walter now?"

"At home, probably slobbering all over your leather couch."

"He can't get up there on his own, so Beckett made him a little staircase," Sierra said, the proud light in her eyes as she looked at him making his heart swell. "It's adorable."

"Well it's either that, or goodbye leather couches," Beckett said, making light of it. Truth was, the dog deserved to sleep on a couch for however long he had left on this earth.

"I want to meet him," his dad said.

"I guess I could bring him by sometime," Beckett said, unsure how the hospital would feel about it.

"He'd be a great therapy dog," Sierra said. "He's really calm, seems to love people in spite of all he's been through."

"Good. Bring him in," his dad said, aiming a grin at him. "I always wanted to be a grandpa. Congratulations, fur daddy."

They stayed to visit another forty-five minutes or so. Sierra managed to coax his dad into eating half his soup that she reheated for him, a few bites of the fruit cup and a quarter of the cupcake. When his dad began to grow tired, Beckett took his cue to leave, promising to bring Walter in the next day.

Sierra walked close beside him on the way back to his truck. Beckett was aware of every tiny thing about her, from her scent to the different shades of brown in her hair as the sun glinted on it. The urge to wrap his arm around her shoulders was so strong he had to take a step away from her as they walked. There was no way he could do it without it ending up with his tongue in her mouth.

"Thanks for coming," he said. "He wouldn't have eaten anything for me."

"I was happy to come." She glanced over at him. "You're a good son."

Beckett shrugged. "He's my dad." And he was a great one. The rock of the family. Beckett's hero.

She closed the distance between them, slipped her arm through his and leaned her head on his shoulder, the sweet scent of her shampoo swirling around him. Beckett suppressed a growl of longing. It was all he could do not to stop and drag her into his arms, cover that sweet mouth with his and to hell with the risk to their friendship, or Noah's.

"I hate that a man as good as him is going through this," she said.

That cooled the heat burning beneath his skin. "Me too."

He didn't want to take her back to her car, but he drove her to it anyway. He wanted more time with her. A little more time spent without the ghosts in his head and maybe he could wrestle with whether to risk everything he'd built with her and her family for a chance at making her his.

You already know the answer. You can't go there with her.

They arrived at her car all too soon. "Thanks for the ride," she said with a smile, and hopped out.

Beckett watched her walk to her vehicle, feeling like he was being torn in two, his heart at war with his conscience.

Fuck it. I can't let her go.

He rolled down his window. "I've got an apple pie at home. Feel like a slice?" he found himself asking. It was a lame offer, but it was the only thing that came to mind besides tasting that ripe, sexy mouth and then doing everything in his power to rock her world. Damn, there were so many things he would love to do to her.

Her smile only made the fire inside him burn hotter. "Sure, I'd like that. I'll follow you."

By the time they made it to his place he was rock hard in his jeans from thinking about all the things he could do to her, his whole body taut with repressed need. Except when he pulled up to his house, he spotted a flash of pink out on the front porch.

"Is that Ella?" Sierra asked, frowning as she got out of her car behind him.

"Looks like." She'd probably come over to spend time with the dog. He hoped Tiana knew about it.

"I thought she was supposed to be at home after school today?"

"She was." He was going to find out what was going on.

Sure enough, they found Walter lying next to Ella on the porch. She must have used the spare key to let him out.

"Hi, Mr. Beckett, Miss Sierra," Ella said, stroking one

of Walter's long ears. "I brought Walter a cookie, and we got him something else on the way to school this morning, too." She turned to the dog. "Walter, look up. Walter," she coaxed, trying valiantly to snap her fingers above his head.

Walter reluctantly lifted his head and looked up, and Beckett spotted the red and blue plaid bow tie she'd put on his collar.

Ella grinned at him and Sierra. "What do you think? So handsome."

Sierra chuckled. "Very distinguished."

"Do you like it, Mr. Beckett?"

He thought it was ridiculous, but he wasn't going to say that to her, especially not when those big blue eyes were fixed on him like that. "Yeah, I do."

He wanted privacy with Sierra but Ella seemed in no hurry to leave. "I thought you were supposed to go home after school today?" he said to her. Normally Tiana didn't get home until six-thirty or so.

Ella shrugged and kept petting Walter. "My mom's working late tonight to cover for one of her friends."

Oh. "What about her boyfriend? Isn't he there?"

"Yes."

Beckett shared a look with Sierra. Clearly Ella didn't want to go home, even though that's where she was supposed to be right now. Was she lonely? Wasn't comfortable around the boyfriend maybe?

"Are you hungry?" Sierra asked her.

Ella lifted a shoulder. "A little. It's okay, though. I'll just wait here until my mom comes home."

"Don't be silly, come inside," Beckett told her, opening the door. In the kitchen he got her a glass of milk and a couple of cookies from a package in the pantry.

She sat in a chair at the table, gaze on her plate, one leg swinging back and forth idly, a distant expression on her face.

Beckett glanced at Sierra, who shrugged and spoke. "So, Ella. Are you supposed to be home for dinner today?"

The girl nodded, staring at her untouched cookie.

Beckett frowned. "Instead you came here."

"I went home, but after I dropped my backpack off I came straight here to see Walter."

It sounded like an excuse to him. "You didn't want to hang out with your mom's boyfriend?"

At that Ella's gaze darted up to him, her expression freezing. Then she quickly lowered her gaze.

Beckett's instincts were jangling now. Something wasn't right. "Ella? What's wrong?" When she didn't answer he crossed to her and sat in the chair beside her. He consciously gentled his voice before speaking. "If something's wrong, you can tell me."

She bit her lip, seemed to hunch in on herself. "He came into the bathroom while I was having my bath one night," she finally whispered in a rush.

For a moment Beckett wasn't sure he'd heard her right, because the words were drowned beneath the sudden rush of blood pulsing in his ears. He forced back the shock, the red-hot tide of anger and kept his voice level even though his entire body was rigid. "By accident?" If it wasn't... He curled his fingers into his palms, squeezed.

Ella didn't answer. Wouldn't look at him, her gaze glued to her untouched cookies.

"On purpose?" he asked, needing to know exactly what had happened.

She nodded and his stomach clamped tight, his fingers now denting his palms.

He sat up straight, his heart beating faster, anger and protectiveness swirling through him. Ella wasn't the type of kid to make this shit up. And now it made way too much sense why she'd been hanging out here after school, rather than going home if there was a chance the boyfriend might be there.

"Did he touch you?" he bit out, his voice sharp.

She hunched in more on herself. "No."

Beckett was even more uneasy now. There was more to this. He was certain of it.

Sierra shot him an anxious look and crouched down beside Ella's chair. "Ella, whatever happened was not your fault. You understand that, right?"

Ella gave a reluctant nod, still looking ashamed and uncomfortable.

Sierra watched her with a calm expression belied by the worry in her eyes. "Honey, please talk to us so we can help."

Ella darted a glance at her, then up to Beckett before lowering her gaze back to the plate. For a long moment she sat there, frozen, her hands clenched together in her lap. "He showed me his privates," she whispered in a shaky voice.

Beckett's lungs seized and he tensed like someone had sucker punched him in the gut. Mother*fucker*.

Outrage flashed in Sierra's eyes but she stayed where she was, maintained her outward calm. "He did?"

Ella nodded, her cheeks bright red, humiliation stamped all over her face. "And then he…rubbed himself in front of me."

Beckett felt sick as he envisioned it.

"He… He wanted me to touch it, but I wouldn't. I shut my eyes."

There was pain in Sierra's eyes now. Pain that told Beckett she was remembering something hurtful. "Did you tell your mom?"

Ella shook her head, looking miserable as tears slid down her cheeks. "He said if I told anyone, he'd kill her."

Bright red fury pulsed through Beckett's bloodstream, so powerful it all but stole his breath. Every muscle in his body was wire-tight as he thought about that son of a bitch violating Ella's innocence that way. As he remembered all the horrific abuse and injustice toward children he'd seen overseas.

He was on his feet without realizing it. "Stay here with Ella," he growled to Sierra, already heading for the front door. His body was locked and loaded, spoiling for a fight with the predator down the lane.

"Beckett, wait," she called out, but he didn't stop or look back.

His mind spun, his usual control rapidly slipping away as the seconds passed. He hadn't been able to do anything to protect those kids overseas.

Never again. He could and *would* do something about this. He would protect Ella now and make her abuser pay for what he'd done, see that he was brought to justice.

He jumped off his top step and took off in a run the moment his feet hit the front lawn, racing across the grass toward the path that cut through the forest in a shortcut to Tiana and Ella's house.

The bastard's SUV was parked out front.

Beckett slowed to a lope as he reached the driveway and leaped up onto the front porch. He was breathing hard as he hit the bell, not because he was winded, but because of the fury roaring like lava through his veins.

For one moment he considered kicking the door in, but managed to rein in the impulse at the last moment as footsteps sounded in the hallway.

The door opened. Brian blinked at him in surprise, then frowned, presumably because of the lethal expression on Beckett's face. "Hey. What—"

Beckett pulled back his arm and slammed his fist into the middle of the asshole's face.

Bone crunched as Brian's head snapped back. He screeched and hit the floor on his knees, both hands cupped around his nose and mouth as blood began to pour from between his fingers. "Fuck! What the *fuck*?"

Beckett grabbed the front of Brian's shirt, jerked upward. "You sick son of a bitch," he snarled. Seams ripped as Beckett drew his fist back again, ready to deliver another dose of medicinal justice.

"Beckett, no! Don't."

He had just enough control left for Sierra's voice behind him to stop him. But he didn't let Brian go. Instead he fisted the front of the asshole's shirt and glared down at him, his chest heaving. One punch wasn't enough to satisfy him or ease the rage pumping through his system. A busted lip and nose was only a fraction of the pain this motherfucker deserved.

"Beckett." Sierra's feet thudded lightly on the wooden front steps as she ran up them. She set a hand on his back, her touch light, tentative. "No more. Don't ruin your life over this piece of crap."

"Excuse me?" Brian said.

Beckett clenched his jaw. It would feel so goddamn good to hit him again, to beat him until he couldn't get up.

"What the fuck is *wrong* with you, man?" Brian yelled, grabbing hold of Beckett's wrist with one bloody hand and trying to wrench out of his grip.

Not happening. This fucker wasn't going anywhere but to jail. "Call your brother," he said to Sierra, his voice low, dangerous. "Get him over here *now.*" *Before I kill this fucker with my bare hands.* Thankfully she didn't interfere further and did as he said, walking back down the front steps as she spoke to Noah.

"Let me *go*, asshole," Brian yelled, still struggling, blood dripping down his chin, staining his shirt and splattering over Beckett's fist. "I'm pressing charges."

"Shut. Up," Beckett snarled, giving him a warning shake that made Brian go still. This son of a bitch had showed his junk to Ella? Had blackmailed her into silence by threatening to kill Tiana if she told anyone? Fuck that. Fuck *him*. And what the hell else had he done? Ella might not have told them everything. "Did you touch her?"

"Who? What the fuck are you *talking* about, you psycho?"

"You know exactly who," he growled. "Did you touch Ella, you sick motherfucker?"

The man's green eyes widened slightly and he paled beneath the blood spatters on his face. "*What*? What did she tell you?" He tried to shake his head. "Whatever she said, it's a lie. She's fucking *lying*."

The urge to smash the fucker's face in was so strong Beckett struggled for breath for a moment. It took him several seconds to get control. "If you come near her again, I'll fucking tear you apart. Do you understand?" Holding Brian's gaze, he let the other man see the killer inside him, the deadly promise beneath the words. "I can kill you fifty different ways and make it look like an accident. No one will ever find your body. Feel me? You go near her again, you even *talk* to her again, and I'll put you down like the animal you are. That's a promise, and I swear to God, I'll keep it."

Brian gulped, then launched into an outraged tirade that Beckett paid no attention to whatsoever. He was focused on holding this predator in place where the asshole couldn't hurt anyone else, listening behind him as Sierra continued speaking to her brother.

"He's on his way," she said to him a moment later. "Should be here in under ten minutes."

Beckett glared down at Brian in warning. "You move from this spot, I'll break another few bones in your face." He shoved Brian onto his ass on the entry floor and folded his arms, silently daring him to run.

Brian squawked and immediately tried to scramble to his feet but stopped when Beckett uncrossed his arms and took a menacing step forward.

They held a short staring contest until the coward looked away, unable to take the accusation and strength of Beckett's gaze. Oh yeah, this bastard was guilty. Sierra waited behind him out on the porch, pacing back and forth.

Finally Noah showed up. He loped up the front steps in his uniform, stopped in the doorway to take in the scene with a single glance. "Well. Evening, folks. What've we got here?"

"This asshole showed up on the doorstep and punched me in the face as soon as I opened it," Brian accused, thrusting a finger at Beckett. "He broke my goddamn nose, flung all kinds of disgusting accusations at me—"

Noah held up his hand and looked at Beckett. "Why'd you punch him?"

"Because he deserved it."

Amusement glittered in Noah's eyes but he kept his game face professionally in place. "Enlighten me."

Beckett told him, and the tightening of Noah's lips as he turned back to stare down at Brian was reassurance enough that this bastard was going in for questioning.

Noah did his job, listening to everyone's side of the story as he took their statements separately, making notes and calling it in to dispatch before hauling Brian to his feet and slapping on the cuffs.

"What?" Brian spluttered, twisting around to look at Noah in disbelief. "Are you fucking serious?"

"I've got two witnesses who said the exact same thing, and Ella's version of events. I'm going to talk to her next. For now, you're coming in for questioning while we investigate this further."

"What about them? He assaulted me without provocation, and she saw it," he said, jutting his jaw out.

"They're coming in too," Noah said.

A car pulled up in the driveway. Beckett and Noah turned around as Tiana climbed from her vehicle, her expression worried, auburn hair flying around her shoulders as she hurried toward them. "What's going on?

What's happened?" Her gaze darted back and forth between them. "Is Ella okay?"

Beckett stepped forward to meet her. "Not exactly."

"Where is she?"

"My house. She's safe, I promise."

She relaxed a little, only to gasp when she saw Noah walking Brian out of the house in handcuffs, her boyfriend's face and chest covered in blood. "What the...?"

Brian didn't waste any time protesting his innocence. "Don't listen to them, babe," he said earnestly. "It's all lies, I swear. I didn't do it."

She remained unmoving beside Beckett, a dozen yards away from Noah. "Didn't do *what*?" She peered up at him, her mismatched eyes searching his. "Beckett? What didn't he do?"

"I'll talk to you in private, ma'am," Noah said. "Right after I put him in the back of my patrol car."

Noah ignored Brian's sputtered protests, put him in the back and shut the door. Then he came back to them, took Tiana by the arm and led her a discreet distance away.

Beckett knew the moment his friend told her the important bit, because Tiana gasped and clapped her hands over her mouth in horror. Her gaze shot to Beckett, shock and fear there. Looking to him for confirmation or denial.

Beckett nodded once. "It's true. I'm sorry."

Her hands lowered slowly from her face. She was pale, but there was no mistaking the lethal wrath in her expression as she swung her gaze toward the patrol car.

Then she wrenched away from Noah and bolted right for it, murder in her eyes.

Chapter Twelve

Sierra bit back a protest as Tiana whirled and tore toward Noah's cruiser. Her brother cursed and started after Tiana, clearly about to intervene, but Beckett caught his arm.

"Give her a second," Beckett murmured. "I wanna see this."

Noah shook his head and yanked free. "Yeah, not happening."

He caught Tiana a foot away from the rear door. Inside, Brian immediately started shaking his head and babbling, his voice muffled by the window, but they could still hear him. The bastard was proclaiming his innocence, insisting Ella was lying.

He made Sierra want to throw up. This entire incident had shaken her, dredging up things she would rather forget.

"I didn't do it," Brian argued, eyes wide, wearing an innocent expression that had no doubt worked in his favor in the past. "I would never—"

Tiana slammed both hands against the window, making Brian duck back as though he was afraid she would shatter the glass. "You disgusting pig of a *bastard*," she choked out, and hit the window again.

Noah grabbed her, hauled her backward. She resisted and kept yelling, her words devolving into grunted curse words and threats as she vented her anger on her daughter's abuser.

Noah sighed. "Tiana, stop. I need you to calm down."

Tiana didn't. She ignored Noah as he dragged her farther away from the patrol car and kept on shouting at Brian. Threatening to cut off his balls if he ever came near her or her daughter ever again.

Sierra officially loved her.

Noah finally dragged her far enough away that she stopped shouting, and let her go, watching her warily. "I know this is hard. I know you're upset," he began.

Tiana straightened a few feet from her and Beckett, looking traumatized. "Oh, God," she cried, her face twisting with grief. "I need to see Ella. I need to see my baby."

Sierra rushed over and drew her into a hug, unable to stand it. "It's okay. It's okay, we'll take you to see her."

Noah shot her a grateful look. "I'm taking him into the station for questioning." Then to Tiana, "You'll need to bring your daughter over after that. I need to get her official statement."

Sierra nodded as Tiana did the same, willing away the queasiness in the pit of her stomach.

"You stupid prick," Brian was yelling at Beckett from inside the car, his bloody face twisted with anger. "I'll ruin you for this! I'm pressing charges—gonna sue your ass for—"

"Charges for what? For exposing you as a pedophile?" Beckett shot back.

His eyes bulged. "For assault, asshole, and libel. My lawyer will crush you. He—"

"There was no witness during the assault," Noah said. "For all I know, you tripped and fell on your face on the way to the door."

Brian's face twisted as he stared at Noah. "Fuck you. Fuck *all* of you. You can't prove anything, it's Ella's word against mine. I'm a respected banker. No one's gonna believe I would ever do anything like that. They're not gonna take an eight-year-old's word over mine."

"That's up to the judge when you go to trial," Noah said, and turned his back on Brian. Taking a calming breath, he faced them. "I'll contact a social worker, have them meet us at the station when you're ready to bring Ella in," he said to Tiana, who was still huddled in Sierra's arms. She nodded once but didn't look at him, her shoulders shaking with her quiet sobs.

"We'll take her to my place so she can see Ella," Beckett said.

Noah nodded. "I'll call you later. You'll both have to come down and give your official statements too."

After he left, a resounding silence filled the yard, broken only by Tiana's tears and the distant sigh of the sea. Sierra's heart went out to her. To learn her daughter had been violated in this way was horrible. She just hoped it hadn't gone any farther than Ella had told them.

Finally, Tiana drew in a shuddering breath and stepped away, wiping her face with her hands. "I didn't know. I swear to God, I had no idea he would do something like that. If I had, I would never have had anything to do with him. I would never have let him near my daughter."

"We know that," Beckett said, his deep voice calm. "It sounds like we stopped this before any real damage was done. At least, I hope we did."

"I need to see Ella. Right now."

Beckett nodded and came over to slide an arm around Tiana's shoulders, and Sierra got a good look at his right hand. Three of his knuckles were cracked and already swelling, though he didn't seem to notice or care. "Come on, we'll drive you up."

They got into her car for the short drive up the lane. When they pulled up beside the house, Tiana jumped out and ran for the steps. "Ella? Ella, baby."

Ella appeared on the front porch, her expression uncertain, Walter at her feet. "Mama?"

Tiana took the steps three at a time and engulfed her daughter in a big hug. "Oh, baby, I'm so sorry. I had no idea what was going on." She hugged Ella for a long time, then knelt and took her daughter's face in her hands. "God, sweetheart, I feel sick about everything. Why didn't you tell me about Brian?"

Sierra leaned into Beckett, a faint shudder of relief wrapping around her when he slid a solid arm about her waist and drew her to him. She felt so incredibly safe with him holding her.

Oh, man, that was bad. If she'd thought she was in trouble with him before, now that she'd seen the extent of his protective streak, she was done for.

Ella peered around her mother's shoulder to look at her and Beckett. "I...was scared."

Tiana made a choked sound and hugged her tighter. "I'm sorry. Nobody will ever do anything like that to you again, I promise. He's never going to see you again."

"Is he still at our house?"

"No, baby. The sheriff came and took him away."

Ella seemed to droop in relief. "So I won't have to see him ever again?"

"Only if a judge wants you to tell your story in court."

"Let's go inside." Beckett let them in the front door and got them settled at the kitchen table with some leftover cupcakes.

When Noah called to say Brian was being held overnight and asked Tiana to bring Ella down to talk to him and the social worker, Beckett stood. "I'll drive you down. Sierra and I have to go in and give our official statements anyhow."

"No." Tiana put a hand on his forearm, her smile wobbly but with an underlying firmness to it. "You've done more than enough for us already. I'm okay now. I'm calm enough to drive us. But thank you. For everything."

Beckett inclined his head.

Ella took her mother's hand and walked with her to the door, pausing there to look back at Beckett. "Can I still come and visit Walter?"

He smiled and Sierra's breath hitched at the softness on that hard face. "Of course you can. Anytime you want."

The grateful smile on that little face hurt Sierra's heart.

She stood on the porch with him as Tiana and Ella got into the car and drove away. Honeysuckle perfumed the air, a slight breeze wafting along the porch.

In the sudden quiet, she looked up at him. His profile looked hard enough to be carved out of granite. She studied it, following each line and wishing she could secretly take a picture.

"You okay?" she asked finally.

She'd never seen him lose control like that before. Beckett was always calm. Seeing him lose it had scared her a little. While she hadn't actually seen the punch that had done so much damage to Brian's lying face, it had obviously packed a lot of power. If she hadn't called out to him when she had, if he hadn't listened to her, he might be in a cell right now, facing charges for aggravated assault or worse.

Beckett nodded once, staring up the empty driveway toward the lane, the muscles in his jaw flexing beneath the heavy stubble there. "I couldn't stand knowing that asshole defiled her that way. Or the thought of him getting away with it."

"I get it." The justice system was a sad joke a lot of the time. It seemed like the victims were punished instead of the criminals.

She stepped in front of him, drawing his full attention. The anger was gone from his gaze now, but there was something in his eyes that made him look...haunted. Even though she didn't know what had caused them, she wanted to wipe those shadows away forever because she couldn't stand to see him hurting.

Sensing he needed comfort too, she cradled the side of his face with her palm, his whiskers prickling her skin. Something flared in his eyes for a moment, then his face went carefully blank. She hated that he felt the need to hide from her in any way, even as it reminded her of all she risked emotionally by pining for a man who would probably never fully let her in.

There were so many things she wanted to say, beginning with what a good man he was, to protect Ella the way he had. How much she admired him. How much she cared about and wanted him. Except that would only make him retreat from her more, and she was afraid to voice the depth of her feelings aloud. So her only remaining option was action.

Her heart began to pound.

Before she could chicken out or give herself the chance to overthink it, she went on tiptoe and brushed her lips across his. A soft caress meant to soothe even as it lit her senses up. She'd wanted to kiss him for so damn long.

Beckett stiffened. It was subtle, but she felt it, heard the rumble of protest issuing from his throat.

Hurt and humiliation pierced her. It was as if all of her buried insecurities had just been proven right. He didn't want her. She was a friend to him and nothing more and she'd just made a fool of herself.

Closing her eyes, she allowed herself only another moment to savor the feel of his mouth against hers before she eased back, sparing herself the formal rejection she was certain was coming. But as she turned to walk away he snagged her wrist, stopping her.

And what she saw when she looked up at him stole her breath.

Beckett's dark eyes blazed with raw hunger, his entire face taut as he stared down at her.

Sierra's pulse skittered in her throat. Had she been wrong? Her gaze dipped to his mouth once more, the tension crackling between them like live electricity as she anticipated feeling his lips on hers.

"Don't," he rasped out with a shake of his head, the warning in his voice clear.

She met his stare, unsure what to think. The mixed signals he was sending confused the hell out of her. "Why not?"

"Because." A muscle bunched in his jaw, his eyes burning with suppressed need she would give anything to satisfy.

No. Because wasn't an answer. She needed to know the reason why. "Because I'm still Noah's little sister to you?"

He huffed out a bitter laugh. "Not even close."

The tiny bubble of hope she'd been suppressing swelled in her chest. Sensing she could break through his defenses if she just pushed a little harder, she cocked her head to study him. "I'm a grown woman, Beckett."

His gaze lingered on her mouth. "I noticed."

The underlying heat in his tone, the way his eyes darkened, made that bubble expand. "Good. It's about time."

He didn't answer.

She pushed again, the depth of her feelings throwing caution aside. "And since we're being honest, I've wanted you for years."

Shock flashed across his face. "What?"

Oh, please. She held back a snort. "No way you never noticed. None." He was a Green Beret. He saw everything, details most people would miss. There was zero chance she had hidden everything well enough for him not to notice.

He shook his head, stepped back to run a hand through his hair in agitation. His knuckles were bloody, already turning color. "We can't. You and I are a really bad idea."

Maybe. Crossing the line was a huge risk for both of them. Still, she'd exposed too much to turn back now. She'd already laid herself bare. "Why not? Because you're Noah's best friend? Because I'm too young for you?"

"No." He seemed to force himself to meet her gaze, and the look in his eyes made her heart thud. He wanted her, but refused to allow himself to go there.

Well, she refused to let this go. "Tell me why, Beckett."

He made a frustrated sound and growled, "Because of *this*." His hands locked around her upper arms as he spun them around and pinned her up against the side of the house with his powerful body.

Sierra gasped, her whole being going hot, then weak at the way he caged her in with his hands on either side of her head.

His dark eyes burned with a raging hunger as he towered over her, the muscles in his arms and shoulders taut, the unmistakable bulge of his erection shoved against her abdomen. His lips were inches above her own, his clean scent filling her lungs.

She shivered, paralyzed, every nerve ending coming to sudden, painful life, unfulfilled need making her ache inside. Oh, God, she needed him so badly, had no idea he'd wanted her this much...

And then his mouth was on hers, those big, strong hands diving into her hair, gripping tight. She moaned and automatically arched into him, her tingling breasts hitting the solid wall of his chest as she reached for his broad shoulders. She'd dreamed of this for so long, could hardly believe it was happening.

Beckett tightened his hold on her, asserting his dominance and control. Her lips parted beneath the demanding stroke of his tongue and then it slid between them, caressing hers with such skill it tore a whimper of longing from her. It was so much more than she'd imagined it would be. She'd sensed this in him, this forceful, slightly rough edge as a lover.

It turned her into a puddle of need.

Beckett didn't just kiss her. He took possession of her with a masterful blend of dominance and seduction that made her tremble. Her insides liquefied beneath the white-hot tide of desire that swept through her, her entire body humming with need.

Far too soon he abruptly broke the kiss to stare down at her, breathing hard, his expression almost angry. Her legs were so weak they were barely keeping her upright, her lungs fighting for air. Holy God, what he could do to her with a single kiss.

He shook his head once, that haunted look back in his eyes. "You think you want me, but you don't know what you're asking for. You have no idea the things I want to do to you," he rasped out. "The things I've wanted to do for years now, and don't dare, because of what you and your family mean to me. I can't risk wrecking that. Because if I ever crossed that line with you, I wouldn't be able to hold back and I wouldn't let you go. Understand?"

Holy hell. She fought off a moan of surrender, arched a taunting eyebrow instead. "Is that supposed to scare me off? Because you're just turning me on more."

A warning growl rumbled in his chest, his gaze all but singeing her face. "Don't push me, sweetness. Not on this."

Her belly did a tight, backward flip as a scorching wave of heat flooded her. Making her skin tingle, her tight nipples ache. Making her want to keep taunting him, find out what it would take to break the last link in his iron control. To see what would happen when it did, because every fiber in her being told her it would be amazing.

"I don't want you to hold back," she whispered, desperate for more, for the release only he could give her.

"Well you should. Because if I don't it would ruin everything."

There was a chance it might. But it was so damn hard to think straight with all the images his earlier words had brought to life in her head.

Erotic, vivid images of the two of them together, naked. Beckett's brooding intensity transformed into the kind of rough-edged passion that made her heart thud and her knees go rubbery.

His hands in her hair, their mouths fused together, that big, powerful body stretching out on top of her. His weight pressing her down into his bed upstairs, or pinning her fully here against the wall as he kissed her again, but this time with his hands and mouth easing the ache in her breasts and between her thighs.

Before she could think of a good comeback or put her mouth on his again he backed off, his expression dark, as though pissed at himself. "Go home, Sierra. It's been a hell of a night and I don't trust myself right now." He stalked past her to the door and walked through it without a backward glance, the screen door slamming against the frame.

Cold suffused her, dousing her arousal. For a moment she almost went after him, the frustration all but choking her. That look on his face, though. That disappointed look that bordered on self-disgust because of what he'd just done and said, made her hesitate.

If she pushed him now while he was at his limit, she could get him to give her what she wanted.

But not all of him. And when it was over, he would regret it and do everything in his power to avoid her from then on.

Nothing was worth that. She wouldn't risk losing him now, when she'd finally managed to put some cracks in his formidable emotional armor. He meant too much to her. She wanted everything he had to give.

Drawing a deep, steadying breath, she ordered her racing heart to slow and made herself walk to her car. They both needed time to regroup. For now she had no choice but to honor his request and let him go.

But this powerful attraction between them was too strong to deny, and it wasn't going away.

The shitty thing was, she had no idea what the hell she was supposed to do about that.

Chapter Thirteen

"**D**id you hear about the incident last night?" the waitress said as she poured coffee into the mug, an excited gleam in her eyes.

Isabelle apparently had a load of fresh gossip and couldn't wait to share it.

As usual, the diner seemed to be the hotbed of town chatter. If you wanted to know what was going on around here, newcomer or not, you found out pretty fast, even without asking. "No, what?"

"Beckett Hollister assaulted someone last night."

No way. "What?"

She nodded, her eyes gleaming with excitement. "It's true. I heard someone tell the story this morning. Beckett heard there was a pedophile living down the street from him. He went over there and punched the guy's face in. Broke his nose, almost knocked a few teeth out."

That didn't sound like Hollister. The man was tightly controlled. He'd had to be to get where he'd wound up in the Special Forces community. "Was he arrested?"

"Who, Beckett?" She scoffed as though the mere idea was ridiculous. "No, but the sheriff came and arrested the pervert. I heard Beckett and Sierra are down there giving their statements this morning. Personally, I hope the creep rots in jail," she added, her expression hard. "You got kids?"

"No." It hurt to say it out loud. *But I would have if Hollister hadn't taken everything from me.*

"Well I do, and the thought of someone like that living in our community just makes my skin crawl."

That was something they could agree on.

"Everyone's talking about what Beckett did. We think he should run for mayor."

Mayor? What a fucking joke. "You're kidding, right?"

Isabelle frowned in surprise. "No, why?"

"Nothing. Forget it. Have a nice day."

Taking the hint, Isabelle moved on to the next table, where she immediately started talking about Hollister and what a hero he was to the new customers.

Jesus. It was sickening to know just how badly Hollister had duped the people in this community. It was like they were all brainwashed. Couldn't anyone see what a coward he actually was? Did *no* one in this miserable fucking excuse for a town know what he *hadn't* done, and what it had cost?

No. Because no one *wanted* to see it.

The pedophile angle could be useful, though. Chances were the suspect would be released on bail until the trial— if there was evidence enough against him to warrant one. So he would be loose in the community again, maybe even already.

Yeah, this might help. Finding out the guy's name shouldn't be hard. Not when gossip spread like literal wildfire in this town. And pinning Hollister's murder on a child predator could work. He had a grudge against Hollister too, with a busted nose and a few loose teeth to prove it. Once Hollister died, people would immediately suspect him. So would the police, as long as there weren't any witnesses around to say otherwise.

That would buy the real killer enough time to skip town and disappear.

A few bills tossed onto the table paid for breakfast, and the warm, salt-tinged air outside cleared the mind. Knowing the end to all this was so close brought a much needed sense of peace.

The need for revenge was too powerful to back out of this now. Hollister had to suffer for what he'd done, and now there was someone else to pin the killing on.

****

"You let him go?" Sierra said, her face full of shock and disappointment as she stared at him.

"Yes, it's the law," Noah muttered, not liking it any more than her.

"Well the law sucks," she said with a scowl, folding her arms across her chest.

"Yeah, sometimes it does." Sometimes more than others.

God, this day. It had been shitty from the start when he'd woken up to find a pipe had burst in the kitchen, and had gone downhill from there. All after the long night he'd pulled, dealing with the Ella Fitzgerald case.

Upon arriving at the office this morning he'd found a report from the FBI about another young woman who had gone missing from the neighboring county. Five women over the past five years. The Feds suspected a serial killer was at work, but so far they had no evidence or leads and not much to link the disappearances yet—not even the remains of any of the victims. Noah hated that the monster's hunting ground was so close to home.

But there were all kinds of monsters in this world. Including the pedophile he'd been forced to release from the holding cell a couple hours ago.

"He's been charged, but the court date isn't for another

ten days from now, and he was able to post bail." No surprise, given that Brian was a successful banker and had no priors. It turned Noah's stomach to let a sicko like that loose in his community, but he was sworn to uphold the law and had to obey the rules, even if the rules sucked.

Still, part of him wished he'd let Tiana take a few swings at the asshole last night, instead of intervening the way his badge and position mandated.

Sierra kept staring at him. Almost as if she expected him to change things somehow.

He would if he could have. "Look, I know how much this must upset you, but there was nothing more I could do. How are you doing, anyway?" he asked in a softer tone. She and Beckett had just finished giving their official statements about last night, and it must have stirred up a lot of shit for her.

She lost the glare, lowered her gaze. "I'm okay."

Beckett was in the other room waiting for her, so Noah didn't mind digging a little while they had the privacy. "You sure?"

"Yeah. I've been thinking a lot about Heather, though."

"Me too." He'd never forget that day. Neither of them would. "How's Ella, do you know?"

"Her mom's taking her to a counseling appointment this morning."

"That's good. Tiana seems like a great mom."

"Beckett seems to think so. It's not easy, being a single parent. She's doing the best she can, and she clearly would do anything for her daughter."

"Yes." Noah had thought about Ella a lot over the past sixteen hours. About what would have happened if she hadn't told Beckett and Sierra what Brian had done. The bastard would no doubt have taken things further, and would have kept abusing her for as long as possible all while pretending to be the doting boyfriend Tiana thought he was.

Fucking gross. And given his and Sierra's own experience with a child predator they had both trusted, yeah, he was glad Beckett had busted the bastard's nose.

Sierra sighed. "I'm just glad we found out what was going on before it was too late."

"Me too."

"What about you?" She eyed him with the knowing stare that only a sibling could bestow. "I know abuse calls are the worst for you."

"Part of the job." Unfortunately, even a place as small and safe as Crimson Point wasn't spared domestic and sexual abuse cases. But that shit involving kids was always tough for him to compartmentalize.

"You working a full shift today?"

"Yep. You?"

She glanced back toward the door. "Technically I've booked the whole weekend off, but we'll see. I think I'll go to Beckett's for a while after this, though. This whole thing bothered him more than he's letting on, I can tell."

He could already see where this was going. Sierra had a big heart and thought she could help everyone. "Yeah, good luck with getting him to talk about it."

Good luck with getting Beck to talk about *anything* that bothered him.

He and Noah had been best friends since kindergarten, and Noah could count on one hand how many times Beckett had opened up to him about something that bothered him. Beck liked to handle everything on his own. "I didn't even find out about the divorce until it was all over with." And he also never talked about what had happened overseas.

"Challenge accepted," Sierra said with a determined smile that almost made Noah a little sorry for Beckett. "And you weren't exactly an open book when you broke up with Katherine, either."

Noah grunted. "That was different." Her betrayal had cut deep. So deep he'd become a serial dater in the years since she'd left Crimson for the bright lights of New York City.

"Yeah, because it happened to *you*," Sierra pointed out. "Call me if you need anything else."

"I will." He hugged her goodbye and settled behind his desk to make a dent in the files that had piled up on him.

Calls were sparse throughout the day, and nothing more came in about the missing women case. It took most of his shift to get through them and file the last of the paperwork so he could finally head outside and climb into his patrol car.

He thought about grabbing takeout from one of the restaurants in town on the way home, but didn't feel like stopping, or calling any of the women he'd gone out with recently. He'd go home, grill himself a steak and make a baked potato to go with it, then sit out on the back porch and enjoy some quiet for a while. His elderly neighbor had moved out of her house several weeks ago and the little cottage had been empty ever since. Several people had come to look at it but so far no one had put in an offer that he knew of, so he had extra privacy.

It was kind of nice not to have neighbors for a change.

He took a right onto Front Street, now bathed in shades of purple and blue with the twilight. Most of the shops and businesses were closed except for the bar and a few restaurants.

A flicker of light from behind an abandoned building up the block caught his attention. He slowed as he approached the old diner that had been empty for more than a year now. With the weather warming up it wasn't unheard of for vandals to migrate into the area and break into empty places, sometimes simply to crash, others to strip copper pipe or wiring and sell it for cash. He'd better check it out.

He parked along the curb and got out, alerting dispatch to what was going on. One hand on the butt of his service weapon, he walked alongside the shingled building. The light flickered again from behind it, and he heard someone moving around in the back alley. "Hello?" he called out.

"Hi," a feminine voice answered cautiously. The light shifted, and something metal clanked.

Noah rounded the corner and stopped when he saw the young woman climbing down a ladder, paint roller in her hand. The first thing he noticed was her breasts, but he quickly tore his gaze upward. Her deep blond hair was pulled up in a messy bun, her jeans and shirt splattered with paint.

She stepped off the bottom rung and gave him a polite but wary smile. "Hello."

He swept his gaze over her, taking in the curvy shape of her body in the paint-smeared clothes. She had a smudge of it across her cheekbone too. "Hi. I saw a light on back here and thought I should check it out." He eyed her. It was getting dark fast and she seemed to be alone. "Are you with a painting company, or...?"

"I'm the new owner." Her accent was pure Midwest. She swept an errant lock of hair away from her cheek and tucked it behind her ear. "Bought it last week. Are you the sheriff?"

"Yes. Noah Buchanan."

"Poppy Larsen," she said, holding out a hand.

He looked down at it, at the paint all over her skin.

"Sorry." She laughed softly and wiped the front and back of it against the leg of her jeans before offering it again. "Nice to meet you."

"You as well," he said, shaking and releasing it as he sized her up. He'd been a cop for so long that he was a little suspicious by nature. Not much happened around here that he didn't know about, and the rest he found out eventually. She definitely wasn't a vandal, though.

Vandals didn't work late fixing up a place. "I hadn't heard this place had sold."

"Everything was finalized last night. The paperwork went through this morning, so I wanted to get cracking on the renovations."

Huh. He would check that with the local real estate agent in the morning, and see what he could find out about the deal and Poppy. "Are you doing them yourself?"

"Mostly."

Big project for one person. The interior of the diner was straight out of the fifties, and not in a good way. "What's it going to be?"

"A bookstore and café-slash-tea room. I plan to have it open in time for the Fourth of July."

Well that was…ambitious, given that it was only a few weeks away. "How long have you been in town?" He hadn't heard any talk in town about a newcomer, and that was damn unusual.

"I came out here a few weeks ago and just fell in love with it. I bought this place, and I put an offer in on an old cottage yesterday down on Honeysuckle Lane."

"Two-story with gray shingle siding?"

She stilled, watching him more intently. "Yes, you know it?"

"I live next door."

Her eyes widened, and in the lantern light hanging from the ladder he saw that they were a rich, deep brown. "Oh. Well then we might be neighbors if all goes well."

If so, his neighborhood just got a major upgrade. "Looks like." To keep from staring at her, he tipped his head back to examine the back of the building. She had finished about two-thirds of her first coat, a soft blue color. "How much longer are you planning on working?"

"I want to get this coat finished at least. After I get the outside done, I'm starting demo on the inside. Hopefully tomorrow afternoon."

Noah stared at her in surprise. "Have you got a contractor to help you out? If not, my best friend owns a contracting business here in town. He's a stand-up guy. I'm sure he could take on some of the work for you."

A tiny frown appeared in the center of her forehead. "Really? I'll think about it, thanks. But I'm on a pretty tight budget, so I'm going to have to do most of the work myself."

Noah nodded, even more curious about her. No way she was even thirty, and she wasn't wearing a wedding band. Where had she gotten the money to buy this place? "Okay. His name's Beckett Hollister, if you change your mind. Tell him I referred you."

"I will."

He should leave, but instead found himself hesitating. This whole thing felt weird. She literally had no one helping her? "You're doing all of this by hand? You don't have a sprayer?"

"No."

Well that was just wrong. And crazy. "I've got one at home you can borrow. I'll go grab it and bring it back for you."

She blinked at him, her surprise clear. "Really?"

"Yeah. You're a Crimson Pointer now, and we take care of our own."

"Oh," she said softly, a touched smile curving her mouth. "That's really nice of you, thanks."

She seemed caught off guard by his offer. He understood. He was wary of strangers too. "It's no big deal. I'll be back in a bit." That way he could find out more about her, get a better feel for who she was. "Don't fall off that ladder while I'm gone."

"I won't."

He drove home, changed quickly, then grabbed the sprayer and a few trim brushes from his garage before heading back. Half an hour ago he'd been beat and ready to hole up for the night, but now he had plenty of energy back. Who was Poppy Larsen, and what was her story?

She had almost finished the bottom of the east side of the building when he got there.

"Reinforcements have arrived," he announced as he came up the sidewalk, and began setting up the work light and sprayer. He could help her out, dig into her background a little *and* have something to distract him from his shitty day. Win-win.

"You don't have to do that," she protested, setting her roller down and hurrying over to him. "It's more than enough that you're lending it to me in the first place."

"I'm happy to help. Had nothing to do tonight anyway," he said, filling the reservoir. Nothing besides drink beer alone and wish he could have done more to keep Brian locked up.

"Well, wow, I didn't expect this." She seemed uncomfortable with accepting his help.

"Might as well get used to it. People around here help each other out."

"That's nice to hear."

"So, Poppy. Where are you from?" he asked as he took the ladder around to the side of the building and adjusted the light so he could see the wall better.

"South Dakota. You?"

He climbed to the top so he could start painting in the gable. "Born and raised right here."

"Yeah? You're lucky."

He adjusted the nozzle and made his first pass, testing the spray pattern, making sure he didn't drip. "I am. It's a great place to live. You'll love it." This place was in his blood and he intended to stay forever. That decision had meant making certain sacrifices, including losing the woman he'd once planned to spend the rest of his life with and raise a family with, but he didn't regret his choice. Crimson was home and always would be.

"I'm looking forward to it."

Within an hour they had finished the edges and trim by hand, making small talk but mostly painting in silence. She was a hard worker, and a bit of a perfectionist, working out here as darkness fell with only the work light to see by. She was also guarded, giving him the bare minimum whenever he asked her questions. He didn't blame her, but something about her and her situation had his cop instincts jangling.

Poppy seemed sweet enough on the surface, but she was hiding something. He was certain of it.

Once they were done he climbed down from the ladder and did a walk around to make sure they had good coverage. "Looks pretty decent, but you may have some touch-ups to do come daylight."

"I don't care, this was just so nice of you, thank you. You've saved me hours and hours of work."

"My pleasure." He wiped his hands on a rag, eyed her with a newfound respect. He sincerely hoped her business did well here. "My sister Sierra is the vet in town," he said, gesturing across and down the street to her clinic. "She's a big bookworm, so I'll tell her about your place. She can help spread the word."

"That would be great." She stood, stretched her back, unconsciously giving him an eyeful of the full curves of her breasts as they pushed against the fabric of her shirt. "I'm guessing you're not much into tea parties, but do you like pie, Sheriff?"

"I love pie." Who didn't?

"What kind?"

"Any kind." His mom's pumpkin pie was famous in these parts, but he wasn't fussy.

"But what's your favorite?"

"Cherry, I guess. The sour kind."

She nodded. "Okay. As soon as I get my new appliances installed, I'll make you one."

That was sweet, but he didn't want anything in return. "You don't have to make me a pie."

"Well you're getting one. And free coffee at the shop for life." She gestured to the building. "It would have taken me the rest of the night and most of tomorrow to get the second coat done. You're a life saver."

"You're welcome. And talk to Beckett if you decide you want a professional hand."

"I will." She gathered up her roller and brushes and turned to offer him her hand. "Well. See you around the 'hood."

He nodded. "Maybe even over the fence." That would be a nice change in scenery.

A dimple appeared in her cheek as she smiled back at him. She was adorable in a girl-next-door way with her hair mussed and paint-stained clothes. He could just imagine how gorgeous she would be cleaned up. But looks—and people—could be deceiving. "Maybe."

Potential neighbor, buddy, and she's hiding something. So back that train of thought up the tracks.

He drove home, deep in thought.

Everyone had secrets. He just hoped Poppy's wouldn't bring trouble to Crimson Point.

Chapter Fourteen

This was a really bad idea. Probably the worst Beckett had had in a while.

But he was doing it anyway, because he owed Sierra an apology that needed to be delivered in private, and because he didn't want things to be weird between them going forward.

Though kissing his best friend's little sister definitely made things weird.

That kiss two nights ago had been a serious wake-up call. No matter how much he wanted her, he couldn't risk ruining the most important relationships in his life by taking things any farther. That's what he'd brought her here to say.

"Come on in," he told Sierra, who followed him into his kitchen.

He hadn't slept for shit after she left the other night, cursing himself for what he'd said and done—for wanting way more—and stewing about what had happened to Ella. He'd had multiple nightmares, to the point where he'd finally downed half a bottle of Jack to make himself pass out.

Last night had been the same, except for the alcohol.

He'd opted for a pot of hot coffee instead, and catching up on work. She'd been on his mind constantly. This morning they'd both spent another few hours at the sheriff's department, answering more questions and giving their official statements before heading to work. Now it was early afternoon.

Can we talk?

Her text an hour ago had frozen him on the way out of a jobsite. He'd wanted to say no. Almost had. After the other night, it was dangerous for them to be here alone. His defenses against her were already too weak. But they needed to talk things through and limit the damage done. He owed her at least that much.

She stopped in front of the sink and turned to face him. "Let me see your hand." She held out hers expectantly, palm up. She'd been a bit shaken when everything had first happened the other night, but seemed fine today.

"My hand's fine."

She arched an eyebrow and wiggled her fingers. "As a medical professional, I'll be the judge of that."

Resigned, he stuck out his hand for her to examine. "Nothing's broken." He'd broken plenty of bones to know the difference.

She grasped it gently, checking it. And just that innocent touch turned him on. "I agree, I don't think there's any fractures," she said, taking a closer look at his knuckles. "But it's swollen and bruised and gonna be sore for at least a week. Come with me."

Before he could protest she'd curled her fingers around his wrist and led him over to the couch. Across the room, Walter stopped snoring long enough to open one eye and look at him from the dog bed Beckett had put in front of the fireplace, then went right back to sleep.

"He's such a character," Sierra said with a chuckle.

"Yeah. He's got so much personality," he said in a bland tone.

"Okay, sit," she ordered him, tugging on his wrist. He sat, albeit reluctantly, stayed put while she went back to the kitchen and came back a minute later with a makeshift icepack, some water and ibuprofen.

"You're making a big deal out of nothing," he muttered.

"Beckett." She gave him a hard look. "Do me a favor, take the damn pill and be quiet."

He made a face but took the pill and allowed her to wrap his hand up with the ice on the back of it. She sank beside him onto the couch, and even though he'd already decided on his course of action for them he was still torn between grabbing her and kissing her until she melted, and getting up and walking away.

Putting distance between them was the smart thing to do, but then, nobody had ever accused him of being a genius. "So about the other night," he began.

She set an elbow on the back of the couch and propped her head in her hand. "Which part?"

Damn, she apparently wasn't going to make this easy on him. He'd start at the beginning. "Sorry I lost my cool like that. With Brian." Well, that she'd seen it. He definitely didn't regret punching that asshole.

"Don't be sorry. I'm glad we caught him in time. Mostly I'm glad he's been charged, and you haven't."

"I knew she wasn't hanging around here just for the hell of it. Just never imagined it was because of anything like that." Shit, he should have figured it out sooner. All the signs were there. How had he not put the pieces together?

"Me either." She shook her head. "I hate thinking about what would have happened if she hadn't told us."

"I know. What about you, you okay?" His gut told him the incident had dredged up something ugly for her.

She nodded but looked at the floor rather than at him. "It just...brought up some things for me."

His focus sharpened. "What things?"

Her eyes were so incredibly blue. "Did Noah ever tell you about our Uncle Tom?"

"No."

"He was a friend of my parents, not really our uncle. Anyway…" She blew out a breath. "Something about him always gave me the creeps. The way he looked at me, the feeling I got when he hugged me."

Beckett's insides tightened. He already didn't like where this was going.

"I never said anything, because I thought it was just me. Then one weekend, he babysat us while my parents were out of town. My best friend was staying over with us. He knew her, and I didn't like the way he looked at her either. In the middle of the night I heard him come down the hall and I was sure he was coming to my room."

He forced himself to remain still. To not react even though a growl was building in his throat.

"But he walked past, to the room where my friend was sleeping. She always liked to stay in the guest room because we had a four-poster bed in there. I usually slept in it with her when she stayed over, but that night for some reason I wanted to be in my own room. I heard him open the guestroom door." She swallowed, tucked her knees up. "I heard muffled cries. I was scared, so I ran to get Noah."

"How old were you?"

"Eight."

Hell.

"I followed Noah to the door. And when he threw it open, we saw Uncle Tom holding my naked friend in front of him on the bed. He had a hand over her mouth and the other around her neck. His pants were down. We got there literally seconds before he raped her."

"Jesus Christ."

"Yeah. It was awful. Noah went crazy and attacked

him. Tom ran out, bleeding. The police found him a mile from our house. They hauled Noah and me in for questioning while my friend went to the hospital. Everything was a mess. My friend was never the same again."

He could imagine. "What did your parents do?"

"After Tom was arrested they severed ties with him and we never saw him again. There was some friction between our parents and Noah for a while after. And with me, too, because they refused to talk about it. They wanted to just move on and pretend it never happened."

Beckett had never known that. It shocked him, actually. The Buchanans had always seemed like the ideal family to him.

"Tom was arrested for raping another girl about a decade ago. I heard he died in jail a few years back. Hanged himself."

"He never touched you?" It was killing him.

She shook her head, adamant. "No. At least, not in an overtly sexual way. But whenever he did, it made my skin crawl. Even as a child I sensed his intent, saw something wrong in the way he looked at me. Hearing Ella the other night made me furious and sick, because it made me feel helpless all over again."

Beckett's free hand curled into a fist and he clenched his molars together. Yeah. He knew how that felt.

She gave him a startled look. "Are you grinding your teeth?"

He grunted. It burned him to know she had ever gone through anything like that, even more so because the offender had been a family friend. Beckett had never heard the story before.

"Noah was my protector, even back then."

"Good thing I didn't know about Tom at the time," Beckett said. He would have been the same age as Noah at the time it happened. He would have torn Tom apart.

"Me too. After what I saw last night, I can just imagine what you would've done if he'd attacked me."

"I would *always* protect you," he said, looking deep into her eyes. "If you were ever in trouble, I would be there. I'd do whatever it took to make sure you were safe." *Even if it's me I need to protect you from.*

Her expression softened, a little smile playing about the edges of her mouth that he wanted to feel under his. That taste the other night hadn't been enough. Not nearly enough. And he was afraid that when it came to her, nothing ever would be. Another reason to shore up the crumbling boundary between them. "I know you would. And I love that about you. That you care more than you let people think you do."

She wasn't wrong, but she didn't really understand. He sighed. "I've seen things happen to kids that I can't forget." He wasn't going to elaborate, because he didn't want her to have the same images in her head that haunted him. "Things I couldn't do anything about at the time. It made me feel sick inside."

She searched his eyes. "While you were overseas?"

He nodded. "You saw Ella the other night. The way she wouldn't look at us. As though she was ashamed. As though it was her fault." He pushed out a deep breath, the cold in his hand becoming an ache now. "What happened over there stayed with me. It drove us all crazy not to be able to protect those kids, or at least stop the abuse. Trust me, I would have shot every last one of those sick bastards if it wouldn't have landed me and my guys in Leavenworth for the rest of our lives."

She reached for his uninjured hand, curled her fingers around it. "I'm sorry. Ella was lucky. And to be honest, I was damn relieved that her mom believed us right away. Sometimes the parents side with the abuser and make everything worse."

"True. Tiana's a great mom." One side of his mouth

160

kicked up. "And I'd be lying if I said I didn't wish your brother had let her have a go at the guy."

She smiled. "Yeah, I wish he had too." Then she tipped her head to the side, considering him for a long moment. "You look like you need a hug."

He stiffened, opened his mouth to protest, but she was already winding her arms around his neck and resting her head on his shoulder.

At the feel of her, the walls around his heart crumbled a little more. He'd had a bitch of a past forty-eight hours, and only Sierra had made it bearable. But blurring the line between friends and lovers any more wasn't fair to her. She didn't know the truth about him. Wouldn't want him if she understood just how badly his soul was stained, all the baggage he carted around.

He wouldn't do that to her. Letting her go and putting some distance between them was the right thing to do. It was what he'd meant to do when he'd agreed to come back here and talk.

Except now that she was holding him, it was the last thing he wanted to do, and he was scrambling to recall all the reasons why he should pull away.

She smelled incredible, felt perfect pressed against his side, and dammit, he was so damn tired of holding back. Of punishing himself for his failures and carrying his heavy load alone.

Shit.

With a sigh he wound his arms around her and turned slightly, bringing her against his chest. She made a contented sound and snuggled closer, making his heart squeeze.

This was exactly what he'd needed, and again he found himself questioning all the reasons why he should stay away from her. They had history together, a lifetime of friendship—his intentionally pulling away the past while notwithstanding—solidified by his bond to her brother and parents. She also didn't fully understand what she would be getting into by entering a relationship with him.

But dammit, his desire for her was too strong, and threatened to overtake everything else, even his fear of losing her and her family. He could almost feel the battle slipping away from him. And he was so damn afraid of losing her forever if he did.

"If I tried to warn you away from me again, would it make any difference?" he asked, pretty sure he already knew the answer.

"None at all. But your voice is damn sexy, so if you still feel the need to, go ahead."

He almost grinned, but sobered fast. "There are things about me you don't know. And if you did, they'd change the way you see me." She deserved more than him.

She pulled back to look at him. "No they wouldn't." She said it immediately, her expression serious but calm.

Yes, they would. God, he had to tell her at least some of it, try to make her understand what he meant. "I...struggle sometimes." Jesus, it was hard to say that aloud. Especially to her, when she was the one whose admiration he craved the most.

"With what?"

Where to start? "Fitting back into society. With things I've seen and done. Things I couldn't do." He hated telling her even that much but she deserved to know. "I have nightmares. Adjusting to life back here is harder than I expected. I'm not the same guy you grew up with."

"I know you're not," she said softly. "The same as I know that neither of us are perfect. But I still want a chance with you anyway."

She said it with such conviction that all his remaining arguments died in his throat. His heart thudded against his ribs as he stared at her. The pull between them, their connection was so damn strong, but he didn't want to fuck this up and lose her as well as Noah if it turned out he was more than she could handle and less than she deserved.

As though she sensed him wavering, Sierra looked him dead in the eye as she continued. "We've known each other for a long time. I understand you better than most people, even if I don't know all your secrets. But if you ever decide you want to tell me about them, I'll be here to listen. The only thing I couldn't stand is you continuing to shut me out."

Beckett's chest constricted and he couldn't look away.

Christ. With those four sentences she'd essentially rigged his protective walls with explosives and detonated them. It seemed like he'd been swimming against the current for so long now, trying to keep away from her, outdistance her and outrun the inevitable.

He'd failed. And now he needed her too badly to push her away. Strong as he was, he wasn't strong enough to stay away. He couldn't stop this any longer.

Pushing his free hand into her hair, he slid his fingers through the soft, silky tresses before burying his nose in them, breathing her in. Heat and arousal swept through him in a rush, along with a sense of rightness. It scared the shit out of him.

"Are you sure this is what you want?" he made himself ask in a last ditch attempt to give her an out, brushing her hair away from her cheek. He was territorial as hell and wouldn't apologize for it. It was only fair to warn her of that. "Because if we take things any farther, there's no going back. You'll be mine and no one else's."

None of that was romantic or remotely politically correct, but he didn't give a shit because that was how he felt. If she wasn't on board with that, better to end this now before they both did something they would regret later.

Surprise flitted across her face, then a smile of pure female satisfaction that made his gut clench and his heart pound. "That's an awfully possessive thing to say for an aloof guy like you."

He snorted. "Trust me, I'm anything but aloof when it comes to you."

Something close to triumph flared in her eyes. "I've wanted to be yours for a damn long time, Beckett." She smiled. "But I know you're going to be more than worth the wait."

Lust and possessiveness hit him so hard his whole body tightened. When it came to getting something he wanted, Beckett didn't play fair. He wanted Sierra, no holds barred.

Starting right now, he would make her his.

"Sweetness, I'll make sure of that," he said, and leaned her backward to stretch her out and press her into the cushions.

SIERRA'S HEART THUDDED in a relentless rhythm against her ribs as Beckett stared down at her with so much hunger in his eyes it made her insides clench. She was all in, for better or worse, and now there was no going back.

Without a word he grasped the bottom of his shirt and methodically began peeling it upward. The abrupt change in him startled her a little, but not enough to stop this. She'd wanted him for so long and he would never do this with her just for kicks.

She pushed up onto her elbows, her mouth going dry as each inch of his bare torso was revealed to her ravenous gaze. Up, up the fabric moved, exposing bronzed skin and sculpted muscles of a man who had spent his entire adult life honing his body into a lethal weapon.

Her gaze snagged on the design displayed on the well-developed slope of his left pec. She'd never seen the tattoo before. *Molon Labe* was written in an old script beneath a distinctly Pacific Northwest native-stylized eagle. Beautiful and unique. It would look gorgeous as a framed black-and-white photograph.

Then he dragged the shirt over his head, and all she could do was gape at the beauty of his muscled arms and shoulders. It had been years since she'd seen him without a shirt on down at the beach when he'd first joined the military. He'd looked sexy as hell back then, but now... Now he took her breath away.

She sat up and reached for him, eager to touch him, feel all that power beneath her fingertips. His smooth skin was hot, the right side of his ribs nicked here and there by what she could only assume were shrapnel scars.

Before she could look her fill, Beckett cupped a big hand around the back of her head and brought his mouth down on hers. He'd taken her off guard the other night. This time she was ready. Or she thought she was.

She expected him to take. To dominate. Instead he explored, slowly stretching out on top of her until he pressed her down into the cushions.

She gasped at the feel of his warm, hard body blanketing her, his weight pinning her in place as he sucked at her top lip, then her bottom one. He slid his tongue across them, delved inside gently, the velvet caress igniting a shockwave of need inside her. And then his hips settled between hers, the hard ridge of his erection pressing into her core through her jeans and she couldn't help the moan that spilled out of her.

Oh my God...

Beckett delved deeper, stroking and caressing with his tongue while she clung to his shoulders, ran her hands up and down the ridged power of his back. She was melting from the inside out, her insides quaking. Making out with him was a thousand times better than she had dreamed it would be, and finally having him reach for her made tears prick the backs of her eyes.

He pushed up on one arm to reach for the bottom of her shirt, still kissing her. She helped him, fighting a tiny jangle of nerves as they pulled the material up and over her head. His eyes darkened as he stared down at the deep blue satin cradling the mounds of her breasts.

But instead of tugging the bra aside as she'd expected, he trailed his fingers lightly over her chin, down her throat to her collarbones. That tender, tantalizing touch was so unexpected after the rough edge he'd shown her two nights ago.

The pads of his fingers grazed oh-so-softly across her skin, making her nipples pebble and her core throb. His touch drifted down into the valley between her breasts, his expression absorbed as he mapped the curve of her right breast, then the left.

He didn't undo her bra. Rather, he skimmed his fingers down the midline of her body, over her stomach, coming up onto his knees to dip beneath the waistband of her jeans. "Let me see you," he said, his voice husky. "I've imagined what you look like for way too long."

His words turned her heart over even as they injected another shot of arousal through her body. The thought of being naked while he was still partially dressed was a little unsettling, but she'd wanted this forever and wouldn't deny him anything. She undid the button, lifted her hips so he could help her work the denim over and down her legs.

A low, throttled groan rolled out of his throat as he took her in, lying there against the leather in nothing but her matching bra and thong. "Sweetness, you don't know how beautiful you are to me," he breathed, and bent forward to press his lips just above her navel.

Sweetness. The word itself, and the low, intimate tone he used hit her like an arrow to the heart.

She clenched her fingers in his short hair, his heavy stubble scraping her tender skin. Then he started kissing his way upward and her eyes drifted closed just as his lips and tongue stroked the curve of her breast. His clever fingers slipped around beneath her to undo the bra. One light tug at the front and she was bared to his gaze.

Beckett made a low, hungry sound, his hands coming up to cradle the soft mounds. She gasped, bit her lip as he ran his thumbs across her hard nipples, sending pleasure zinging through her veins.

Her fingers tightened in his hair, a groan of relief and pleasure coming out of her when he surrounded one tight point with the soft, wet heat of his mouth. Sierra held him to her while the restless ache between her legs turned into a relentless throb.

He seemed in no hurry, totally absorbed as he sucked first one side, then the other, using his fingers to tease the one his mouth had just vacated. All the while he kept her anchored in place with his hips, and the inability to move only heightened everything.

Heat shot through her, the scent of leather and man swirling around her while she drowned in decadent pleasure. One hand blindly sought his hip, curved around the taut muscles of his ass and pulled, needing more pressure. He gave it to her, settling the ridge of his erection tight to her core and moving his hips in slow circles while his mouth continued to drive her insane.

"I need more," she finally pleaded, voice tight. Her heart thundered out of control, all her senses overloaded.

"I know what you need," he said, easing his body to the side a little, capturing her lips to smother her cry of protest at the loss of his weight and the pressure where she needed it most.

He leaned over her, looming there while his tongue teased hers. His hand drifted down, his callused palm sliding over her belly, over the top of one thigh before his fingertips brushed up the sensitive inside to cup the center of her thong.

She hitched in a breath, her whole body tightening, raw need pulsing through her. "Beckett…"

"I've got you," he murmured, his mouth moving to the side of her neck, finding a spot that made her shiver as his fingers stroked the lace over her wet core, making her entire body sizzle. "Lie still for me."

God, he had her, all right. Maybe more than he realized. She almost felt like she was having an out of body experience, finally getting to live the culmination of all her secret fantasies.

A tiny part of her brain buzzed, warning her that moving this fast wasn't a good idea, but she was too keyed up now, ready to explode. He couldn't leave her like this.

Beckett's teeth closed gently over her skin, his lips sucking, tongue laving as his fingers slipped beneath the lace into her slick folds. A soft cry spilled from her as he teased her with tiny motions, gliding slow and easy up and down, moving a little higher with each stroke until finally he brushed the swollen knot of her clit.

His mouth was there to capture her whimper, his tongue sinking in to twine with hers. Sierra was lost in a haze of sensation, her skin hypersensitive, his touch between her legs too perfect to bear.

"Did you ever think about me when you touched yourself?" he murmured.

Blood rushed to her face but she was comforted that he couldn't see it because he was too busy teasing her lips. "Yes."

"How often?"

She groaned and strained to lift her hips, needing more pressure from his fingers. She'd thought he would be rough and demanding. This tenderness was almost torture. "All the time," she gasped, on some level knowing she should probably be embarrassed by the admission but at this point she didn't even care.

He rewarded her with a growl of approval and a caress of such pinpoint precision she forgot to breathe. "That's so hot. I thought of you so many times too," he said.

Really? "You did?" she managed to gasp out.

"Yeah." Then he bent and captured her nipple with his mouth.

Ohhh...

Sierra trembled under the dual lash of pleasure and squeezed her eyes shut.

This was a thousand times better than all the times she'd touched herself while thinking of him. And picturing Beckett stroking himself while thinking about her was insanely hot. He was still intense, but far more patient now than she'd expected. In fact, at the moment he seemed determined to make her crazy, each stroke of his fingers and tongue pushing her closer to the edge.

She made a choked sound, burning, and he was the only one who could extinguish the flames. "God, Beckett, I'm..."

"Gonna come for me? Yeah, you are," he said, his lips brushing her sensitive nipple as he spoke. "When I've decided you're ready."

Oh, God. She wanted to look at him but didn't have the strength to peel her eyes open. Her body throbbed all over, frantic for release. "Just don't stop," she blurted, desperate.

"Hmm," he mused, never stopping. "Don't like being teased?"

"Not today," she gasped out, tugging harder on his hair. *Do something.*

He growled. "I'm gonna make it so good, sweetness," he said in a low, possessive tone that sent a delicious shiver through her. She loved that he called her that. "I'm gonna make you crave me."

The dark promise almost pushed her over the edge. *I already do.*

His fingers slid down, adding pressure at her entrance, then eased inside her and stroked, his thumb settling directly over her clit. Unable to speak, she held on for dear life.

The pleasure intensified with each skillful caress of his fingers and tongue, until her incoherent moans filled the air. "Please, I can't—"

"Lie still." This time there was steel beneath the velvet command.

She quivered, fighting to obey when all she wanted to do was writhe. He didn't stop. Didn't tease now, just maintained that exact pressure and rhythm to push her over the edge.

Sierra's whole body contracted in the instant before the orgasm hit. She cried out in ecstasy, her hips rocking against his hand, fingers locked on the back of his head while the pleasure crashed through her. On and on it went, while he drew every last moment of it out.

When it finally ebbed she went limp against the couch, panting, and eased her grip. Beckett lifted his head and braced himself on his forearm to look down at her, a tender possessiveness in his gaze that turned her heart over. He slipped his hand from her panties and curved it around her hip, squeezing with firm pressure.

Mine.

The gesture said it as clearly as if he'd spoken it, and it thrilled her to her toes.

Something fanned over her hair. Startled, she whipped her head to the side to see Walter's face inches from hers, his nose quivering as he sniffed at her, eyes alert, his sausage-shaped body rocking slightly with each wag of his tail. "Oh, God, he's a canine voyeur."

"Walter, get outta here," Beckett said with a rough laugh, shooing the dog away with an authoritative wave of his arm. "Perv," he added as Walter retreated to the edge of the rug and laid down with a bored sigh, staring at them.

Laughing softly, Sierra looked back up at Beckett. He came up on his knees, his heavy thighs straddling hers, and the bulge of his erection was impossible to miss. She leaned up to reach for it but he caught her wrist with a negative sound. Startled, she met his eyes.

"Got a meeting I have to be at in twenty minutes, and then I'm gonna take my dad out for his surprise. He's having a good day. So as much as I hate the idea of getting dressed and leaving things between us like this right now, I have to go." He leaned over to grab his shirt from the floor, and tugged it back on.

"Oh. But what about..." She eyed the front of his jeans, then looked up at him.

"Later," he said, his eyes holding such sensual promise that her belly fluttered. Raising her hand to his mouth, he kissed the palm, then gently nipped the heel. His gaze raked over her, pausing on her bare breasts as a low groan came out of him. "And you know what?"

She barely remembered her own name at the moment. "What?"

The sexy smile he gave her curled her toes. "It's definitely going to be worth the wait."

Chapter Fifteen

Oh, for crying out...

*O*At the resistance on the other end of the leash, Beckett paused in the middle of the hospital hallway and masked his impatience as he stopped to look behind him. "Come on, Walter, we're on a tight timeline here."

The doggy voyeur continued plodding along behind him, taking his sweet-ass time.

Sierra thought he'd make a great therapy dog? He'd just see about that. But damn, Beckett was in a great mood. Best he'd been in in months. Maybe years.

All because of Sierra.

He couldn't stop thinking about her, about the sweet, uninhibited way she'd come undone for him on the couch a few hours ago, and couldn't wait to see her again as soon as he got back from the hospital later this afternoon. His life was far from settled or ironed out, his dad's declining health and the stress of the business weighed on him, but the thought of finally sliding deep inside Sierra filled him with anticipation.

Even if a large part of him was still terrified that he would fuck this up.

It seemed like half an hour had passed before Walter managed to shuffle his way down the rest of the hall. Beckett poked his head into his dad's room and knocked on the open door. "Hey. Brought a special visitor to see you."

His dad perked up and pushed himself upright against the pillows stacked behind him. "Oh?"

Walter waddled into the room and stood there looking like the saddest animal on earth.

His dad cracked a laugh. "Well, Walter. Your pictures didn't do you justice."

"What, he's even uglier in person?"

"Way uglier. Lord, that tongue…"

Walter shifted his gaze from Beckett to his father and back, the end of his tail wagging feebly. "You wanna pet him?" Beckett asked.

"Love to. Come on up here, handsome fella." He patted the covers.

Beckett stooped, bit back a grunt as his back twinged while lifting Walter up onto the foot of the bed. The mutt stood there for a moment looking confused, then extended his head to sniff the hand Beckett's dad held out. Walter's tail wagged a little, then he all but collapsed with a deep groan and rolled to his side for a belly rub.

"And that's Walter," Beckett said, shaking his head. For some reason the dog seemed to get a smile out of pretty much everyone they met.

Walter was a secret charmer. While walking him in town and on the beach this morning before heading to the sheriff's office, Beckett had received more female attention than he had in the past two years, all because of the dog.

"He's scrawny." His dad stroked a hand down Walter's back. "I can feel all his ribs."

"We're working on that. Trying to work on his personality, too."

"I dunno, he kinda reminds me of you."

Beckett shot his dad a mock scowl. "Thanks a lot. You know I look like you, right?"

"Yeah, but old Walter's got that whole grouchy, standoffish vibe going for him." His dad eyed him. "See the resemblance now?"

He chuckled under his breath.

His dad's eyes widened. "Was that almost a laugh?" He looked at Walter in feigned astonishment. "Who is this guy you brought in to see me? Can't be my son."

"Your son is right here, and his hearing still works just fine."

"That's a damn miracle." He continued petting Walter, whose eyes were closed, well on his way back to dreamland.

Beckett glanced at the food tray beside the bed. Half the lunch was gone, and that was better than any other day this week. "How you feeling right now?"

"Not too bad. Got a decent sleep last night."

Perfect. "So I talked to your medical team." He slipped his hands into his pockets. "You up for an adventure right now?"

His father's dark eyes shot to his, curiosity and excitement burning in them. "What kind of an adventure?"

"An out of the hospital, father-son adventure."

"Shit, yes. Get me outta here."

Beckett grinned. "Okay then. You stay and pet Walter while I get everything organized."

It took some doing but the staff was fantastic, loading his dad up with enough pain meds to keep him comfortable for the next few hours. Then they unhooked his IV, dressed him warmly and put him in a wheelchair.

His dad was grinning from ear to ear as Beckett pushed

174

him down the hall, Walter perched morosely in his lap, long ears and tongue dangling. "Yeeehaw," his dad crowed, chortling as Beckett picked up speed and headed for the elevator. "I feel like we're making a prison break."

"We pretty much are."

In the lobby his dad cackled with glee as they headed for the main doors. "Woohoo, *freed*om!" he yelled, drawing everyone's attention. He closed his eyes and tipped his head back when they got outside. "Oh, yeah. Smell that salty air."

This was supposed to be a fun day, something to make his dad smile and make him forget for a few hours that he was dying, but for some reason those words put a lump in Beckett's throat.

He helped his dad into the front passenger seat of his truck, and Walter seemed happy enough to sit in his dad's lap so Beckett left the dog there. "Where are we going?" his dad asked, eager as a puppy as he put on his seatbelt and waited for Beckett to start the engine.

"It's a surprise." One he hoped his dad would love. He'd called a buddy that morning to lock down the favor. Walter seemed to like going for rides in the truck, so...hopefully he'd like this too.

Beckett drove them half an hour south down the coast and took the turnoff toward the water. His dad was still perky, looking around at everything. "Are we here? There's nothing out here."

"You'll see." A few minutes down the road he reached their destination.

His father turned his head to gape at him. "Dune buggying?"

"Yep." He couldn't help but grin. "Haven't done it in ages. At least not outside of A-stan or Syria. Remember the last time we went out?"

"You were about eighteen and full of yourself. As I recall you thought you were such hot shit that you did something stupid and got your buggy stuck at the bottom of the dune. Had to get the owner to come tow you out and he was not happy."

"Nope. But I've learned a trick or two since then. You'll see."

His dad's smile of anticipation was a balm for the soul. "What about the dog?"

"He's coming too. Got it all worked out. Come on, Walter, down you get." He lifted the dog out of the truck, and this time his back didn't twinge.

Walter plopped his butt on the sand and sat there looking sorry for himself, staring up at Beckett with droopy, red-rimmed eyes.

"Come on, you'll like this," Beckett coaxed, tugging on the leash.

Walter sighed, got up and reluctantly followed, resigned to his fate.

Beckett's old high school buddy who ran the place had their dune buggy ready for them. "Thought Walter would appreciate these," he said to Beckett, who grinned.

"Goggles?"

"Doggles."

Ha! "Awesome." Beckett put Walter in the back of the buggy, strapped the seatbelt through his harness and tugged the doggles in place, easing his ears out so they weren't pinched by the elastic straps. Walter stared back at him glumly through the plastic lenses, a canine Eeyore.

He was so damn cute that Beckett pulled out his phone to take some pictures, and texted one to Sierra. *Furry copilot*, he typed. She was running errands right now but would get a kick out of it when she was done.

Beckett helped his dad strap in next, tucked a blanket around him to ward off the chill of the ocean breeze, and handed him a helmet and goggles. "You ready to do this?"

"You bet."

"You gotta tell me if you start to hurt, though."

His dad made a face. "Just drive, junior."

Excitement hummed through Beckett as he buckled in behind the wheel and fired up the engine. He drove them down the path that led to the dunes, and started up the first incline. "How you doing?" he asked his dad, concerned about his pain level. They'd drugged him up pretty good at the hospital, but bouncing around in a dune buggy while full of tumors might be too much even for the meds.

"Great. Don't feel a thing."

Chance he was lying? Ninety-nine percent. But Beckett would have to trust him to speak up if it became too much. "Tell me if you start to hurt anywhere."

His dad waved a hand impatiently. "Shut up and drive, boy."

Yes, sir. At the top of the hill the ocean came into view in the distance, an endless expanse of blue that stretched along the entire horizon where it met the sand.

Grinning, Beckett paused for a moment, met his father's enthusiastic gaze, then gunned it. His dad let out a whoop of pure elation as they raced down the far side of a dune and hurtled up the next one.

He stopped at the crest to check on Walter. To his surprise the dog's mouth was open, his tongue lolling in his near-toothless mouth. It almost looked like he was smiling. "What do you think, Walter?"

Walter wagged his tail.

"Yeah, thatta boy," Beckett praised, and hit the gas. They plunged down the dune, tires spraying sand, then rocketed up the next slope.

"Your driving's sure come a long way," his dad yelled over the wind and noise of the engine. He didn't seem to be in any pain, but he was a tough old bugger. Beckett would keep a close eye on him.

"Had some experience with driving in sand over the years," he yelled back. He aimed for a steep drop and shot toward it, chuckling when his dad grabbed hold of the roll bar. Oh, yeah. This was so much damn fun.

The buggy hurtled down the incline, engine racing as they picked up speed.

A howl sounded from behind him.

Startled, Beckett slowed a little and glanced behind him. Walter was perched on the seat in his harness still wearing his doggles, ears and tongue flying in the wind, his head thrown back and his mouth open as he let out a loud baying sound. And his tail was thumping like mad against the seat.

Beckett laughed and curved up a smaller dune. "Might have created a monster."

"Walter, you *animal*," his dad joked to the dog.

Walter howled again in doggy delight, and they both laughed.

Beckett couldn't remember the last time he'd had this much fun—with the exception of what he'd done to Sierra earlier. Years at least. And when he stopped at the crest of another dune to swap places with his dad, the smile on his old man's gaunt face squeezed Beckett's heart so hard it was as though someone had clamped a vise around it.

"She's all yours," Beckett said, then rounded the front to take the passenger seat and buckle in. "Be gentle with me."

"Not a chance." His dad gunned it and it was Beckett's turn to holler as they raced down the sand.

Rather than go up and down the dunes some more, his father turned them sharply toward the beach. In minutes they were racing along the wet strip of sand just beyond the reach of the rolling waves, the wind whistling through their helmets.

Beckett took out his phone and snapped some pictures of his dad, whose smile was clear even through the helmet visor, then took some of Walter. It looked like the dog was having the time of his life, and maybe he was. Who knew the old timer was an adrenaline junkie at heart?

Wet sand and seawater sprayed up from beneath the back tires as his dad raced them down the beach. Miles and miles of damp sand lay before them, not another soul in sight. God he'd missed this, just hanging with his dad. They'd lost so much time together while Beckett was away on one deployment after the other.

Finally his dad decided he'd had enough fun for the day and turned them back toward the garage. Beckett texted a few more pictures to Sierra, including a selfie of sorts of him and his dad, and Walter unknowingly photobombing in the background, his face visible between the gap in the front seats. They weren't anywhere near the quality that she shot even with her phone, but she'd still like them. A few minutes later she responded.

Omg, that's the cutest thing I've ever seen! Are you guys having fun?

Having a blast, he typed back, smiling to himself. He couldn't wait to see her tonight. To pull her thighs apart and slide his tongue between them, have her hands and mouth all over him. There were so many things he wanted to do to her, and have her do to him in return.

He just hoped the real him didn't make her change her mind about them eventually, because if it did, his whole world would implode.

"Who you texting?" his dad asked as he steered them up the winding path through the smaller dunes tufted with plumes of sea grass.

"Sierra. Thought she'd get a kick out of Walter."

His father eyed him speculatively but didn't comment. Back at the garage Beckett removed Walter's doggles and unstrapped him before setting him on the ground. His dad was slow getting out of the buggy.

"How's your pain level?" Beckett asked.

"It's all right," he replied, slightly stooped over as he headed for the truck.

Beckett glanced at his dad as he drove out of the

parking lot a minute later. He looked exhausted now, lines forming around the sides of his mouth. "Guess we overdid it, huh?"

"Nah. Worth it. Haven't had that much fun in I can't remember since when." He reached over and gripped Beckett's shoulder in a firm grip. "Thank you."

"Thank *you*. It was fun." He was quiet for a while, Walter's rattling snores coming from the back seat. Normally he wasn't one to talk about his personal life, even to his dad, but this was important. His dad knew her, and with time running out, he didn't want to hide anything.

He exhaled. "Sierra and I are seeing each other, Dad." That sounded casual enough, even though he was anything but casual about her.

Those dark, sunken eyes focused on him, and a grin spread across his thin face. "Called that one years ago, my boy. Good for you. What took you so damn long?"

Beckett was so surprised he didn't know how to answer. "Whaddya mean, years?"

"Years. As in a series of three-hundred-and-sixty-five days."

He smothered a chuckle. "You never said anything."

"Neither did you."

Yeah, because he'd felt guilty as hell about it. How in hell had his old man noticed, when he'd barely let himself see it? "It's a big adjustment for both of us. Things are still brand new. Haven't even told Noah yet."

"Better not wait too long. But you and her, it feels good?"

He smiled. "Yeah." Amazing. Beckett refused to let his inner demons destroy his chance at happiness. He'd seen it happen to too many of the guys he'd served with. And he'd watched it happen to Carter all too recently.

"She's a sweetheart, I've always loved her. You better treat her right."

"You know I will." As long as she felt he was worthy of her.

"I do." His dad gave Beckett's shoulder an affectionate shove. "Tell her I said hi and that I'm happy for you both."

"I will." Beckett had a feeling Sierra would be touched by it.

The drive back to the hospital went by far too quickly, but his heart was lighter than it had been in years. Because now he had hope again, and the chance of a future with Sierra to fight for.

He left Walter sleeping in the truck with the windows half open and took his dad inside. A few feet inside the main entrance, his dad stopped, and from the drawn, pinched look on his face, Beckett realized how much the afternoon had exhausted him.

"Here," he said, grabbing an empty wheelchair. Beckett hated to see him in pain. His father eyed it with loathing but lowered into it. "You hungry?"

"No. Just tired."

Up in his dad's room the nurses were there to help him back into bed and restart his IV, along with another dose of pain meds. Beckett hovered nearby, his heart sinking at the sight of his dad lying there so frail and tired, willing the medication to kick in.

When they were alone again his dad motioned to the chair beside the bed. Beckett sat in it, took the hand his father held out to him. "I needed that so damn much," he said to Beckett with a little smile.

"Me too. You feeling any better now?"

His father was quiet a moment, still holding Beckett's hand. "I'm tired." His gaze strayed to the framed picture of Beckett's mom over on the side table. "I miss her so damn much."

An aching lump settled in the back of his throat. He swallowed hard. "I know. I do too."

That deep-set gaze swung back to Beckett, full of

weariness and pain. "You're not too old for me to give you a piece of fatherly advice, are you?"

"No."

His dark eyes were fierce with love and urgency. "Good. Because if Sierra makes you feel the way I felt about your mother, then you damn well hold onto her tight and don't let another day go by without telling her what she means to you. Life's so damn short, son. You'll regret it if you wait."

Beckett looked down at their joined hands. His dad was right, as usual. He squeezed that too-fragile hand gently. "Love you, Dad."

"Love you too."

Beckett sat there quietly until his father was fast asleep. Then, gently withdrawing his hand, he stood and left, the urgent need to see Sierra burning inside him.

Chapter Sixteen

"**M**ac, how the hell are you, man?" Beckett asked, grinning as he tucked his phone between his ear and shoulder and reached for the truck door handle.

While he'd been out with his dad he'd missed four phone calls, including one from a newcomer to the area from South Dakota—Miss Poppy Larsen, who he'd just met with. He wasn't sure how much work he could do for her on her limited budget, but Noah had referred him so he would set up a meeting, crunch some numbers and see what he could do for her.

"I'm doin' awright," Aidan answered in his distinctive Scottish burr. "You?"

"Can't complain. You still in Florida?"

"Aye, and the humidity's already killing me. Not sure I can stand another summer here. Will never ken how the locals can bear it. Now what's all this about a job offer? Did you finally decide to start your own contracting business?"

"Why, you interested?"

Aidan huffed out a laugh. "Depends on what you say next."

"Not the kind of contracting you're used to." Beckett figured that was a good thing. "I need a project manager for my home renovation business. We're slammed, have more work than we can handle right now, and it's only getting busier. You'd be responsible for helping with inspections and quotes, and managing the jobs and crew. And you'd get full benefits after three months."

"I thought Boyd was doing all that for you."

A heavy weight settled in Beckett's chest. "He was, until the other day." He cleared his throat. "I had to let him go."

"Sorry to hear that," Aidan said after a moment's pause. "How is he?"

"Not good. I've had to sever ties with him, it's gone that far."

"Ah, damn. What about Weaver?"

Based on what had happened yesterday, Beckett was pretty sure Jase was done as well. "I think he's reached that point too. To help me out he's temporarily taken on both CFO and project manager roles until I can find someone else."

"And that's where I come in, I suppose?"

"I want guys I can trust with me."

"Well that means a lot coming from you, Yank."

"It should," Beckett teased.

"What's it like there in Oregon?"

"Helluva lot cooler than Florida. A lot like Scotland, actually, except better."

Aidan grunted. "Eh, now yer bum's out the windae."

Beckett chuckled at the Scottish translation of *you're full of shit*. "I've missed your sayings, MacIntyre. So will you think about it? It's a full-time salary position, benefits, the works. With the added bonus that you'd get to work alongside me all week long."

"You trying to entice me, or make me run away screaming?"

"Hey, you seemed to like working under me well enough overseas."

"It was okay. And don't say under like that, it's weird." He paused. "Will there be regular range practice and access to high explosives with this job?"

"I can add that into your weekly schedule if it will help turn the tide in my favor."

"Ah, you know just how to sweet talk a man." He pronounced it like "mon".

God, he'd missed the Scottish bastard's dry sense of humor. "So? What do you think?"

"You know what? I *will* think about it. I need to look up this hometown of yours first, though. What was it again? Red Tide?" He rolled the R.

"No, that's a toxic algae bloom."

"Aye, perfect." He sounded smug.

Beckett shook his head, one side of his mouth turning upward. "It's Crimson Point. And yeah, it's way better than Scotland. Go ahead and look it up. You'll see."

Aidan scoffed. "We'll see about that. All right, I'll let you know by the end of the week if I'm interested or not. Friday?"

It was more than Beckett had actually expected, so he was hopeful because he would love to bring the Scotsman on board. "Sounds good. Take care, laddie," he finished, using his best accent.

"Don't call me that. Only a Scot can call another man that."

"Well now you've gone and hurt my feelings."

"Wait. You have feelings? As in plural? I was sure you used your only one up last year when we were in Syria."

"You mean during the mission when you told me you considered me an honorary Scot?"

Aidan grunted. "Must have been the heat."

Or because we cheated death when I got us all out of there alive by calling in a pinpoint danger close airstrike?

185

Beckett didn't say it, because it was too close to bragging and Aidan remembered that day as well as him. "Don't forget I've got Scottish blood in me from both sides of my tree. How much more Scottish can I get?"

"You could wear a kilt. I would take you much more seriously if you could pull off a kilt without making me laugh."

Beckett huffed a laugh. "Whatever, I'm not wearing a fucking skirt, even for you."

A gasp. "*Skirt*? How dare you. I'll have you know that—"

"Got another call coming in," he lied, enjoying both the banter and Aidan's sputtered outrage. "I'll talk to you Friday."

He hung up, had no sooner set his phone down in the console tray when it rang. Not MacIntyre calling back to argue the prowess and vital historical significance of the kilt.

Sierra.

A smile spread across his face. "Hi, beautiful."

"Wow, hi. I could definitely get used to that greeting."

"It's the truth. You almost finished for the day?" It was nearly four.

"Almost. I just got your flowers. They were waiting for me when I got back from the bank. They're beautiful, thank you."

"You're welcome." He wasn't the romantic type, but since that talk with his father just before leaving he'd felt the need to make a gesture to show her he was thinking of her. If he wanted to hold on to a woman as rare as Sierra, he needed to step up his game. He couldn't just phone that shit in. So he was trying.

"I loved the note even more," she said quietly.

Life is short. Let's not waste any more of it. "I'm glad." His dad's words to him earlier had had a profound effect on him. They had obliterated any remaining hesitation on his part, and pushed him into action. No matter how this played out between him and Sierra, he was going to take the risk and let her in. Or at least try to.

"Looks like you and your dad had an amazing time."

"We did. Think we overdid it, though. He was in pain when I got him back to the hospital, and exhausted. As soon as they gave him another dose of meds he was out."

She made a sympathetic sound. "I'm sure spending the afternoon having fun with you made it more than worth it. Are you headed home now?"

"Just gonna check one of the projects first."

"You up for a dinner date at my place, rather than going out tonight?"

All parts of him were up for that. "Maybe. What are you making?"

"Does it matter, as long as it's edible?"

"I'd rather eat you instead."

She gave a husky laugh. "I'm going to swing by the hospital and visit with Molly for a bit, then grab the groceries on my way home."

"Want me to bring anything?"

"Just have your gorgeous butt there at seven."

"How do you know it's gorgeous when you haven't seen it yet?"

"Hmm, but I plan to tonight."

Hell yes. "If you play your cards right."

"Seven o'clock, sharp."

He loved her sassiness. "Okay. I'll be there."

He drove to the jobsite with a smile on his face, full of anticipation about what tonight would bring. Things were moving fast between them, maybe too fast, but now that they'd crossed the line it was so damn hard to hold himself back with her.

It was a beautiful late spring afternoon. As close to perfect as it could get here on the coast.

Given what a great day he'd had up until now, he

should have known things were too good to last.

After checking in with Jase via phone and talking to the crew on site, Beckett was about to leave when someone came up the stairs. He tensed as Carter came into view. "What are you doing here?"

Carter glanced around, looking even more exhausted than he had the other day. "We alone?"

"Yeah." He folded his arms. "What do you want? I thought I made my position clear the other day." He waited.

There was no anger from Carter this time, however. No cutting or snide-ass remarks. Just a soul-deep sadness in those almost black eyes as he faced Beckett. "I wanted to apologize for what I said."

"You should be apologizing to Weaver, not me."

"I stopped by the office but he wasn't there, or at home. And he isn't taking my calls."

"You surprised?"

"No." Carter broke eye contact and lowered his head a moment before continuing. "Look, I know I haven't been the easiest to deal with lately. I'm...trying to get my life back together."

"What about Molly?"

He shook his head. "She won't talk to me. She's going ahead with the legal separation. We have to both be legal residents in Oregon for six months before she can file for divorce."

Beckett wouldn't say he was sorry. Molly had to do what Molly had to do, and Beckett wanted her to be safe and happy. With Carter, she was neither of those things anymore.

Carter drew a deep breath and seemed to force himself to meet Beckett's gaze. "I came to talk to you about the possibility of getting my job back."

Beckett stared at him. It might have been funny if it wasn't so fucking awkward and sad. "That's not happening."

A spark of anger lit in Carter's eyes. "Beck. I'm begging you, as a friend and someone you served with. As someone who had your back during all those tight spots we got into. Please."

It killed Beckett to have to refuse him. But he didn't have a choice. Carter had been a liability for a while now. He couldn't risk his business or reputation on someone so volatile and unreliable. And there was no easy way to say it. "I'm sorry. I can't." Not even odd jobs or handyman stuff, because he would still have to work with people.

Carter didn't react, just stared at him for a long moment, almost in shock. "So that's it then?"

"I can't. You'll have to look for a job elsewhere."

"Like where, back in Kansas?"

"Why not go home? You've still got family there."

Carter snorted derisively. "They don't give a shit about me. Guess nobody does." He dragged a hand through his hair, his expression full of defeat and desolation.

Beckett had to bite back the words forming on his tongue. *Let me see what I can do.* No. He couldn't risk taking a single step back from his stand on this. Couldn't risk passing his former teammate onto someone else, because Carter was so unstable. Even though it made Beckett feel like shit, Carter would have to fight this looming battle on his own.

"I'm sorry," he said again, unable to keep from saying something to fill the void.

"You're sorry." Bitterness dripped from each word.

"Yes. I am." He pushed out a breath, that damn guilt pricking him. "Look, I'll ask around, keep an ear open for anything that might work for you. If I hear of anything I'll let you know." Though it was gonna be damn hard to find anything that wouldn't require Carter working with other people.

Carter nodded without looking at him. "Yeah. See you

around." He turned and disappeared down the stairs, leaving Beckett's belly feeling like it was full of concrete.

God, he was so tired of feeling like shit for things he'd had to do in the line of duty, and now his career. For some reason it felt like the guilt over this situation with Carter threatened to become the proverbial straw on the camel's back.

Beckett had let a lot of people down during his years of service—unintentionally, though that didn't make anything better. Now he'd done the same to a teammate, a man he'd shed blood, sweat and tears with in the worst circumstances imaginable.

His mood was straight up pissy when he walked out the front door a few minutes later. Carter was nowhere to be seen. Beckett got into his truck, absently reached over to scratch Walter's floppy ear as he started the engine. He needed to go home, have a shower and clear his head before heading over to Sierra's, or he would ruin their night together. Carter was a grown man, and only Carter could fix the mess he was in.

Except Beckett had a bad, gut-deep certainty that things weren't going to get better for his former teammate.

The sight of the old Victorian perched on the cliff filled him with a bittersweet pang when he turned into the driveway. His parents had both loved this place, and so did he. It was home, still held pieces of them here.

His dad hadn't been back here in over two months. The next good day he had, Beckett should bring him back here for a few hours. Let him sit on the back porch in his favorite rocking chair with a beer while Beckett grilled them steaks, and enjoy the view together.

Inside he gave Walter his dinner and jumped into the shower, mentally shoving the meeting with Carter out of his mind. He'd had a great afternoon with his dad, and had a dinner with Sierra to look forward to. Soon he would feel her underneath him again, taste her. Tonight he was staking his claim in the most elemental way possible.

Whatever happened, he needed her tonight.

He changed into fresh jeans and a button-down shirt before heading out the door, checking his phone for messages as he reached the porch.

He'd missed three calls from the hospital while he was getting ready. No one had left a message or text. He frowned, a warning buzz igniting in the pit of his stomach. If it was really important they would have left a message, right?

They called three times in the past twenty minutes.

Icy fingers of unease wrapped around the base of his spine. He called the number back. "This is Beckett Hollister. I missed your calls just now."

"Beckett, hi, this is Nancy." The nurse from his father's floor he'd become friendly with. "You need to come here straight away. I'm afraid your dad's taken a turn for the worse."

Chapter Seventeen

Sierra did her best to conceal her concern, but the plain truth was, Molly looked awful. Dressed in pastel pink scrubs as they sat outside in a small courtyard off the Emergency entrance, her face was pale and drawn, dark shadows beneath her eyes. Her eyes had a dull look to them, as though she hadn't slept in a long time, and little stress lines had formed around them and her mouth.

Seated next to her friend at the small wrought iron café-style table with her soup and sandwich, Sierra waited for her friend to say something, but quickly filled the void when she didn't. "Not hungry?" It was warm out, but the umbrella shaded them from the sun.

Molly gave a tiny shake of her head. "No. Sorry, I'm not the greatest company today."

"That's okay, you don't have to pretend with me."

"I'm glad, because that shit's exhausting," she said, the corners of her lips lifting.

"Did something happen?" Sierra asked, seeing right through the attempt at humor.

Molly dropped the act, her expression sobering. "I filed the separation papers yesterday."

192

She said it with such guilt that it wrenched Sierra's heart. "I'm so sorry, hon. I know how tough that must have been for you." Molly was hard on herself and took her responsibilities seriously, but after what had happened with Carter the other day, it was for the best.

Her friend nodded, lips pressed tight together, her salad untouched in front of her. "They were supposed to serve Carter with them this morning, but I wasn't sure where he was so I don't even know if he got them. I haven't called him because I don't know what to say."

"Is he expecting this?"

"Yes. But it will still hit him hard. Hell, it's hit me hard, and it was my decision."

Molly looked so tired, and after today she had two back-to-back night shifts ahead of her. "What are you planning to do now?"

"Start proceedings for the divorce as soon my six month residency hits, I guess. There's no point in waiting. It's over. It's been over for a long time now." She shook her head, a faraway look in her pretty eyes. "The TBI changed everything so fast. I'm gutted and frustrated that the man I loved has deteriorated to this extent right in front of me, and there's not a damn thing I can do about it."

"Moll, you tried everything."

She groaned. "I also stood up in my church in front of our friends and family and vowed to stay with him through sickness and in health," she murmured, blinking fast.

"But it's your health and safety at risk now too, if you'd stayed," Sierra pointed out. "You didn't have a choice anymore."

Molly nodded absently. "I know. He knows it too, because he doesn't trust himself either. And that's almost the worst part."

It made Sierra cringe to recall the story about Carter

pressing a gun into Molly's hands and ordering her to shoot him if he ever threatened her. How terrifying must that have been? "I feel terrible for him, for what's happened. But I'm glad you're protecting yourself."

"Thanks. Maybe in time I won't feel like the worst person on earth for leaving him. In the meantime I'm just taking one step at a time. I'll help him out as best I can with finances and whatever, but...I can't be with him now."

"I know." She reached across the table to rub Molly's upper arm and give her a reassuring smile. "It's going to be hard at first, but it will get better."

Molly forced a smile, then frowned and fanned her hands in front of her. "Anyway, I don't wanna talk about this anymore." She attempted a smile. "What's new with you?"

Beckett. Except this wasn't the time or place to announce the exciting turn of events in her own life. Not when her best friend was suffering from a broken heart.

"Been busy with work," she said, sidestepping the issue for now. "Hey, you know what we need? We need a full-on girls' night again. We'll go to that spa you love and get our nails done, and I'll even do a yoga class with you. Then I'll order us takeout from that Italian place you love, and we'll grab your favorite treats from Sweet Spot after the spa. We'll go to your place and binge on movies all night. We'll make it a weekend night so I can stay over. We can make up beds in front of the fireplace, then I'll make us French toast in the morning. How's that sound?"

The first stirrings of a real smile lit Molly's face. "I would really love that."

"Me too, it's been too long. You just say when, and we'll make it happen."

"I'll let you know once I get my new work schedule tomorrow. And aw, I love that you would do yoga for me. I know how much you hate it," she said, her eyes now brimming with silent laughter.

Sierra grinned, glad to see a bit of sparkle back in her friend's eyes. Molly would get through this. And Sierra hoped she would be happier for it soon. "Babe, there's not much I *wouldn't* do for you."

They both dug into their late lunches. A few bites in, the sound of running footsteps caught her attention. She and Molly both glanced over in time to see Beckett racing toward the Emergency entrance.

Sierra stood so fast her chair almost toppled over in her haste. "Beckett."

He darted a glance over at her and slowed, and the fear in his eyes sent a jolt of alarm through her. "It's my dad. He's... I don't know what's going on. I gotta go." He turned and rushed through the automatic doors.

God. Sierra looked at Molly. "Should I..."

Molly flapped a hand at her with a worried frown. "Yes, go. I'll meet you up there and find out what's going on."

Sierra hurried for the elevator, dread gathering in the pit of her stomach. Beckett was a private person. This recent change in their relationship was so new and fragile, because she wasn't sure where they stood yet and hadn't talked about it. She didn't want to invade his privacy at a time like this, but she also wanted to be there for him, and if this was as bad as she feared, she didn't want him going through it alone.

When she reached the palliative floor the door to Mr. Hollister's room was shut. A nurse bustled out of it as Sierra approached, stripping off a pair of latex gloves.

Sierra paused there in the hallway, her stomach sinking as she met the nurse's gaze. "Is he..."

The nurse gave her a sympathetic smile. "Won't be long now."

Oh, God. She took a breath to steady herself, even as shock reverberated inside her. How? Beckett had just taken him out, and based on the pictures she'd seen, they'd had a ball together. How could Mr. Hollister have gone downhill so fast?

"Are you a friend of the family?" the nurse asked.

"Yes."

"His son's with him right now. Maybe wait a bit, give him some time alone. This is a shock for him."

Sierra nodded, aching for Beckett. She stood in the hallway for a few minutes, then walked slowly toward the closed door. Footsteps sounded behind her and she glanced back to find Molly coming toward her. "Hey," she said quietly. "What did you find out?"

"It was a stroke," Molly answered, coming to stand in front of her. "Happened less than an hour ago. He was fine, had just finished his lunch when it happened. A nurse was in the room with him. There was nothing anyone could do. He's in a coma now, and not expected to survive the night."

"Ah, shit," she whispered. She wanted to hold Beckett so badly. This was going to slice him bone deep.

Molly drew her into a hug, which was so like her, offering warmth and comfort even when her own world was falling apart. "I'm so sorry. He had a DNR on file. It's just a waiting game now."

Sierra leaned her forehead on her friend's shoulder. "Poor Beckett."

"I know." Molly eased back. "You going in there with him?"

"I'm not sure if he'll want me there."

Molly nodded. "Just give him a little while to himself, maybe. Did you call Noah yet?"

Her brother. She hadn't been thinking. "I'll do that now."

"Okay. I'm due back on shift now, but I'll check back when I can. If you guys need me for anything, have one of the nurses up here page me."

"I will." She dialed her brother as soon as Molly turned to go and told him what was going on. She was still standing in the hallway, hovering near the door when Noah arrived minutes later. "That was fast," she told him, accepting the hug he offered.

"Called in one of my deputies to cover for me." He glanced at the shut door. "How's Beckett?"

"I don't know, I haven't gone in yet. Think we should?"

Noah nodded. "We're family." He strode for the door, Sierra right behind him, her stomach clenched into a giant knot. Noah knocked gently and pushed it open. Beckett glanced up from his father's bedside, his face drawn. "Hey, Beck. You feel like some company?"

Beckett didn't answer. His gaze moved from Noah to her, and the pain embedded there broke her heart. He'd been through so much already with losing his mom as a boy, hadn't had an easy life during his time in Special Forces, and it was hard to see him hurting like this again. She wanted so badly to ease his suffering, to make this more bearable somehow.

"He had a stroke," he said, his voice low and rough.

"I know. Molly got a report and came to tell me." She walked over and lowered herself into the empty chair beside him, careful not to crowd him while Noah did the same on the opposite side of the bed.

Lying so still in the bed, Mr. Hollister appeared to be sleeping. He had no respirator or anything like that hooked up, and the nurses had turned off the heart monitor.

"He has a DNR in place," Beckett finally said a minute later, his strong, bronzed fingers wrapped around his father's frail hand. "He wouldn't want this."

Sierra nodded. "I know." Unable to stand it, she slipped her hand out and curled it around his left one. The only good thing here was that his dad was no longer in any pain.

"We're so sorry, Beck," Noah said in a low voice.

Beckett nodded, still focused on his father. "He was so full of life when we were out on the dunes together. But after I brought him back here he said he was tired. I think... I think maybe he meant he was done fighting."

Sierra swallowed past the growing restriction in her throat. "Maybe."

"What do you need right now?" Noah asked him, leaning forward. "You want me to make some calls, or...?"

"Yeah. Could you call Jase and a few of the crew guys? Let them know I won't be in tomorrow?"

"Of course. Anyone else?"

Beckett shook his head. "Can't think of anyone else right now."

"Okay, man. Back in a bit." Noah rose, squeezed Sierra's shoulder before leaving.

The quiet was stark and oppressive after the door shut behind her brother. She kept her hand curled around Beckett's, feeling helpless.

"He would've hated this, you know," he said. "Us sitting here gawking at him, waiting for him to die."

She winced at his blunt words. "I think it would have brought him a lot of comfort to know you were here with him."

"He stayed with my mom until the end," he said. "I got tired of sitting there, so I left. Wasn't in the room when it happened. But he stayed." His voice thickened. "So I'm staying with him now."

She squeezed his hand, pressed her lips together. It tore her up to see him hurting. This tough, commanding man who meant so much to her. She didn't want to be indelicate, but she had to ask. "What did the doctors say?"

"Could be minutes or hours. Not more than a day, they think."

She nodded and remained silent for a while, just being there with him. For him. "What did he think of Walter, by the way?"

To her surprise, Beckett cracked a quiet laugh. "He got a kick out of him." He shook his head, a faraway look in his eyes. "God, we had fun out there. He loved it. I hate that I left him cooped up in here for so long. I should've taken him out way before then. I should've—" He swallowed, cleared his throat and bowed his head. "I should have done a lot of things differently."

"No. You're an amazing son. He knows how much you love him."

"Hope so. Never told him often enough. I can't even remember what I said before I left earlier—" His voice cracked. He pulled his hand from hers just as Noah opened the door, and turned away from them as though embarrassed, scrubbing his palm over his face.

Sierra met Noah's gaze. Her brother tipped his head to indicate she should follow him out and give Beckett some privacy, then slipped back into the hall.

Torn, Sierra stood, then laid a gentle hand on Beckett's shoulder. His muscles were rock hard beneath her palm. "Tell him you love him now. I'll be right outside if you need me." She started to turn away, bit back a gasp of surprise when his hand flashed out to curl around her wrist. She looked back at him, her heart twisting at the agony etched in his face.

Beckett tugged her toward him. When she stepped into the embrace he drew her into his lap and against his body. He banded both arms around her back, holding on so tight she could barely breathe. "Don't go," he whispered roughly.

The pain in his voice tore her up inside, but him wanting her here knitted it back together again. He was reaching out, when closing up would have been so much easier for him.

She squeezed her eyes shut against the sting of tears and hugged him in return. "Okay," she whispered back. "I'll stay."

She would stay with him as long as he wanted her to.

Chapter Eighteen

The waiting was the worst part.

Beckett shifted in the armchair next to his father's bed and rolled his head from side to side to try and ease the knots in his neck and shoulders. It was mid-morning and somehow his dad was still hanging in there. He'd remained unresponsive throughout the night, his breathing becoming increasingly erratic. And Sierra…

His gaze strayed to where she was curled up on her side on the pullout chair in the corner, a thin hospital blanket draped over her. The stubborn woman had refused to leave, even to go home for a few hours' sleep.

The sight of her melted Beckett's heart. She had stayed. Would have stayed even if they hadn't already crossed the line from friends to lovers.

It meant everything to him.

Though it was a horrible thing to admit, now Beckett just wanted this to be over. His dad had gone through a lot in his life, including losing the only woman he'd ever loved while she was in her prime. He'd never dated anyone after. If this was his time to go, then Beckett didn't want him to suffer a single moment longer than necessary.

A grating rattle sounded as his father's chest slowly expanded. Struggling for breath. God it was hard to

201

watch. His mom had made those exact same sounds in the hours before she passed.

Sierra stirred on her makeshift bed. Her eyes opened. She blinked twice, then immediately sat up, her deep blue gaze darting to his father before swinging to him. "Hey." She sat up, winced and put a hand to her neck. "What time is it?"

"Ten." She'd woken at shift change three hours ago then gone back to sleep. Since then he'd spent way too much time watching her sleep. It was probably borderline creepy, but he'd taken the opportunity to stare, would have curled up behind her and held her except that he refused to leave his father's bedside.

"How's he doing?" she asked softly.

"Same. Breathing's more and more labored all the time."

She made a sympathetic sound. "You didn't sleep, did you?"

"I'll sleep later." He wasn't leaving his father alone for a second.

"And I'm guessing you haven't eaten, either. Feel like some coffee or something?"

He could tell she wanted something to do, to help. "Sure. Thanks."

She popped off the bed and stretched her back, momentarily drawing attention to the prominent curve of her breasts beneath her top. "Back in a bit."

Loneliness hit him when the door shut behind her. He wasn't great with words, preferred to keep his feelings to himself. Now he couldn't.

He focused back on his dad, took that fragile hand in his own, and did the hardest thing he'd ever done. "You don't have to hold on for me," Beckett told him. "I don't want you to suffer anymore. I'll be okay, Dad. But before you go, I want to thank you for all you've done for me. You were the best father I could have ever had."

He swallowed. Shit, he was getting so choked up it was hard to suck air into his lungs. "I'll miss you, but I won't ever forget you. It's okay to let go now. Go see Mom, and give her my love." He swallowed harder, squeezed that limp hand. "Love you, Dad."

For some reason Beckett had thought that would do it, but as the minutes dragged past the tough old bugger still refused to let go. So, more waiting. But at least now Beckett had said all of the things he'd been thinking about throughout the night.

Sierra slipped back in with coffee and donuts. She gave Beckett a soft smile and handed him a cup and plate. "Apple fritters, fresh from the fryer. Your dad's favorite."

His throat was still too thick to answer. He nodded his thanks, accepted the coffee and the donut. They ate in silence, the horrible sounds of his father's dying breaths rattling in the room. Beckett had seen so much death, but witnessing this had him about to crawl out of his skin.

When he set his half-empty cup down Sierra did the same, then got up from her chair and came over to wrap her arms around him from behind. "How you holding up?" she murmured against the top of his head.

It felt so damn good to feel her against him. "I'm okay."

"No you're not. And you don't need to pretend with me."

For some reason that made him crack a slight grin. "Okay. Then I'm the shits. This sucks ass."

"Yeah, it does." She kissed his head, rested her cheek on his hair. "Did you tell him goodbye?"

"Yes. He's just stubborn."

She huffed out a laugh. "See, you come by it honestly."

"Guess so." He caught her upper arm and pulled her around in front of him, then drew her into his lap for a proper hug. She settled against him with a sigh. She felt perfect there, and just holding her eased the weight of his grief. "I told him about us," he said after a long pause.

"You did? What did you say?" Her fingers rubbed gentle patterns over his back.

"I said we were seeing each other. Know what he told me?"

"What?"

"He said 'about time'."

She tipped her head back to peer up at him, surprise lighting the depths of her eyes. "He did?"

He nodded, tucked her hair behind her ear. "He saw it even before I did. You and I together." That was incredible to him.

"Well I'm just glad you finally clued in."

He leaned in, kissed that smiling mouth. A slow, tender kiss that told her without words how much he treasured her, and how much it meant to him that she had stayed here through the toughest night of his life.

A soft knock sounded on the door. Beckett lifted his head just as Noah appeared in the doorway, dressed in his sheriff's uniform. His shocked gaze bounced between him and Sierra for a moment. "Hi. Just thought I'd stop by before I head into the office."

Sierra straightened but didn't jump out of his lap. "Hi."

Noah had to have questions about them, but to his credit he simply put his hands in his pockets and leaned a shoulder against the doorframe. "Any change?"

"Not really," Beckett answered. Once he'd made it clear to Sierra what he wanted and settled everything between them, he would talk to Noah.

A long, wheezing sigh came from his father's lungs, ending in the worst rattle yet. Beckett tensed and Sierra jumped to her feet. "I'll get the nurse," she said, and hurried out of the room, grabbing her brother's arm to tow him with her.

Beckett grasped his father's hand, fighting back the

ribbon of panic trying to wind up his spine. Had he somehow been waiting for Beckett to kiss Sierra in front of him?

Two nurses bustled in, checked his father's vitals and adjusted his meds before leaving. His breathing grew weaker, raspier. Beckett stayed right where he was, tracking the increasingly slow rise and fall of his father's chest.

Death was never pretty. But taking every last breath with the man who had been his parent, friend and mentor, was tough.

Stop, Beckett begged him silently, unable to take any more, about to come apart at the seams. *Let go. Please.*

Finally, his father did.

His chest stopped moving. Beckett swallowed, the prolonged silence echoing in his ears, and shoved back a spurt of fear.

Wait. He bit the impulsive protest back. Saying it was selfish.

He reached for the call button, his entire body numb.

A nurse came in, went straight to his father to check him. She met Beckett's gaze a moment later. "He's gone," she confirmed.

Beckett nodded, unable to find his voice. He'd wanted this to be over, but shit, the staggering finality of it shook him. He cleared his throat. "I just need another minute."

"Of course," she said gently. "Take your time."

When she left, Beckett stared down at his father's hand in his. *Christ, I already miss you.* A deep, searing ache spread beneath the front of his ribs. He pulled in a deep breath, then another. It was over. His dad wouldn't want him to stay here any longer.

Digging deep for the courage to let go, Beckett leaned over and kissed his dad's forehead. "Love you," he murmured, then stood, every muscle protesting the movement after sitting for so long. With one last squeeze of his father's hand, Beckett let go.

Sierra was in the hallway with Noah and Jase when Beckett exited the room. Her eyes were sad. "He's gone?"

Beckett nodded, dropped his head on her shoulder when she came over to wrap her arms around him. He was vaguely aware of Noah and Jase murmuring their condolences, but all he cared about was Sierra holding him. She was the only thing keeping the cracked pieces of his heart together.

After dealing with the administrative stuff at the hospital, Sierra insisted on driving him home despite his protests. In all honesty he was exhausted, so he relented and let her take over, lacing his fingers through hers as she drove.

Another pang of grief hit him when the house came into view up the lane. He fought it off, not willing to face it yet.

The moment he stepped into the house, his defenses slipped. Familiar smells and sights surrounded him, haunting him with so many memories. Some happy. Some sad. Knowing his father would never again step foot in the house, hurt. He'd already known it on one level, but the harsh finality of it was damn hard to accept.

He glanced around. "Where's Walter?"

"Ella's taking care of him for the next couple of days."

He nodded. "That's nice of her."

"You've got a lot of friends, Beckett. They all want to help you."

They can't help me.

Outside in the distance he could hear the muted roar of the ocean. Ceaseless. Rhythmic. Soothing. His dad had loved it. Loved this place, the house, the town and the people in it.

Now this house was Beckett's, and that hurt so damn much it stole his breath. He struggled to contain his emotions. "I'm gonna go take a shower."

Sierra watched him carefully, her eyes sad. "Sure."

He walked to the bathroom like a zombie, stripped and stood under the pounding hot spray in the shower. Exhaustion hit him like an anvil. He washed up, wrapped a towel around his waist and brushed his teeth.

Catching sight of his reflection in the bathroom mirror, he thought about shaving, but he was too damn tired. He needed to crash, and wanted Sierra with him while he did.

When he opened the bathroom door he found her sitting on the edge of his bed, waiting for him. She got up and started toward him, her eyes drifting over his naked chest in a way that made his blood heat. His heart thudded against his breastbone, a strange combination of relief, gratitude and lust slamming into him.

She stopped in front of him, brought her hands up to settle on his naked shoulders. The touch of her soft, warm hands sizzled across his skin, spreading throughout his entire body within the space of a single heartbeat. Eyes searching his, she ran her palms over his shoulders, across his chest, her touch gentle yet possessive.

Need slammed into him, too intense to resist. He buried his hands in her hair and brought his mouth down on hers. She yielded to him with a soft moan, setting his whole body on fire.

He wrapped an arm around her hips, hoisted her off her feet and walked her backward the few paces to his bed. There were so many things he wanted to do to her, things he'd fantasized about and hadn't had the chance to do yesterday. He needed to forget everything for a little while, keep the pain at bay and lose himself in her.

Sierra hooked her legs around his waist and pressed against him, her tongue stroking his. He laid her back and came down on top of her, pinning her beneath him with his weight.

"Need inside you," he rasped out, a little light-headed at having her under him again. He couldn't give her slow and gentle now, he was too amped up. So many months of guilty fantasies were about to come true.

"Yes. Don't make me wait anymore."

No. No more waiting. He was going to make her his right here and now.

Beckett came up on his elbows to give him room to peel her shirt off. She lifted her arms to help him, grasped his towel on the way down and tugged it off him. His cock sprang free, hard and aching.

He hissed a breath between his teeth as her fingers curled around him and stroked. A guttural groan ripped from his throat and for just a moment he bowed his head and allowed himself to savor the pleasure of her touch. Sensation burned up his spine, made his brain go hazy for a moment before he reined himself in.

He needed to taste her. Touch and kiss her all over. Claim her in a way no man ever had or would again.

With single-minded intent he set about getting her naked. The sight of her bared to him completely brought every possessive instinct he had roaring to the surface. He let her explore him at will, the brush of her palms and fingers intensifying the pulse between his legs.

Sierra arched her back and gasped when he cupped her breasts and nuzzled them, stroking his tongue first across one taut, dusky rose nipple, then the other. He sucked them, gentle at first, then harder, letting her feel his hunger for her.

Her hips moved restlessly under him, his cock rubbing between her thighs, and was gratified by the plaintive moan she made when he slid his hand down to cup her sex. She was soft and slick against his palm, his searching fingers.

"Beckett," she whispered, her fingers digging into his scalp as he suckled her. "Now."

"Not yet. Have to get my mouth on you." He released her nipple to lick and kiss his way down the center of her body, his hands curling around her hips while he wedged his shoulders between her thighs. A low, gruff sound came out of him when he saw her glistening folds up close.

Without waiting, he settled his mouth over her, gave her a tender sweep of his tongue that ended over the swollen bud of her clit. Sierra gasped and bit her lip, eyes closed, the muscles in her legs and belly pulling taut. He did it again, again, easing her into it, then delved his tongue inside her, finally tasting her sweetness.

"Ah!" Her hips lifted against his mouth, her hands clutching at his head.

His hands tightened on her hips in a silent command for her to stay still. He tongued her for a few moments, savoring her reaction, then slid upward to focus on the rosy bud at the top of her sex. Licking. Stroking. Sucking softly, using her response to guide him.

When she let out a breathy whimper he slipped a finger partway inside her, pressed upward to rub in shallow strokes along her front wall while he used his lips and tongue to push her to the edge. Her body quivered in his grip, her moans turning to cries.

"Hurry," she panted. "I want you inside me when I—" She shuddered, sank her teeth into her lower lip, her back bowing.

He was too hungry to wait anymore, the need out of control. Knowing he'd brought her this close with his mouth was an insane turn on. He rolled onto one elbow, reached back to dig out a condom from his nightstand and put it on.

Sierra sat up and started to shift to her knees but he stopped her, taking her back down to the bed. He caught her hands in one of his, slowly raised them above her head, asserting his dominance. She gazed up at him trustingly and relaxed, surrendering to him. Her eyes glowed like sapphires in the afternoon light streaming through the open blinds, her legs wound around his hips.

Staring deep into her eyes, he grasped her thigh and lifted it, opening her for him as he positioned his cock against her sex. The sound of their rapid breathing filled the room. He loved that she let him pin her, control her. He needed it. Needed to take her, lose himself in her sweet warmth.

Fingers wound tight around hers, he flexed his hips, sinking a few inches inside her. Heat enveloped him, her body gripping him tight. A low groan rumbled out of him. God, she felt so fucking good…

Her lashes fluttered and she rolled her hips, lifting into him. Fighting him for more.

"Now you're mine," he rasped out, surging forward, burying himself in her slick heat.

Raw, intense pleasure swamped him. He moaned low in his throat and bent to claim her mouth. Sierra whimpered as he plunged his tongue between her lips and began to move his hips, a slow, sultry rocking motion that dragged every sensitive inch of him in and out of her slick core.

Sierra gripped his shoulders and caressed his tongue with hers, clenching around him. He barely had enough sense left to release one of her hands and slide his between them, seeking her clit. He stroked his thumb against it gently, taking his weight on his other forearm as he kept up the slow thrusts that threatened to melt his brain with the incredible friction.

So. Damn. Good.

Too close to the edge already, he let go of her other hand and gripped a fistful of her thick, glossy hair instead, watching her face. Her eyes opened a fraction then closed again on his next inward thrust, her lips parting on a moan so sexy it sent another shudder ripping through him.

She clutched at his back now, rubbing her pelvis against his hand. "I'm…" Whatever she was going to say dissolved into another moan.

God, he wanted to make this last forever, but he couldn't hold out much longer. "Slower," he commanded.

Eyes squeezed shut, face reflecting the strain as she approached release, she nodded.

It nearly killed him to slow down, but each drag of his sensitive flesh against her core made his muscles bunch, the promise of ecstasy so close he could taste it.

"Oh, God, like that," she gasped, whimpering when he dragged the head of his cock in and out over the sweet spot just inside her. Then she tightened around him, cried out as she started to come.

Beckett let his eyes slam shut. He lowered his head, buried his face into her hair and surged deeper, harder. The pleasure rose higher and higher, burning a path of fire up his spine. He cried out as the orgasm hit him, obliterating everything, made all the sweeter because it was Sierra he was buried deep inside.

Lying sprawled on top of her, he fought to catch his breath. Was he crushing her? She soothed that worry by relaxing under him with a sigh, easing her legs down from his hips to tangle with his own, her arms looping around his back.

He let out a low growl of enjoyment when she stroked her hands over his hot, damp skin from neck to the base of his spine. A gentle, comforting caress, but he could feel the possessiveness behind it. She'd wanted to claim him as well, and she had.

"Was that like you imagined it would be?" she murmured, her fingers stroking through his short hair.

"Better." He nuzzled her temple, lower to run his nose along the side of her neck. "So much better."

"Hmm, for me, too." She kissed his temple. "Ready to sleep now?"

"Yeah." He gently rolled off her, dealt with the condom and helped her beneath the covers.

Pulling her to his chest, he wrapped his arms around her back and held her close. She tucked one leg between his and settled her cheek on his chest with a contented sigh that filled him with the first real sense of peace he'd felt in forever.

This was what he'd needed. Sierra. Naked. In his arms.

But the peace didn't last.

Her breathing slowed and deepened as she slipped into sleep. He held her, focused on her sweet warmth and weight, staring out the bedroom window and the view beyond.

The ocean. He could hear it now, a rhythmic sigh as the waves rolled against the shore.

He thought of his dad, of all the times they'd spent on the water together, or on the beach. It was part of them. The beach, the ocean and house were still here, even though he was gone forever.

Christ, he's really gone.

His lungs seized, his heart hitching as the grief he'd shoved down so deep threatened to burst free. Panic sizzled through him.

He didn't realize he'd gone rigid until Sierra stirred slightly. "Beckett?"

He didn't answer. Just pulled her closer and turned his head to bury his face in the curve of her shoulder.

She made a soft, sympathetic sound and curled around him. "I know it hurts. It's going to be okay, baby," she whispered.

Was it? He was lost, far out to sea where no one could save him. And Sierra was his only lifeline.

The crack in the wall where he'd bricked-in his emotions suddenly split open…and came tumbling down.

Holding on tight to the woman who owned his battered, cynical heart, he let the crushing tide of grief carry him away.

Chapter Nineteen

It was full dark now. Was Hollister alone?

A quick check through the binoculars showed Sierra's car was still in Hollister's driveway. It had been all day. She must be staying over.

Were they together? If so, that was new. No one in town had talked about it, but everyone knew Hollister's dad had died this morning.

A light flicked on in the upstairs bedroom window, giving a perfect view inside.

Two figures appeared, silhouettes backlit against the darkness. A large frame that could only be Hollister. Then a smaller, curvy figure.

Sierra.

Hollister lifted an arm and tucked her into his side. For a moment they stood there, looking out at the darkened yard, or maybe the ocean beyond. They were definitely together.

Everything clicked in that instant.

Sierra. She was the answer.

It wasn't enough for Hollister to die. He had to watch Sierra die first. He had to feel the maximum amount of pain possible before he was shot, before his own suffering was over.

The weight of the pistol was comforting, familiar, the distant sigh of the ocean filling the night.

In the window Hollister and Sierra embraced, kissing each other as they stepped away out of view. Between one breath and the next, the upstairs light went out, plunging everything back into darkness.

The soles of the new shoes barely made a sound as they moved from the cover of the trees, over the paved lane to the soft, thick grass of the front lawn.

I have to get Sierra. Have to take her first.

They had no idea someone was outside the house right now, hunting them, the symbol of hatred hidden in the jeans front pocket.

The waiting was over—it was time to dole out the punishment dreamed of for so long.

Attacking them now while together was a huge risk, but it didn't matter. There was nothing left to live for now anyway.

As long as Sierra died in front of Hollister first, whatever happened afterward didn't matter.

****

A sense of impending doom filled Beckett as he stood in the desert, surrounded by darkness. All around him his teammates lay in defensive positions, awaiting the enemy counterattack they all knew was coming.

They were outnumbered ten to one at least. And the closest air assets that might give them a fighting chance at surviving the coming battle were more than twenty minutes out.

"We doing this alone, Cap?" one of the men asked him.

"Help's on the way," he answered, bringing his own weapon up and taking aim across the gulley where the

enemy would be attacking from.

An RPG screamed overhead and detonated behind them. Rock and debris showered down, pelting their backs and legs.

Gunfire erupted across the gulley, shattering the night, glowing tracers lighting up the darkness in streaming arcs of death. His men returned fire, but it was already too late. They were already starting to die.

He ordered a tactical retreat, trying to get them behind better cover. They didn't make it. Just as in the actual mission, they never reached the safety of the ridge.

Faces swirled before him. Bloody faces of his dying teammates. The men he had sworn to look after and bring home to their wives and girlfriends. The doomed hostages from the op in Syria. Their blank eyes stared up at him accusingly, the sounds of their agonized, dying screams still echoing in his ears.

Cole Goodman's face appeared through the smoke and dust, half of it missing from the bullet that had shattered his skull. Blood streamed out of his mouth as he opened it to speak. "You could've saved me and the others," he rasped. "But you stood by and did nothing."

The allegation punched through his chest like a hollow point round. Because it was true.

Goodman's face twisted, shifted as it changed shape and became Carter's. His former teammate's dark brown eyes bored into his, almost lit from within from the madness that was tearing him apart. "You turned your back on me. You have no honor."

Beckett shook his head, started to defend himself, but then he saw his father lying there on the ground, covered in the hospital blanket. His eyes were open, staring up at him. "Gone," he said. "We're all gone now."

Before Beckett's horrified gaze, his father's face began to decompose. He tried to turn away, to close his eyes, but he was trapped, a scream building in his throat at the evidence before him. Everyone he'd loved or was supposed to protect lay dead or dying around him, their blood soaking into the thirsty desert sand...

He jerked awake, his lungs on fire, his heart threatening to explode out of his chest.

Bolting upright, he sucked in a breath of air and wiped a shaking hand over his damp face, nausea rolling in his gut as he swung his legs over the side of the bed.

Before he could stand, the mattress shifted. "Hey. You okay?"

No. Not even close.

He flinched when a gentle hand settled on his sweaty back. Shit, that had been a bad one, and he hated that it had happened in front of Sierra.

She sat up behind him, kept her hand where it was, maintaining contact. She was silent for a few moments, allowing him a little time to try and get a grip on himself. "Bad dream?" she murmured.

There was no way to hide it now. "Yeah," he answered, his voice rough.

"Can I help?"

He shook his head. He didn't mean to shut her out. "I'm gonna take a shower." He was sweaty and gross and needed a few minutes to himself. Sierra seeing him this way was too much, and fueled all his secret fears. She'd already seen him at his weakest and most vulnerable earlier. He was terrified of her learning the truth: that he wasn't the hero she deserved.

Thankfully she didn't say anything or follow him. In the bathroom he locked the door and let out a relieved breath before firing up the shower.

He forced his mind to go blank as he stood under the spray, focused on the warmth of the water, the smell of the soap. Simple things that grounded him in the here and now and helped chase away the jagged splinters of the dream still clinging to his consciousness.

When he stepped back into the bedroom Sierra was lying on her side watching him. She gave him a soft smile and patted the bed next to a plate she'd set there. "You didn't get the chance to eat earlier, so I made you a sandwich."

It was like an invisible hand reached through his ribcage and squeezed his heart. "Thank you." He slid in next to her, hugged her close and brushed a gentle kiss over her mouth, a familiar smoky scent in the air tempting him. "Bacon?"

She pushed at his shoulder. "Yes, a BLT, bacon crispy with extra mayo, just the way you like it. Eat up before it gets soggy."

She was such a sweetheart. And he was a fucking mess. "You want some?"

"Already had one."

He sat up and polished it off in a few bites, then set the plate aside and switched off the lamp. The darkness helped, allowed him to hide a little. He wanted Sierra to see him as strong and capable, not weak and in need of help. "I needed that, thank you."

"You're welcome." She scooted over, plastering her body along his. "You know what? I'm no expert, but I understand what it means to carry guilt around. It's exhausting. And the only way to unload it is to forgive yourself." She kissed him softly. "Whatever happened, please try to forgive yourself."

He didn't know if he could do that, but her words resonated deep inside him.

He sank into the kiss, letting the stroke of her hands and the press of her body soothe him, thankful she wasn't pushing him to talk or making a big deal about it. He tucked her in close to his chest and sighed, breathing in her scent as they both drifted back to sleep.

Walter's deep, sharp bark made his eyes fly open in the darkness sometime later. Beckett tensed and waited, listening.

The dog barked again, this time a series of them that ended in a low, warning growl.

"What is it?" Sierra whispered. "Do you hear anything?"

Beckett was already sliding out of bed. During his missions overseas, he'd learned to implicitly trust the working dogs' instincts. "Stay here." He set a hand on Sierra's shoulder to keep her where she was, then tugged on a pair of jeans and hurried downstairs.

Walter was by the front door looking through the right panel window beside it. Ears perked, tail straight out, intent on something outside.

Beckett stepped up close to him. "See something, buddy?" Probably a raccoon, or maybe a cougar. They were rare in the area now, but it still happened occasionally.

He peered out the window in the top half of the door, checking the porch and front yard. A shadow moved at the edge of his peripheral vision. He snapped his head to the left to get a better look, caught something moving back into the trees across the road.

A warning tingle prickled the back of his neck. The shadow had been big. Might even have been human.

Moving quietly, he retrieved his pistol from the locker in the den, then slipped out the side door to look around. The porch was empty. Nothing had been disturbed. But as the clouds parted overhead, the moonlight slanted across the lawn in a swath of silver.

A sheen of dew on the newly-trimmed lawn glistened in the light, except for the small, darker patches revealing the footprints.

One set that led from the road right up to the garden bed at the edge of the side porch, then back again.

Beckett firmed his grip on his pistol and swept his gaze back to the deep shadows across the road where the forest had swallowed whoever it was. Could have been a kid looking for an easy target to rob.

Or something more sinister. Like a certain pedophile now back amongst the population.

Taking a step toward the railing, his bare foot landed on something. He looked down, saw the bits of whatever it was scattered on the porch floor.

Crouching down, he ignored the twinge in his low back and picked up one of the pieces. Part of what appeared to be a patch. Gathering more of them, his gut dropped when he recognized it.

A 3rd Special Forces Group patch. Cut into pieces and dumped here for him to find.

He shoved to his feet, his gaze snapping back to the forest. Jesus Christ. Carter. Had to be. Was he drunk? Coming here in the middle of the night to leave this as a giant fuck you? It made no goddamn sense.

He thought of the note he'd found on his windshield. *You have no honor.* Had that been Carter too?

Beckett stared at the distant tree line. He would have gone in there after him, but Carter was gone now and there was no way Beckett was leaving Sierra alone here undefended, just in case.

A bone deep weariness crashed into him, the cut-up patch a blow he had no defense against. He picked up the pieces, slipped back inside and checked to make sure all the doors and windows were locked before dumping the patch in the garbage. Anger began to burn away the hurt.

Walter shuffled up to him. Beckett reached down to stroke the dog's head. "Good boy." If not for him, Beckett would have slept through the incident.

The dog stared up at him, illuminated by a shaft of moonlight that spilled across the hardwood floor.

Beckett nodded at the staircase. "Come on," he said, picking up Walter's memory foam bed before heading upstairs, the shuffle of paws following him up the wooden treads. With the dog here to alert them, Beckett felt more at ease and willing to relax his guard a little.

Sierra was wide awake in his bed, waiting for him. "Everything okay?" she asked as he set Walter's bed on the floor.

"Yeah, it's fine," he said, and silently laid his pistol on the nightstand before sliding in next to her. Telling Sierra what he'd found would only upset her.

Near the door, Walter curled up on his bed and let out a deep sigh.

Beckett turned Sierra onto her side and tucked her into him, wrapping an arm around her ribs. She was what mattered. Carter could go fuck himself.

Chapter Twenty

Beckett had never planned a funeral before. He'd had no idea how much work was involved, even for a simple service like this one.

He finished a call with the funeral home director and sat back in the kitchen chair with a sigh to rub at his tired eyes. Sleep was an uphill battle for him right now, even though Carter hadn't returned since the other night. Having Walter sleep in the room with him and Sierra had helped, but hadn't banished the ghosts.

Sprawled out on his side near the front door, the dog cracked one eye open and looked up at him.

"You're a good boy, Walter." The dog thumped his tail on the floor once as if to say 'I know' and closed his eye.

It was way too damn quiet in the house.

Sierra was at her clinic for a couple of hours to finish up some things before the service. She'd spent the last two nights with him and he already missed her. This place felt empty without her in it.

Over the past two days she'd helped him out with many of the final arrangements his dad had gone over with him. Even though it was just a matter of executing his wishes, it was still a lot to get done in a short amount of time. He'd been so busy with all of that and various administrative things for work projects during the days, he and Sierra had only seen each other when he'd come home late at night to crawl into bed beside her.

A text came in. *Missing you.* She sent a picture of her blowing a kiss at the camera.

It made him smile even though his heart was heavy. *Miss you too. See you soon.*

Once this was over and he saw his father through this final step, he was making Sierra his priority.

He loved her. Loved her so much his heart could barely withstand it. He was going to tell her tonight, start fresh once all of this was behind them, and then they could make plans for the future. Their future, and he would have to learn to live with the risks involved.

But first, he had to lay his father to rest.

He went upstairs to shower and dress, then went into the master bedroom. It was exactly as his dad had left it, the double-wedding ring quilt spread neatly over the king-size bed, his bottle of cologne sitting on top of the bureau next to their wedding photo and another of them as a family.

Beckett paused in front of it. He'd been around eight or so in this one, taken down at the beach below the house, all of them standing on a large driftwood log that had washed up on the sand. Beckett stood between his parents, their arms around his shoulders, all of them grinning at the camera as the sun set in front of them.

All three of them without a worry in the world. All three of them oblivious to the pain life had in store for them.

He crossed to the walk-in closet and opened it. His dad had emptied it of all his wife's things a few years after she had died. Now the racks and shelves were full of his modest clothes, mostly flannel shirts, a couple of polos. One suit jacket he'd had for probably twenty-five years.

The faint scent of his dad's cologne wafted up, stirring

emotions and memories. Beckett reached for the drawer where his dad's tie collection was kept. Four neatly-coiled ties sat in it. He knew exactly which one he was going to wear. His dad's favorite—his "lucky" tie he wore to every important business meeting, and every Christmas dinner.

Beckett put on the bright red tie. He smoothed the tail down, added the clip to keep it close to his shirt placket and slid on his tailored jacket over top.

Back downstairs he put Walter's leash on him and walked him down to Tiana and Ella's place, promising to pick him up the next morning.

"We're really sorry about your dad, Mr. Beckett," Ella told him, and handed him a card she'd made.

It showed a stick figure of whom he assumed must be him, standing with his head bowed, his mouth downturned and big blue teardrops dripping from his eyes. Walter sat at his feet, gazing up at him with big googly eyes, his tongue sticking out the side of his mouth, large red hearts rising in a line above his head. A stick drawing of Ella next to Beckett appeared to be hugging him around the waist.

He couldn't help but smile, even as a pang hit him. "Thank you. That's real nice of you."

Mirroring the drawing, the little girl stepped forward to hug him. Beckett bent and gently returned it while Tiana watched them with a soft smile.

In his truck he set the card in the tray at the front of the console and drove to the funeral home. The director was there to meet him with the usual condolences, then led him back into a room where an urn was waiting on a small marble table.

The sight of it hit him hard. For a moment it was as though all the air was sucked out of the room. Finally his lungs opened again. He walked forward and picked up the urn, fighting the wave of grief that threatened to smother him.

His father's ashes. This was all that remained of him.

In a half-daze he walked outside into the bright spring sunshine and set the urn on the front passenger seat of his truck. "One last ride after this, Dad, then you'll be home forever."

When he pulled into the full church parking lot a few minutes later, Sierra was there waiting for him. Just the sight of her filled him to bursting, eased the ache in his heart.

She enveloped him in a big, warm hug the moment he stepped out of his truck. "Missed you," she murmured, leaning up to kiss him.

He gathered her to him with an arm around her waist and cupped the back of her neck with his free hand. "Missed you too, sweetness." He kissed her, slow and firm, a gentle claiming until the world and everything but her faded away.

A discreet cough brought his head up. Noah stood a few yards away, wearing a tailored suit and an awkward expression. Molly and Jase were there too, staring at them wide-eyed. "Hey," Noah said. "So I'm guessing you guys are…" He cleared his throat.

"Yes," Sierra said, cuddling into Beckett's side. "We are."

Noah nodded. "Ah. So…huh."

Beckett would talk to him later, but not until after he'd bared his heart to Sierra. "Thanks for coming."

Noah nodded. "Of course. Your dad was one of the best men I ever knew."

Yes. He had been. That was something Beckett would always be proud of.

Sierra glanced past him into the truck. "Aww," she said softly, her eyes filling when she saw the urn sitting there.

"Yeah. The guest of honor," he said, turning to lean over and lift it out.

Sierra put her hands out for it and looked up at him. Beckett gently handed it to her, his heart squeezing when she hugged it to her and murmured, "Hey, Mr. H. The gang's all here for you. And don't worry," she added in a whisper, shooting a loaded look at him. "I'm going to take care of Beckett for you."

God, he loved her. He wanted a life with her. A future that now seemed more possible than he could have imagined a week ago.

"I brought you something," she said, indicating the small purse slung over her shoulder. "It's in the big pocket."

Beckett unzipped it and pulled out a rectangular-shaped wrapped parcel.

"You can open it later if you don't want to now."

He turned it over and tore a corner free, a sweet, stinging pain hitting him when he saw the photo she'd framed. She had taken the selfie of him, his dad and Walter that he'd sent her, professionally edited it to adjust the lighting. His dad looked so damn happy, and Walter so ridiculous in his doggles, it made him laugh in spite of the hurt. "Thank you. I love it."

I love you.

He wasn't going to tell her that in front of everyone. When he told her it should be while they were alone.

"You're welcome. It was too good a shot not to frame up, and I wanted you to have this to remember your fun day together." She brushed a kiss over his mouth and drew back to give him a supportive smile.

He drew a steadying breath, grateful to have her beside him through this. "Let's get this done."

Sierra and his friends walked with him to the church's front door. Stepping inside, he damn near choked up.

Every single guy from the construction crews he ran was there, along with most of the townspeople. Even former neighbors who had moved out of the area years ago, and the nurses from the palliative floor who had cared for his father.

And Carter.

Beckett spotted him over in the far corner. His former teammate had shaved and even worn a suit for the occasion. He stood alone in the back, his gaze full of undisguised yearning as he stared at Molly, then it shifted to Beckett and filled with regret.

So many unspoken things passed between them as they stared at each other.

Beckett forgave him for the things he'd done. Because Carter had shown up here today to support him and honor his father, even after all that had happened between them. That was what mattered.

Throat tight, Beckett walked straight up to him and pulled him into a hug. "Thanks for coming, man. Means a lot."

"Wouldn't have missed it," Carter said, his voice thick. There wasn't a hint of booze on him.

Beckett leaned back to look into those clear, almost black eyes, slapped a rock hard shoulder. One side of Carter's mouth pulled up in a half-grin, and he nodded once.

No more grudges. They couldn't go back to who or what they'd been before, but now they could at least both move forward without bad blood between them.

The moment was over in an instant, because a line of people waited to speak to Beckett. He finally put a stop to it by setting his father's urn on a podium up front and waited beside it while everyone took their seats.

Sierra, Noah, Jase and Molly sat in the front row reserved for family. Carter sat a few rows back with some of the nurses. It was standing room only in the church, and Beckett was overwhelmed by the show of respect and support the town was giving him and his dad.

The service was short and to the point. Beckett read a

eulogy he'd prepared, managed to keep his voice even throughout the whole thing before taking his seat beside Sierra, who immediately reached for his hand and twined her fingers through his.

A few people came up to tell funny stories or say how much his dad had meant to them and the town. A short reception followed, passing by in a blur of faces and condolences. He shook hands, accepted hugs from the women, but really he just wanted out of there so he could breathe again.

Finally, the last guest left, and it was just him, Sierra, Noah, Jase and Molly. Carter had slipped out without saying goodbye, and Beckett didn't blame him. Had to be hard on him and Molly to see each other.

"Where to now, your place?" Jase asked him, putting his flat cap back on as they left the church.

Beckett nodded and slid an arm around Sierra's waist. "He wanted to be scattered on the bank and from the point at the lighthouse." The same as they'd done with Beckett's mother's ashes so many years before.

"We'll meet you there."

Everyone assembled in the backyard as Beckett carried the urn toward the bank. His friends stood behind him as he scattered a handful of ash along the edge of the garden where it met the bank. From there it was only a few minutes' walk up to the path that led to the lighthouse.

He took Sierra's hand, held it until they reached their destination. He stood beside her at the edge of the point for a long moment, taking in the sweeping view of the ocean as the waves crashed against the rocks below. His dad had loved the ocean. Now he would be a part of it and this place forever.

Opening the urn one last time, he stepped to the edge and flung the contents in an arc. The wind caught the plume of ash and whipped it into the air, carrying it out to meet the waves, the slight salt spray tingling against his skin. "Bye, Dad," he murmured, hoping that wherever his father's spirit was, he was at peace.

Sierra came up behind him to wrap her arms around his waist. And suddenly Beckett felt strangely at peace as well. "He'll never really leave you," she said over the wind.

He squeezed her arms. "No." Then he turned and drew her to him, hugged her tight. "Thank you."

She kissed him, her eyes shining with what he dared to hope was love. "Ready to head back?"

He nodded and captured her hand for the walk back to the house.

Jase came up to hook a casual arm around Beckett's neck. "Come on, buddy. We're taking you to the Sea Hag for a toast to your dad."

"Okay." His dad would've liked that. He glanced at Sierra. "You coming too?"

She leaned her head on his shoulder. "Sure."

Chapter Twenty-One

Sierra walked up to Beckett's back porch with Molly while the guys headed out to the bar. It was three in the afternoon. After meeting them at the bar she would run to the market and grab something to make dinner for her and Beckett. He'd had a long, tough week and she wanted to pamper him.

"You want to come with me to the Hag, or do you have plans?" she asked Molly.

"Wish I could, but I have to get to work."

"I thought you had the day off?"

"Switched a shift with someone so I could make it to the funeral."

Sierra stopped to face her. It had to have been tough on her to see Carter there. "You okay?"

Molly didn't pretend to misunderstand what she meant. "Yeah. I wasn't expecting to see him there today. He looked good." There was a wistfulness to her voice that tugged at Sierra's heart. "Like the old Carter."

She gave a sad smile. "He did."

"I can't let that make me question my decision," Molly said, shaking her head firmly. "I gotta stand my ground and move forward, no backsliding."

"You do. But I know that doesn't make it any easier. You sure you don't have time for a cup of coffee or something before you head in?"

"No, I can't." Then Molly shot her a narrow-eyed look and whacked her arm.

Sierra's eyes went wide. "What the heck was that for?"

"For not telling me about you and Beckett. What's going on between you two, anyway?"

"What do you think?"

"I think you've been holding out on me."

Sierra chuckled. She wasn't exactly sure what Beckett had in mind for them, but she sure as hell knew what she wanted. Him and no one else, forever. God, she hoped he wouldn't break her heart. He was dealing with so much right now. "It just kind of happened."

"Yeah? When? Because you didn't say anything when I saw you the other day."

"It was sudden. And it took both of us by surprise."

Molly gave her an *oh, please* look. "I don't think so. You've had a thing for him for a long time."

Sierra gaped at her. "What? How did you know?"

Molly rolled her eyes. "Girl, I'm not blind, even if he was. But I'm glad he's seeing things straight now." She nudged Sierra with an elbow. "So? Is it serious?"

"It better be. It's all happened so fast, and with his dad dying we haven't really talked about us yet." She'd been hoping to do that either tonight or tomorrow. "As you may have noticed, Beckett's not the most talkative guy, especially when it comes to feelings." He was still guarded around her sometimes but he'd made an effort to open up to her about certain things. If he kept doing that, she could handle whatever else life threw at them.

"Well I hope it all works out for you guys. I love you both to death, and I want to see you happy."

"We love you too, and I'll keep you posted." She held out her arms. "Now gimme a hug." Molly gave the best hugs. Well, apart from Beckett, but they were totally different kinds of hugs. Molly's hugs filled her with a contented warmth. Beckett's made her entire body hum and turned her heart to mush.

Molly squeezed her tight, rocking from side to side a bit. "Love you."

Sierra hugged her hard. "Love you too. I'll call you tomorrow, so we can schedule that girls' night."

"That's a plan. I'm gonna need an update about you guys asap. And I want *all* the details. You can't leave anything out."

She snickered. "You're so dirty."

Molly grinned. "You know it."

Just as she stepped back, her phone rang. It was Macy, from the clinic. "Hey. What's up?"

"I just got a call about an emergency from one of our new patients. Sadie, the female Golden Retriever you saw last week for the first time got hit by a car."

"Oh, no."

"The owner can't risk taking her all the way to the emergency clinic, so she called here. Can you come in?"

"Of course, tell her to come in right away. I'll be there in ten minutes."

Molly raised her eyebrows. "You on call?"

"Yes, my business partner is out of town, and the patient is too critical to transport the distance to the emergency clinic. I gotta go."

"Yeah, go." Molly waved her past and Sierra rushed to her car.

She pulled into the clinic parking lot several minutes later and slid into the space beside Macy's car. After sending Beckett a quick text, she headed inside.

Emergency patient. Not sure when I'll be done. Will swing by bar after if there's time. Xo

Macy was waiting for her with an update. "Apparently the dog's conscious, but in a lot of pain. She's bleeding from the mouth, can't stand. Natalie should be here with her any minute. I've got everything set up in the OR."

"Great, I'll get ready." In the back she assembled what she might need for surgery and put on her scrubs.

"She's here," Macy called.

Sierra stepped through the exam room door in time to see Natalie walk in. Her face was drawn, expression set as she took in the two of them, and she was alone.

"Where's Sadie?" Sierra asked in concern. Still in the car? "Do you need help bringing her in?"

"No." Natalie shut the clinic door behind her and reached back to twist the lock.

Startled, Sierra stopped where she was. What—

Her heart seized when Natalie raised a pistol at her. Macy gasped and froze by the desk.

Sierra gaped at the weapon, heart thudding in her ears. "What are you...?" She didn't understand what was happening. Couldn't get another word out, her throat constricting as fear detonated inside her.

Natalie's eyes glittered with pure hatred as she stared at her. "You're coming with me. And there can't be any witnesses."

Before Sierra could react, the woman turned the weapon on Macy. Macy let out a panicked cry and started to duck behind the desk, but it was too late.

Sierra jolted as the gunshot exploded through the room, staring in horror as Macy crumpled to the floor. Blood spread across her chest, splattered all over the floor and wall behind her. Her eyes were open, fixed on Sierra in shock, agony twisting her face as she lay there, unmoving.

Oh, Jesus... Sierra took a lurching step toward her, needing to stop the bleeding.

"Stop." Natalie turned the gun on her.

Sierra jerked to a halt, afraid to move.

"Don't touch her. Step away." She waved the pistol to

the left.

Sierra took two shuffling steps away from Macy, unable to tear her gaze away from the end of the muzzle. Why? Why had she done this?

"My fiancé's name was Cole Goodman. That name ring a bell?"

Slowly, Sierra shook her head.

"Your man never mentioned it to you? Why am I not surprised?" She waved the pistol impatiently, motioning toward her. "You're coming with me. Now."

For a split second Sierra considered whirling and making a run for it. But she'd never make it. The door was too far away. She'd be shot down before she'd even made it two steps.

As if reading her thoughts, Natalie's hard gaze turned icy. "Don't even think about it. I need you alive. For now."

At those ominous words Sierra took an involuntary step backward, flinched as Natalie's other hand whipped up. Before Sierra could even discern what was in the woman's grip this time, Natalie lunged over and thrust her hand out, hitting Sierra in the side of the neck with something.

Hot, electric pain radiated through every part of her. Her muscles convulsed, her entire body out of control, then went limp.

She hit the floor on her side, unable to move or even draw a breath. She was dimly aware of her arms being wrenched behind her, and something being fastened around her wrists. Her muscles refused to obey her silent command to move. To fight.

She was powerless to do anything at all as Natalie dragged her past Macy's body and out the back of the clinic.

****

The Sea Hag hadn't changed a bit in the past twenty years. Beckett glanced around the familiar space. This had been his dad's favorite spot in town to grab a cold one after a long day at work or out on the water, and he'd often stop in on his way home. Being here now was bittersweet, but fitting.

He slid onto a stool beside Noah and ordered himself his dad's favorite beer. The place was full of tradespeople and work colleagues, all here to raise a glass to his father's memory because Jase had previously organized it.

Only thing missing was Sierra.

"It's on the house," the bartender told him, sliding the cold bottle across the bar to him.

"Thanks, Gus."

"My pleasure."

"Sierra not coming?" Noah asked him.

"She got called in for an emergency at the clinic. Might stop by if she's done in time."

Noah nodded, leaned a forearm on the polished bar to give him a rueful look. "So. You and my sister, huh?"

Beckett covered a wince as he took a swallow of beer. He'd intended to have this conversation in a day or two, once he'd settled everything with Sierra, but he wasn't going to sidestep it if Noah wanted to talk now. They'd been friends for over thirty years. Beckett owed it to him to be straight. "Yeah."

"How long has that been going on?"

"A few days."

Noah's eyebrows shot up. "For real? Well no wonder I didn't know."

"You okay with it?" Not that it really mattered to him whether Noah was or not. He wasn't giving Sierra up for anyone, even his best friend.

"It's gonna take me a while. Just make sure you're not taking advantage of her, okay? You're dealing with a lot right now."

Beckett wasn't offended. If anything, he was glad to see Noah being protective of Sierra. "I get it. I'm gonna talk to her tonight about everything." He would go against his nature, even though it made him squirm inside, and verbally lay it all on the line for her.

He was going to risk everything and bare his past because his love and need for her were stronger than his fear.

Noah considered him for a long moment, then nodded. "Okay." He lifted his bottle. "Here's to you guys. And, as her big brother, I feel compelled to add the obligatory 'if you hurt her I kill you' thing. No offense."

"None taken. And I wouldn't expect any less," Beckett said with a smile, and tapped his beer to Noah's.

"Whoa, what's all this seriousness going on?" Jase asked, sliding onto the stool to Beckett's left. "What'd I miss?"

"Nothing," Noah answered. "Just warning Beck not to break my sister's heart."

Jase nodded in approval. "Good. If he does, I'll hold him for you so you can beat his sorry ass."

Beckett snorted. "You and what army?"

Jase raised his eyebrows. "That a challenge, old man? You're almost forty and you've got a bad back. And I would use any and all weapons at my disposal."

"Yeah, and you'd have to use every last one of them to have a prayer at pinning me," Beckett said, shooting Jase a grin as he climbed off his stool to face the room.

Everyone seemed to have a drink in hand, so he raised his arm and called out in his officer's voice to get the room's attention. "I'd like to thank you all for coming. I appreciate it, and it would have meant a lot to my dad." He raised his beer in salute. "Here's to Jase for setting this up, and to my father. Cheers."

"Cheers," everyone chorused, and drank.

He lost track of time as the minutes slipped past, but stopped accepting drinks from people after the third beer and went around the room to shoot the shit with the guests. The guys from his crews told funny stories about his dad, or recalled sweet gestures he'd performed over the years.

An unexpected bonus would show up on a paycheck when someone fell on hard times. A gift certificate for an anniversary meal out with the wife would appear in someone's toolkit when things were tight financially.

Hearing them filled Beckett with pride as much as they made him ache.

When his phone buzzed in his pocket he pulled it out, surprised to see that more than an hour had passed already. But Sierra wasn't texting to say she was on her way.

Done at clinic. Tiana called to say Ella and Walter are missing. Gone to look in the woods out back of her place. Can you help search?

What the hell? He immediately dialed her number. It rang three times before going to voicemail. He shot her a text. *On my way.*

Excusing himself from the guests he was visiting, he hurried back to the bar to grab his suit jacket where Noah and Jase were talking. "Sierra says Ella and Walter are missing. She and Tiana are looking in the woods out behind their place right now. You hear anything about it?" he asked Noah.

Noah pulled out his own phone, checked it. "No messages. I'll call the station." He spoke to someone briefly, then hung up and shook his head. "Tiana didn't call it in. Must have just happened."

Beckett fished his keys from his pocket. It was his dog Ella had been walking, and he adored that little girl. Had she gotten lost, maybe? "I'm gonna go help look for her." Hopefully she'd just wandered off a little too far and

236

wasn't hurt or anything. Or maybe she'd twisted an ankle or something and couldn't walk out on her own.

"I'll meet you there," Noah said.

"Okay."

"I'm in too," Jase said, hopping off his stool to join them as Beckett strode for the door.

Chapter Twenty-Two

"Ah, looks like Beckett's going to meet us at our final destination," Natalie announced from behind the wheel, her voice smug.

No!

Sierra yanked to free her bound hands where they were tied behind her, but there was no give and the duct tape across her mouth kept her from saying anything. After tying her up in the backseat of the car, Natalie had taken Sierra's phone and used her thumbprint to unlock it.

There was nothing Sierra could do to escape or stop Natalie from texting Beckett. No way to warn him that it was a trap. Her only hope now was that someone had heard the gunshot inside the clinic and called for help. Then maybe someone would find her before it was too late.

Natalie—if that was even her name—was fucking crazy. She'd killed Macy. Presumably wanting to do the same to her and Beckett. Sierra had to get out of this car if she wanted to live, make a run for it and get as far away from this psycho as possible. But how? God, she had to find a way...

The light streaming through the windows changed abruptly, darkening to dappled shade. She twisted her head to the side to look up at the window. Tall trees bordered the road, thick with late spring foliage. Where was Natalie taking her? And why?

Her wrists were already raw from twisting against the cord binding them, but she didn't stop trying to get free. She didn't understand any of this. Who the hell was Cole Goodman? She'd never heard of him. Beckett had never mentioned him. This was all some hideous nightmare.

"I bet you're like all the others around here, aren't you?" Natalie said as she continued driving. "Every single one of you in this pathetic town is a brainwashed loser."

What the hell was she raving about?

"You all think Hollister's a hero. What a joke. And you're worst of all, because now you're fucking him."

Had she been spying on them? Sierra tuned most of it out, concentrating on finding a way out of this mess. If someone had heard the gunshot, they would have called it in. Noah would respond, find Macy's body and see Sierra was missing. He and Beckett would search for her. They would find her and deal with Natalie.

The tires bumped as the car drove over something. Sierra bounced against the seat, wincing as the motion jolted her raw wrists.

"Well I've got news for you about your man," Natalie went on, the car picking up speed now. "He's the opposite of a hero. Heroes have honor, and Hollister has none."

Sierra suppressed a snarl of frustration, her fingers twisting at the cord. If she could just get her freaking hands free she could try to save herself. Steal this bitch's gun and shut her up until help arrived.

"Did he tell you about his last op in Syria in November?"

November.

The word made her pause. Beckett had come home at Thanksgiving, and she had known something was wrong. He'd told her and Noah he was getting out of the military, and she'd assumed it was because his father was terminal. But was there more? If Natalie was telling the truth about this, it fit. Something he'd seen or done overseas had shaken Beckett badly on his last deployment. Something that still haunted him to the point of nightmares.

"I'm betting not," Natalie said with a derisive snort. "But today he's going to pay for what he did there. And he's finally about to feel what it's been like for me all these months."

The car slowed again, then made a left turn and drove over a bumpy road before turning up a path in the forest. Natalie parked and got out. "End of the line for you," she said as she opened the back door.

A dark wave of fear rolled through Sierra. She darted a look past Natalie. All around them was forest. Towering evergreens that blocked out the sky and dense undergrowth of ferns and brush, the sent of it filling the air. They were deep enough in that no one would be able to see the car from the road. Or hear a gunshot.

Her heart began to pound harder. Then Natalie leaned in and reached out to undo the knots holding Sierra's hands to the metal seat anchor.

Sierra kept constant pressure on the cord, waiting for the first measure of give. She was only going to have one chance to use the element of surprise.

The instant she felt some slack in her bonds, she drew her knees up and slammed her feet as hard as she could into Natalie's chest. The cramped position didn't give her full leverage, but it was enough to knock Natalie on her ass.

The woman let out a surprised grunt and flailed her arms out to break her fall as she hit the ground.

Heart in her throat, Sierra scrambled to her knees and lunged for the opposite door, swiveling to reach back, her hands still bound behind her.

"You stupid bitch," Natalie snarled.

Get out! Hurry! Sierra fumbled with the handle, the position of her bound hands making it awkward. Just as Natalie jumped up and grabbed for Sierra's left leg, she managed to pull the handle and open the door. Sierra toppled out, landing hard on her side on the carpet of leaves and fir needles.

Rolling to her feet, she spun around and ran through the trees, heading for the edge of the road.

She only made it three strides before Natalie tackled her.

They hit the ground with a bone-jarring thud, Natalie on top, her weight knocking the breath out of Sierra's lungs. Before she could marshal the strength to fight back, Natalie had a knee dug into the middle of her back and an arm shoved across Sierra's nape, immobilizing her.

"Stay still," Natalie snapped, pivoting to seize Sierra's ankles. Sierra kicked and flailed, almost managed to throw the crazy bitch off, but Natalie yanked a piece of cord around her ankles, immobilizing her again.

Sierra screamed in frustration against her gag, shaking all over.

"Now get up." Natalie seized a handful of Sierra's hair and yanked.

Pain exploded across her scalp as hair tore free. Natalie wrenched her head up, forcing her off the ground, and Sierra had no choice but to follow. But once on her feet, she dug her heels into the loamy ground. If she was going to die, she was going down fighting.

"Move," Natalie commanded, shoving her forward by her bound wrists. With her feet hobbled, Sierra stumbled and fell to her knees, only to be brought upright again by another vicious yank on her hair.

She clenched her teeth against the pain, refused to take another step. The duct tape smothered a painful gasp as Natalie plowed a fist into Sierra's kidney. Her knees buckled, a haze of pain suffocating her.

"I said *move*, bitch." Natalie dragged her upright and forced her forward.

A growl of fury built in Sierra's throat. She twisted around to bash her head into Natalie, but the bite of cold metal against her temple stopped her cold. Her heart careened in her chest as her gaze locked on the pistol.

Natalie jammed the muzzle into her head. "I'll fucking shoot you right here if you give me any more trouble, do you understand?"

Sierra didn't move, too afraid to even breathe.

"Don't bother wasting your energy, because you're just gonna piss me off more and I might decide to pull the trigger early." She pressed her face close to Sierra's, her voice holding a deadly edge. "I'm former Army, sweetheart. You're not getting away from me. And I've waited too fucking long for this day to let you ruin everything now."

She gave Sierra another rough shove, forcing her forward one hobbling step at a time. "Your boyfriend's coming. And we need to be ready when he gets here."

****

Beckett parked out front of his house and dialed Sierra's number again. Her voicemail picked up just as Jase and Noah pulled into the driveway.

"You reach her?" Noah asked, stepping out of his cruiser.

"No, and not Tiana, either. Her car's not in her driveway and no one answered the door when I went there."

"I couldn't reach Sierra either. They must be deep in the woods."

Hell. "Sierra said she was looking back here," he said, indicating the forest down the lane. "Let's do a grid search." He started across the lawn, the others following.

A phone rang behind him. He stopped, looked over his shoulder as Noah answered his cell.

Whatever the person said made Noah's head jerk up, his stare locking with Beckett's.

The hair on the back of Beckett's neck stood on end. *Sierra.*

"I'll call you back," Noah said to the caller, then lowered the phone and spoke to Beckett, his expression tense. "One of my deputies responded to a report of shots fired on Front Street a little while ago. It was Sierra's clinic. Her assistant is dead. They found Sierra's purse but she's missing."

The bottom fell out of Beckett's stomach. *Jesus Christ.* He pulled out his phone, showed it to Noah. "The text came from her phone."

Noah met his eyes, anger burning bright. "Whoever took her must have sent it. They want you."

"Well they're gonna get me." He turned and ran for the house. Inside, he grabbed his pistol, a full mag, and his dad's hunting rifle. When he jogged down the front steps a minute later he found Noah waiting there with his service rifle. Beckett handed Jase his dad's. "Let's go."

"Beck, let me and my guys handle this," Noah said. "They're on the way now."

"Fuck that, I'm not waiting for anything," he shot back, already striding across the yard, Jase right behind him. "I'm going after Sierra." And God help whoever had taken her.

Noah cursed and hurried after him.

He made it to the lane in seconds, in full battle mode, already scanning the trees for signs of movement or recent disturbance. He took the lead, automatically slipping back into his role as commander. Someone had taken Sierra. He would hunt them down.

"Jase, take the left. Noah, the right. I'm going in there," he said, pointing to an area of forest ahead of him.

The three of them fanned out and began their search. Beckett's pulse quickened slightly, all his senses heightened as they entered the dense woods. He lost sight of his friends within moments and kept going. Noah and Jase were pros and could handle themselves. He could hunt without worrying about them.

A quarter mile into the bush, a flash of movement to his right snagged his attention. On instinct he ducked back behind a thick cedar trunk and dropped to one knee, pistol up and ready to fire.

"Hollister."

The female voice coming from the dense tangle of brush startled him for a moment. The kidnapper was a woman? "Where's Sierra?" he demanded.

"Right here. Show yourself, you cowardly son of a bitch."

The insult barely registered, all his focus on his target and getting Sierra home safe. The speaker was moving, circling slowly to the right, deeper into the woods.

Beckett angled his body, anticipating her movements. "I need to see Sierra," he called out.

She had to be alive. He fought to keep his heart rate down, his breathing steady, and refused to let himself think the worst. If this bitch had hurt Sierra…

"Here," the woman called out, almost straight ahead of him now.

A moment later something moved behind the leafy screen of trees. Branches trembled.

And then through a gap in the leaves a pair of wide, familiar blue eyes stared back at him.

"Sierra," he rasped out, the fear on her face slicing through him like a razor blade. He couldn't see much of her, but from the angle of her shoulders her arms appeared to be bound behind her, and the tape across her mouth prevented her from speaking.

But the terror in her eyes sent an icy wave through him.

"Are you okay?" he demanded.

She didn't answer, and then the breeze moved a branch obscuring the rest of her face from view and he saw why.

A hand held the muzzle of a pistol to her temple.

"Drop your weapon," the woman threatened.

Christ. With no clear shot, Beckett didn't have much choice, but damned if he was going to drop his weapon. "It's gonna be okay, sweetness," he told her, hoping she believed him. The sight of that pistol against her head made him insane, but he had to keep calm to save her, and he wanted to reassure her. "Just stay still."

She stared back at him with heartbreaking eyes, unmoving.

A bitter laugh floated out from behind the screen of leaves. "But it's not going to be okay. Not for her, and not for you." The woman with the pistol stepped out from behind cover, staying behind Sierra, using the woman he loved as a shield.

Beckett held that hate-filled stare, memorizing her face. He had never seen her before.

"Drop your weapon!" she yelled at him.

"Who are you?" he demanded. He still didn't have a clear shot, so he slowly lowered his weapon. Jase and Noah were nearby, but if they spooked her she might pull the trigger. He had to keep her talking, distract her.

The woman's lips twisted into a sneer. "I'm Cole Goodman's fiancée."

Every muscle in his body contracted, shock squeezing all the air from his lungs. Jesus fucking Christ. *How*? It couldn't be.

"Didn't think you'd ever have to face me, huh? Well here I am."

His jaw clenched. "Let her go."

"Not a fucking chance, you gutless bastard," she snapped, a wild glitter in her eyes. "You let him die. You sat up there in your nice, safe position on that ridge with your team and watched the whole thing without even trying to stop it. You let them all die."

Each word hit him as if it was a separate bullet, but he refused to let it show. How did she know what had happened?

"I'm former Army too, and I have connections of my own. So yeah, I found out what happened that day. But your cowardly actions didn't just kill Cole." She shook her head, eyes glittering with unshed tears, voice shaking as she continued. "I lost my fiancé, and four days later I lost our baby, too. The only part of him I had left. Well fuck you, Captain Hollister. I'm going to kill your girlfriend while you watch, so you can feel the same pain I did, and then you can finally rot in hell where you—"

"Beck?" The familiar voice came from off to the left. Far away enough that Noah must not have heard the woman ranting.

Shit. Beckett darted a glance to the left as the woman spun to face the direction of Noah's voice. He had to answer. "To your right," he called back, firming his grip on the pistol. He would have only a second to aim and fire if he got a shot.

The woman jerked back around to face Beckett, face pale and pinched, Sierra still held in front of the woman, the pistol muzzle to her head.

"I'm not alone," Beckett said in a calm voice, fighting the urge to charge. With that pistol against Sierra's temple, only a headshot would end this before the woman could fire, and he didn't have the angle. Might not get it. "I've got the sheriff and another vet with me, and they're armed. So put the pistol down and let Sierra go. Let her go and we'll talk."

"You think I'd want to talk to you?" The woman's mouth tightened, fury burning in her fanatical gaze. "Fuck. You."

She was going to pull the trigger. He could see it in her

eyes.

A howl of pain and fury gathered in his chest.

"Drop your weapon and put your hands up. Now," Jase said, appearing out of the trees to the right.

The woman whipped to face Jase, giving Beckett a target for a fleeting moment.

Blocking out that it was Sierra she was holding, he raised his weapon and fired.

The shot exploded through the forest as a mist of blood spattered the leaves. The woman dropped, dragging Sierra to the ground with her.

Beckett charged forward, heart in his throat.

The soles of his shoes thudded against the forest floor as he ran at the kidnapper, weapon up, finger on the trigger. From the corner of his eye he saw Jase rushing toward him but he wasn't taking his eye off the woman. She lay crumpled on the ground with her eyes half-open, a hole just above her left eye.

Before he could reach her Sierra twisted away from the woman and rolled to her bound feet, but stumbled and fell in her haste to get away.

"Sierra." Beckett shoved his weapon into the back of his waistband and skidded to his knees in front of her to gather her up in his arms. "Christ. *Christ.*"

She made a choked sound and buried her face in his shoulder. Beckett fought to get his breathing under control as he fumbled with the cord binding her wrists behind her. As soon as it came loose he reached up and pulled the tape off her mouth as quickly and gently as he could.

"Beckett," she whispered, and grabbed him tight.

"Shh, I've got you. I've got you. Everything's okay now." Beckett crushed her to him with a groan, burying one hand in her hair, keeping her face tucked tight to his shoulder to prevent her from seeing the woman's body beside them.

Jase and Noah reached them almost simultaneously, scanning the area for more threats. "Are you okay?" Jase asked her.

Beckett closed his eyes. Jesus, he'd come so close to losing her. But he couldn't handle thinking about that right now. He had to take care of Sierra. "She's okay," he told them. "She's all right."

"Was she alone?" Noah demanded.

"Yes," Sierra answered, holding on tight. "Oh, God, she sh-shot Macy."

It was over.

"I've got you," Beckett murmured against her hair. "I'm getting you out of here right now."

He scooped Sierra up in his arms and started away from the body, carrying her through the forest as fast as he could. Noah and Jase could handle everything else. Beckett's only concern right now was Sierra and getting her the hell out of here.

Chapter Twenty-Three

"**S**ierra. Look at me, sweetness."

It was the endearment that managed to penetrate the numbing fog of shock enveloping her. She forced her eyes open and lifted her head from Beckett's shoulder to look into his face.

His harsh expression eased a fraction as he scanned her anxiously. "Are you hurt?"

She shook her head once. "N-no. Just c-cold." She was shaking apart, her teeth chattering even though she was in Beckett's arms, safe in his living room with the spring sunshine streaming through the windows.

He lifted her off his lap and set her next to him on the couch to reach down and untie her ankles. As soon as she was free he sat back up and took her face in his hands, studying her.

She wrapped her fingers around his thick wrists, needing the anchor. Staring into his worried dark eyes, all the fear she'd been battling collapsed under a rush of combined relief and sadness. She crumpled.

Beckett made a low sound and cupped the back of her head as she buried her face in his neck, the tears breaking free. He didn't try to quiet her or tell her not to cry, simply

249

held her, rocking her slightly from side to side while she fought to come to terms with what she'd just survived.

She was glad Natalie was dead, but she would never forget what had happened today, or those endless moments while she'd stared across the space at Beckett and thought she was about to die while he watched...

She shuddered, gulped in a choppy breath. "I couldn't d-do anything," she gasped out. That's what bothered her the most. She hadn't been able to do a goddamn thing to stop it—any of it—or protect either of them.

"I know."

"I t-tried," she said, needing him to know that. The thought of him thinking she was weak and useless in that kind of situation was beyond bearing. "I f-fought her. But I...c-couldn't get away."

"Don't," he said softly. "Don't blame yourself. This wasn't your fault. None of it. And you were so goddamn brave, you did exactly what I asked you to." He rested his cheek on the top of her head.

"She k-killed Macy. Shot her dead right in f-front of me, like she was nothing."

"I know. I'm so damn sorry."

Oh, God, it was all so awful. And Beckett... He'd just had his father's funeral hours ago. Now this. She shuddered.

"You're safe now. It's all over, and I've got you."

Sierra gulped in a steadying breath, let it ripple through her, her jerky muscles slowly relaxing. She blocked out all the awful memories and focused on Beckett.

His clean, masculine scent. The heat of his body. The feel of his strong arms around her and the steady thump of his heart beneath her ear.

He had her. Wouldn't let anything happen to her. She was safe now. They both were.

They looked up at the sound of footsteps on the front porch. Noah walked in, Jase right behind him.

Sierra sat up, reached for her brother as he knelt in front of her to pull her into a hug. "You all right, honey?"

"I'm okay," she whispered. Easing back, she searched his face, worried. "What happens now?"

He smoothed a hand over her hair. "My guys have taken over so I could come check on you. I know you're not up to it right now, but I'm going to need you to come in so we can get a full report on record." He glanced at Beckett. "Sure she doesn't need an ambulance?"

"No," she protested, leaning closer to Beckett. "I'm fine. Scrapes and bruises, nothing else."

Her brother studied her for a long moment, then relented with a nod. "All right." He stood and spoke to Beckett. "I gotta get back to the scene. Need to talk to you first, though. Alone."

Sierra bit back the protest that wanted to burst free. Beckett had killed Natalie. Under the circumstances he wouldn't be in any trouble legally, but as sheriff, Noah had to make sure this was all handled according to procedure, no matter if Beckett was his best friend or she was his sister.

Beckett kissed her cheek, his lips warm, chasing away more of the chill. "Sit tight. Be back in a few minutes," he murmured, and eased her off his lap. "Jase, you stay with her."

"Hey, angel face," Jase said, sinking down beside her and wrapping an arm around her shoulders. "You hanging in there?"

"Yes." For the most part. She just couldn't believe this had happened, and wanted the whole nightmare to be over with. She had so many questions, most of them for Beckett. The timing was beyond shitty. How much could a man take before he broke?

"I've called Molly. She's on her way right now."

Sierra nodded, a heavy weight of fatigue beginning to settle over her. She sighed and leaned into Jase's strong body, beginning to shut down inside. "I want a shower," she mumbled. She might have blood spatter on her. She shivered.

"You can take one as soon as Molly gets here."

Thankfully Molly arrived a few minutes later and immediately took charge. She followed Sierra upstairs while she showered and dressed, then wrapped her up in a blanket without any fuss and brought her some sweetened tea to help counteract the adrenaline crash. Sierra sat with her and Jase until Beckett came back half an hour later.

Her friends immediately got up to make room for him, but Beckett didn't sit next to her on the couch. Instead he bundled her up, blanket and all, and carried her upstairs.

He laid her down on his bed, stretched out beside her and pulled her into his body. Sierra groaned and wiggled in closer, starving for the contact. His arms locked around her, hard, and the fierce pressure was exactly what she needed. The anxiety began to bleed away, her pulse slowing.

Her mind refused to stay quiet, however. "Was it true?" she finally asked him in the quiet. Jase and Molly were both still downstairs, she hadn't heard either of them leave, but they wouldn't disturb them here. "What Natalie said? She said that was her name. I don't know if she was lying or not. Was it true? About you letting her fiancé and the others die?"

He stilled, his whole body going rigid.

A few beats of silence passed. Sierra heaved a sigh, dread and annoyance filling her. "Beckett. I need you to talk to me. I can't do this if you won't talk to me."

She was about to push away from him and roll over when he finally spoke. "Yeah. It's true."

The admission surprised her. She kept her face tucked into his shoulder, instinctively knowing that looking him in the eye would make it impossible for him to talk about this. She needed him to tell her this. "What happened?"

"It was during my final deployment, in Syria. Jase was with me. We were on an op to observe American hostages. Cole Goodman was one of them. Army vet." He was quiet a moment. "We might have been able to stop it, or at least mitigate the body count, but command refused our request to intervene. So we stayed put and watched through our binos while they all died by firing squad."

Sierra winced. God, that must have been awful. "Is that what you dream about when you have nightmares?"

"Partly. But that wasn't the first time I've watched people die without stopping it. And there were plenty of others I tried to save and couldn't." He swallowed. "That's what I dream about."

She reached a hand around him to stroke his back. His muscles were rigid. "I'm so sorry. I didn't know."

"I didn't want you to know. Ever. None of this was ever supposed to touch you," he said, a dark edge to his voice.

Sierra heard the self-hatred in it. "What happened today wasn't your fault."

He snorted. "Yes it was."

"No." She refused to let him do this to himself. Squeezing him tighter, she implored him to see reason. "You followed orders and took care of your men. If you'd disobeyed you would have been up for a court martial."

"Maybe, but then none of this would have happened. Macy would still be alive, and you wouldn't have been taken captive and held at gunpoint."

He wasn't going to listen to her, no matter what she said. But she had to try. "Natalie made her choice when she pulled that trigger. But how did she know about you? How did she find out what happened?"

"I don't know, but I'm gonna find out. That mission was highly classified. Someone must have leaked the intel to her. Maybe someone in intelligence. Maybe a politician, who knows."

"I'm glad she's dead. But I'm sorry you were the one who had to do it." And thank God he hadn't missed. That had been one hell of a precise shot he'd delivered. A few inches off and he might have hit her instead.

"I'm not." He rolled away from her a little, cupped her cheek in his hand to look into her eyes. "I told you, I would do anything to protect you. Anything. If that means laying down my own life, then so be it."

Tears burned her eyes. "Don't say that. Losing you would kill me."

"You're not going to lose me. Even if you deserve a helluva lot better than me."

She shot him an outraged look. "Don't say that either. It insults both of us, because it's not true. At *all*."

He shook his head once, his gaze softening. "Sierra, I love you. I'm *in* love with you, and I can't imagine my life without you in it. There's nothing I wouldn't do to keep you safe."

She hitched in a breath, the tears breaking free. "I love you too. Have for a long time." She grabbed him, hugged him tight. "And you just turned the worst day of my life into the best one."

****

Beckett had never been more thankful for anything in his life as he lay holding Sierra while the afternoon light began to fade outside the bedroom windows. She dozed for a bit, but there was no way he could sleep after what had happened.

She loved him. She loved him even though he still wasn't sure he deserved it, and he'd damn near lost her today.

After a time she stirred, and he knew the moment it all came rushing back to her because she sucked in a sharp breath. "Hey," he murmured, kissing her forehead, his hands stroking up and down her spine. "I'm here."

She melted into his hold. "What time is it?"

"Almost seven. You hungry?"

"No."

"We need to go in and talk to Noah. You up to it?" They should have gone immediately but Noah had bent the rules for them. Especially for Beckett, because of their long friendship and because he'd saved Sierra.

She sighed. "Yes. I'd rather get it over with."

When she was ready he took her into town to talk to Noah. After giving their statements and wrapping everything up, as expected there were no charges laid and they were both free to go. He called his former superiors, alerting them to what Natalie Tenant had done and found out. They had promised to look into it and inform him of what they found.

Beckett took Sierra straight back to his place, where Jase had dropped off the takeout Beckett had asked him to pick up from her favorite restaurant. Sierra took a long, hot shower, ate with him at the kitchen table, and then crawled into his lap to wrap her arms around his neck. Beckett scooped an arm under her butt and carried her upstairs, his mouth finding hers while she twined her legs around his waist.

By the time he reached his room he was rock hard and desperate to be inside her. They undressed each other, stroked and tasted and teased until neither of them could take it anymore.

Beckett gathered her beneath him, settled between her open thighs and propped himself up on his forearms to gaze down at her. She was a gift he had never expected to receive, one that had almost been taken from him today. He needed to bury himself deep inside her to ease the beast roaring inside him.

"I love you, Sierra." More than he could ever express

in words.

A soft smile spread across her face. "Show me."

He did. With every kiss, every stroke of his hands and surge of his hips.

He worshipped her, brought her to the edge twice, waiting until she was gasping and pleading before he slid his thumb over the swollen bud of her clit and stroked his cock along her inner sweet spot. She moved underneath him like a gentle wave, her face so beautiful as she came undone, her body locked around him.

Raw possessiveness exploded inside him. She was *his*, and no one was taking her from him. Ever. "All mine, sweetness," he ground out, the pleasure of being held within her like this turning his voice guttural.

"Yes." Those gorgeous deep blue eyes focused on his, full of love and a possessiveness all their own. "And you're mine."

A growl ripped out of him, primal and fierce. He took her mouth, drove into her again and again as release seared along his nerve endings. She held him tight, thighs locked around his waist, fingers digging into his scalp.

And while he lay helpless in her arms recovering, she enfolded him with her body and covered his neck, shoulders and face with sweet kisses that made his heart clench. Her words from earlier came back to him.

This had been his worst day too, but had somehow ended up his best. All because of her.

Lifting his head to look down at her, he stroked his fingers through her soft hair. She knew the worst about him now, and hadn't turned away. Instead she'd opened her heart even wider and tucked him inside it. "Just so we're clear, I want forever with you. A family someday, the works."

A smile tugged at the corner of her mouth, even as her eyebrows drew together in a frown. "Are you asking, or telling?"

"Whichever gets me the answer I want."

Her teeth flashed white in the growing darkness as she grinned up at him. "Well, if you're asking, then my answer is yes. Because that sounds perfect to me."

Beckett growled in triumph and sealed her promise with a deep, thorough kiss.

Epilogue

Five weeks later

Sierra paused in the midst of rinsing off the colander full of fresh local strawberries to glance out the window above the sink. She smiled as she glimpsed Beckett's truck pull into the driveway, back from getting groceries.

It was her birthday. They were hosting a summer barbecue tonight and she was making her grandmother's from-scratch strawberry shortcakes for dessert. A domestic goddess she was not, but Beckett didn't seem to mind, and besides, this recipe was pretty much foolproof.

She set the berries aside and cleared the island to begin making the shortcake biscuits, filled with a sense of newly found peace. The first week or two after the kidnapping hadn't been easy. She'd had her share of bad dreams but they were starting to lessen now, and at least now when either of them had a bad night they had each other to turn to for comfort.

As for the question of how Natalie had found out what happened in Syria that day, Beckett had been informed that she had used her fiancé's life insurance settlement to bribe someone in Army Intelligence. That officer had since been removed from duty, charged, and was awaiting trial.

Now Sierra and Beckett could officially move on with their lives, and they hadn't wasted any time in doing so.

Officially moving in with him here two weeks ago had come as a bit of a shock to their friends and her family, but it was the right decision and she had no regrets. She also didn't care what anyone else thought about it. She loved her little cottage but she loved Beckett more, and now they were creating a life together in the home that meant so much to him and always had to his parents.

Light footsteps pattered on the back porch. Ella appeared on the other side of the screen door, back from walking the dog, her face worried. "Miss Sierra? Can you come out and help me with Walter? He won't get up."

Frowning, Sierra grabbed a kitchen towel and dried her hands. "Why, did he hurt himself on your walk?"

"I'm not sure. He's lying down on the grass and I can't get him to move."

Was he being lazy? Or was something wrong?

Sierra dropped the towel, headed for the back door and walked out onto the porch into the warm summer evening air. Walter was old. She hated to think his body was giving out on him now. He deserved at least a couple more years in a home where he was loved and spoiled beyond rotten before he left this earth.

"Where is he?" she asked Ella, scanning the side yard. He was nowhere to be seen.

"Over here," Ella said, and scampered around the side of the house and out of view.

Sierra hurried after her, barefoot, already mentally listing some possibilities as to what the problem might be. Degenerative disc disease? The start of congestive heart failure? Cancer?

She rounded the corner, the summer grass soft beneath her feet. She hadn't been back to the clinic since the shooting, doing house calls instead until Beckett and his crew could change the space enough to hopefully not remind her of the attack every time she walked through the door, but if Walter needed medical treatment, then she would take him in.

At the start of the front lawn, she stopped short at the sight that greeted her.

Ella stood off to one side near the lane with her mother. Jase, Molly and Noah were fanned out behind Beckett, who stood in the middle of the lawn, Walter seated at his feet. Someone had brushed his ears out, and he was wearing his red plaid bow tie. Carter was conspicuously absent. No one had seen or heard from him in weeks.

"Happy birthday!" everyone chorused.

She laughed, relieved that Walter seemed okay. "Well thank you." Why were they all standing around watching her like that? It was weird. She glanced from Beckett to Ella and back, just to make sure she hadn't missed something. "So, Walter looks okay to me."

"He's fine." A smile playing around the edges of his mouth, Beckett raised a hand and crooked a finger at her. The sexy sparkle in his eyes made her tummy flutter. He was bossy in the bedroom, definitely liked control and to dish out orders, but it worked for her. It *really* worked for her.

What was he doing, though? Sierra approached cautiously, half expecting some kind of prank. The audience made her nervous. "What are you up to?"

"Come here and find out."

When she reached him, he took her face in his hands and kissed her, long and slow. Her eyes flew open when Ella groaned and muttered something that included the word inappropriate, and Jase's distinctive whistle of approval sounded.

She broke the kiss, her cheeks growing hot. Lord, Noah must be really damn uncomfortable right now. And what was with Beckett? PDAs weren't his thing at *all*, let alone in front of her brother and their friends. "Beckett, what—"

She didn't finish. Because he grasped both her hands and sank onto one knee in front of her.

Sierra's eyes widened. "What are...?" She was afraid to say it out loud, in case it jinxed everything. But this couldn't be happening. Could it?

His dark gaze delved into hers. "I love you, sweetness. I want forever with you."

Oh, my God, he was proposing here in front of everyone.

She gaped down at him, mouth open in shock. They'd talked about getting married one day, and maybe having kids, but she'd never dreamed he would do this so fast. Let alone so publicly.

He chuckled at the look on her face. "Look at Walter."

Wait, Walter? Confused, she lowered her gaze to the dog, who was staring up at her with an expression of total boredom on his droopy face. He didn't get excited about much, except for treats and trips in the truck or on the ride-on mower Beckett liked to drive around. Not a dune buggy, but Walter didn't seem to mind.

"He doesn't know any tricks. Or if he does, he's too stubborn to do them. But I know how much you love him in spite of his bad attitude, and I know that also goes for me too, so I let him help me a little."

Sierra scanned the dog, still not understanding. What was she looking for? Maybe Beckett wasn't proposing, and she was an idiot.

Walter chose that moment to flop to the ground and roll to his side with a loud groan, his protruding tongue lying on the grass, red-rimmed eyes gazing up at her. *Just kill me now and end my humiliation*, his expression said.

"Walter, you're killin' me," Beckett muttered, and reached for the dog while everyone laughed. He hauled Walter back upright, holding the dog by the chest so he couldn't lie back down again.

Sierra stifled a giggle. They looked too ridiculous.

Beckett shook his head, his eyes glinting up at her with silent laughter. "Stop laughing and look down." He tapped his finger on the bow tie.

And then Sierra saw it. A round diamond nestled into the center of a red ribbon that someone had woven into the shape of a rose. Beckett had pinned it to Walter's bow tie.

"This was my mother's," he explained as he unfastened the rose ribbon, his strong fingers untying the knot as deftly as he'd freed her from her bonds on that awful day over a month ago. Hands that had protected and comforted her, given her pleasure that stole her breath, and would always be there to hold and support her when she needed it.

"We'll get it set into a ring you love this week," he said, "but I wanted to do this today with everyone here to witness it."

He held up the diamond, and the symbolism in the act wasn't lost on her.

Beckett was essentially holding his heart out to her. This strong, incredibly private man jaded by the warrior's life that had made him, was down on one knee in front of her. Making himself vulnerable to her, exposing his tender insides to her and everyone watching. To publicly prove just how deep his love ran for her, and how much she meant to him.

Oh, my God, she loved him so damn much.

Love shone in his eyes, the late afternoon sunlight turning the black coffee irises into shades of dark chocolate and burnt toffee. "Sierra, will you marry me?"

Her throat closed up. She put a hand to her mouth and

nodded, reaching for the diamond while her vision blurred. "Yes," she choked out. This was everything she'd ever dreamed of, and more. "Now get up here and kiss me." She yanked on his hand, reaching for him as he stood and wrapped his arms around her, their friends cheering in the background.

Released from being held against his will, Walter flopped back down to the ground and rolled to his side with another groan. Sierra laughed in the instant before Beckett's lips came down on hers.

He kissed her, then nuzzled her cheek, his chest vibrating with silent laughter. "Are you mad that I asked you in front of everyone?"

She shook her head. She understood why he'd done it, and the intent behind it meant the world to her. "No. This was perfect."

Life was rarely perfect. But sometimes, it was just right.

She and Beckett were just right for each other. That was the only thing that truly mattered.

—The End—

Dear reader,

Thank you for reading *Fractured Honor*. I hope you enjoyed it. If you'd like to stay in touch with me and be the first to learn about new releases you can:

Join my newsletter at:
http://kayleacross.com/v2/newsletter/

Find me on Facebook:
https://www.facebook.com/KayleaCrossAuthor/

Follow me on Twitter:
https://twitter.com/kayleacross

Follow me on Instagram:
https://www.instagram.com/kaylea_cross_author/

Also, please consider leaving a review at your favorite online book retailer. It helps other readers discover new books.

Happy reading,
Kaylea

Excerpt from
Buried Lies
Crimson Point Series

By Kaylea Cross
Copyright © 2018 Kaylea Cross

Chapter One

For some, gardening was good for the soul. For him, it was a necessity.

It kept him sane. Silenced the insidious voice in his head—at least temporarily.

He paused in the strip of lawn between two flowerbeds to draw in a deep breath, the air faintly tinged by the salty tang of the sea just over a mile away. *Heaven.*

This was his favorite place on earth, and his favorite time of day. After a solid eight hours of honest, physical work, he could come here and let the world fall away while he enjoyed all his flowers.

His beautiful, secret flowers.

Late afternoon sunlight slanted down on him between the tall evergreens that bordered the edge of the property as he strode from the gardening shed with his tools. He'd bought the half-acre nestled into a band of forest bordering a vineyard outside the town limit years ago, before he'd started his garden.

Back then it had just been a place to build his refuge, a spot all his own where he could camp in a location no one would bother him, but over the past few years it had become so much more important. Here he had absolute privacy, no one around to see what he was doing. He could simply be himself and let the mask drop.

It had been over a month since he'd last been here. Weeds had sprung up in a few of the beds, and he still needed to remove the pipe sticking out of the newest one.

Birds chirped overhead, the only sound out here, even

the muted crash of the sea absent this far from the beach. It was so quiet here now, so different from the last time he had been here a month-and-a-half ago.

He paused to admire his latest addition, remembering the day he'd planted it. The sense of satisfaction that had encompassed him from having finally, *finally* finished his secret garden.

Graphic images flooded his brain, triggering the usual response. He fought it, tried to stop the pictures running in his head, shove them down deep where they belonged. If he wasn't careful, they would control him instead of the other way around.

He shook himself. Work. Physical exertion always helped clear his mind and kept the terrible need away.

Most of the time.

The blade of the shovel sank deep into the soil he'd amended in late spring, in preparation for his newest addition. He sang quietly as he worked, to keep his mind busy along with his hands.

After digging out the soil surrounding the pipe, it came out easily. Still singing to himself, he set it aside and filled in the hole. Then he pulled out the weeds that threatened to ruin his masterpiece and raked the rich, dark earth in between the perennials and annuals until the bed was pristine once more.

Now all that remained in the bed were the flowers and its crowning glory. And this particular variety of pink peonies was as beautiful as it was rare.

He'd planted them to remind him of the pretty brunette with the pink dress. The fabric had been the exact shade of the petals. He'd taken great pains to find a match, using his job to contact nurseries all up and down the Oregon Coast to find it. And the day he'd brought it here to plant it...

Images fractured in his head, getting all mixed up. He shook his head, trying to clear the cloud of confusion. The look of delicious terror on her face. A swirl of pink fabric. Peony petals shivering in the breeze. The sound of her muffled screams, growing fainter and fainter…

No.

No, no, no, it was too soon. Much too soon.

But it was too late to stop the inevitable.

The sudden rise of excitement shot through him like a lightning strike, stronger than ever before. His heart rate doubled. His breathing turned harsh and erratic. Sweat popped out across his skin, his hands trembling.

His body tightened. Hardened.

He clenched his teeth and gripped the shovel handle until his knuckles ached, swallowing hard. Fighting the powerful swell of arousal. The burning need to undo his pants and stroke himself to relieve the sudden pressure in his groin.

His whole body shook as he rode it out, until finally after endless minutes, it passed. He had no idea how long he'd been standing there, battling the raging need. His breathing was still harsh as his gaze strayed back to the gorgeous pink peonies, their petals all but glowing in a shaft of golden sunlight.

It was like a sign from above. The dark urges had only gone away for a few weeks this time and now they were back, more powerful than ever.

It frightened and electrified him at the same time.

He glanced around, taking slow, calming breaths. There were more weeds to be pulled in the other beds, but he couldn't tend to them now, he was too shaken. Instead he gathered his tools up and carried them back to the shed, a hollow, heavy regret mixing with the heady sense of anticipation humming through him.

His secret garden wasn't complete after all.

Now he would have to break his most important rule of allowing himself only one perfect victim per year. Hunting again so soon would increase the risk of getting caught, but maybe that would make this one last kill that much more fulfilling.

Maybe this next one would satisfy him enough to forever silence the hungry monster that never gave him rest. Maybe it would finally bring him peace so he could stop.

****

Noah Buchanan jerked awake when the generator started up next door.

What the hell?

He rolled over to squint at the bedside clock. "You gotta be freaking *kidding* me," he muttered.

It was seven-twelve on a Saturday morning. Wasn't there an unspoken rule everybody understood that you had to be quiet until at least nine on the weekends? As a matter of common courtesy?

His new neighbor was from South Dakota. Maybe they didn't have that rule there.

Noah sighed, trying to remember if he had any earplugs lying around. Thanks to yet another file sent over from the FBI on the latest missing women case from six weeks ago, then a domestic disturbance call just prior to the end of his shift, he'd only gotten home an hour ago. That meant he'd been asleep for probably twenty minutes, max.

Outside, the generator got louder.

"Noooo," he groaned. So much for sleep. What the hell was she doing over there, anyway?

He growled as he sat up and scrubbed a hand over his face. He'd showered as soon as he'd gotten home but hadn't shaved, because he'd thought he would have plenty of time to do it *after* he'd had at least four or five hours of sleep. Silly him.

Grabbing a pair of jeans from the chair in the corner,

he dragged them on over top of his boxers and stumbled down the hall toward the kitchen. Through the wide window above the sink he caught a flash of blond hair over the back fence. Definitely his new neighbor.

Since sleep was no longer an option, he hit the button on the coffee maker on his way to the back door. Barefoot, he stepped outside into the warm late-June morning and headed across the back lawn, the grass soft and slightly damp beneath his soles.

He stopped at the neck-high cedar fence that separated the properties, and the moment he saw his sexy new neighbor at the far side of her yard, he suddenly wasn't annoyed anymore.

Poppy stood in profile to him as she raised the wand of the power washer and started on her back fence. She was young, maybe mid-twenties. She wore a tiny pair of frayed cutoff shorts and a string bikini top that framed full, round breasts, leaving her midriff and long legs bare.

Christ. It took superhuman effort to drag his eyes up to her face.

Her honey-blond hair was up in a ponytail, and he could see the wires from the earbuds she had in. Completely absorbed in her task, she had no idea he was standing there staring at her.

As a cop, it was hardwired in him to be cynical. He'd kept an eye on Poppy Larsen since the night he'd met her when she'd first come to town. It seemed odd to him that she'd shown up all by herself and decided to open a business here. So far he hadn't managed to dig up anything of interest about her, but everyone had secrets. He wondered what her real story was.

She continued washing her fence down, making a thorough job of it. On the one hand Noah had to admire her work ethic. But why the hell was she power washing her fence at this hour on a Saturday morning?

He stood there for another minute admiring the view,

since she couldn't see him, then ambled down to the west end of the fence. Resting his forearms on the top of it, he waited for her to notice him.

It was almost comical when she did.

Poppy did a double take and whirled to face him, pressure washer wand still in hand, her chocolate-brown eyes widening in surprise. Her creamy skin glistened with drops of water, and her nipples stood out beneath the triangles of her bikini top.

And suddenly Noah was grateful for the fence blocking his lower body, since half of his blood supply was currently rushing to his groin. A reaction he'd never had while waiting to talk with the elderly woman who had owned the cottage until a couple of months ago.

Quickly shutting off the generator, Poppy yanked the earbuds out of her ears and crossed her arms over her chest, slightly turning her body away as though she was self-conscious.

Now that was a damn shame. The woman had absolutely nothing to be self-conscious about.

"Hi," she blurted, looking both embarrassed and alarmed. "Oh my gosh, I'm so sorry. I didn't see your patrol car in the driveway when I checked a little while ago, so I assumed you weren't home yet. I was hoping to be done by the time you got home." She angled more away from him, until she faced her back porch.

Ah, well, now he couldn't be mad. "Yeah, my cruiser's getting serviced, so one of my deputies drove me home at the end of my shift."

"Oh." She winced. "Did I wake you up?"

Yes, but now he wasn't sorry. "It's okay."

"I'll put this away until this afternoon," she went on, turning to pull the washer into a corner, and giving him a spectacular view of her legs and backside. He'd only seen her a few times since the night he'd first met her in town, and she'd always been in jeans and a T-shirt that hid all the glorious curves on display right now. "I'm really sorry."

"Really, it's okay."

She glanced back at him. "Hang on a sec, I'll be right out," she said, and hurried to her back porch. The screen door to the house banged shut, then she reappeared thirty seconds later holding a plate and wearing a plaid flannel shirt that hid her breasts from view.

Noah was sorry she'd covered up, but sorrier still that she'd done it because he'd made her uncomfortable. He was used to women trying to get and hold his attention, not hide their bodies.

"Peace offering," she said with a little smile as she crossed to the fence, holding up a plate she must have grabbed inside, loaded with pastries. Up close he noticed the light smattering of freckles across her cheeks and the bridge of her nose. And her dark-chocolate eyes had the tiniest amount of gold around the pupils.

"What are these?" he asked, perusing his options. They smelled fantastic.

"They're freshly made, from my shop. Grand opening was last weekend."

"I know." He knew everything that happened in his town. And he still considered her to be an outsider, someone to be wary of. Even though she had a sexy body and smile and brought him freshly baked pastries.

Selecting what appeared to be a bit of chocolate croissant, he focused back on her.

Poppy Larsen was a mystery to him. She'd up and moved here from South Dakota, fallen in love with Crimson Point and bought her shop, then this cottage, all within a matter of weeks. There was no ring on her finger, no tan lines to suggest she'd worn one recently, and the way she'd covered up so quickly just now told him she might even be a little on the shy side.

She had a wholesomeness about her—literally the girl

next door—except for that killer body he now couldn't get out of his head. And for damn sure he'd never lived next door to anyone he'd had such a visceral reaction to before. He wasn't sure he liked it.

"How's business going so far?" he asked, going for polite and professional even though the front of his jeans were still tight. He was the town sheriff, and they lived next door to one another. He wanted them to have a friendly neighbor relationship.

She made a face, the bridge of her nose wrinkling adorably. "Honestly? It could be better. I'm going to try some different events to see if I can pull in more customers."

"It'll get a lot busier in town starting in the next few weeks. Tourist season hits full force around the Fourth of July and holds until Labor Day. I bet business will pick up for you in no time."

"Sure hope so. I've leveraged everything I have into the shop, and this place." She nodded at the whitewashed, shingled cottage behind her.

Whatever else Poppy Larsen was, she was a damn hard worker. She'd done most of the renos on the shop herself, due to budget constraints, and apparently was committed to rolling up her sleeves at home as well. "Are you planning to paint the fence once you're done washing it?" It was yellowed and peeling in places.

"Yeah, it needs a new coat of paint, and so does the cottage. Everything's peeling. I'll get to the landscaping later."

She intended to do all of that in addition to running her own business that had just opened? "You can borrow my sprayer again. And the lady you bought this place from had a landscaper come take care of the yard once a week during spring and summer, then do a cleanup a few times over the fall and winter. We get big windstorms here in the winter, so you'll have a lot of downed branches from the trees."

He nodded at the tall cedars and firs bordering the east side of her property. "I can get you the guy's name and number if you're interested. He's pretty reasonable, and he has a lot of clients here in the area, including Beckett." Noah's best friend, and future brother-in-law. Damn, that sounded weird.

"Have you used him?"

"No, but my yard's way smaller than yours, and I don't have many trees."

"Okay, that would be great if you could give me his number. Thank you." Poppy considered him for a moment. "I was thinking of hosting a poker night this coming Thursday down at the shop. I'm getting a liquor license for special events like that. Do you or anyone you know like to play?"

Noah blocked a frown from forming. Poker at a bookshop-slash-tearoom? "I know some guys."

She beamed at him, her sunny smile transforming her entire face. And it had already been pretty before. "Great. I'll be doing board game nights there as well. Dungeons and Dragons, things like that. And by the way, I haven't forgotten that I promised you a cherry pie for helping me paint the shop. I just haven't had the chance to make it yet."

His lips quirked. "I wouldn't say no to a cherry pie, but I don't want you to go to any trouble. You're really busy."

She shrugged. "I'll fit it in. I always keep my promises."

"Well that's nice to hear. Since we're neighbors, and all."

Her eyes sparkled at him. Not flirtatious, however. Warm. Sincere. "Exactly."

No flirting *and* she'd been in a rush to cover up. He was getting more curious about her by the minute. She also made it hard to stay suspicious of her and her background. "Tell you what. I'll make some calls and see if I can get a couple of my buddies to come out on Thursday."

"That'd be great, thank you."

"No problem. And don't hold off on the power washing on my account. I'm up now."

"You sure?"

"Positive."

"All right." She held up the plate, raised her tawny eyebrows. "Want anything else?"

Oh, he did. But it wasn't on the menu, and wasn't going to be. "I'm good. Gimme a couple minutes to make some calls and I'll let you know about Thursday."

The first person he called was Beckett.

"It's not even seven-thirty in the morning," his best friend grumbled. Noah's sister, Sierra, had moved in with him just over a month ago. "Better be important."

"I thought anything after oh-four-hundred was considered sleeping in for a Green Beret."

"Former Green Beret. Now that I'm a civilian again, I remembered how much I love sleeping. So, what's up?"

"You, me and Weaver, poker game this Thursday night."

"Poker? Man, we haven't done that in years. At your place?" Beckett asked.

"Seven at the new bookshop in town. Whale's Tale."

"Whale's Tale? What?"

"Just be there. We still on for tonight?" They were having a barbecue at Beckett and Sierra's.

Beckett grunted. "If you hang up right now and let your sister and me get back to sleep, then yeah."

Now that was a mental image Noah didn't need. He loved them both, but even after a few weeks to adjust, it was still weird to think of them getting married and having a family together someday. "Fine. But next time you see your yard guy, can you have him call me? My neighbor might be interested in hiring him."

"I'll text him. *If* you hang up right now."

"Fine. See you later." He hung up and called Weaver, a former teammate of Beckett's, who was much perkier than Beckett had been.

Noah ended the call and walked back to the fence. Poppy had hauled the power washer over to the far corner, still wearing her shirt over her bikini top. Noah flagged her down before she could fire it up. "The three of us are in for Thursday night."

Her face lit up. "That's fantastic, thank you. If you think of anyone else, please let them know."

"Will do." He turned and headed back toward his house, in a far better mood than he'd been ten minutes ago. And maybe, if he was lucky, Poppy would decide to take that flannel shirt off once he went back inside. Then he could enjoy his morning coffee while standing in front of the kitchen window and admire the view.

Yep, no doubt about it. Lingering cynicism aside, his neighborhood had gotten a major upgrade the day she'd moved in next door.

coming November 2018

About the Author

NY Times and USA Today Bestselling author Kaylea Cross writes edge-of-your-seat military romantic suspense. Her work has won many awards, including the Daphne du Maurier Award of Excellence, and has been nominated multiple times for the National Readers' Choice Awards. A Registered Massage Therapist by trade, Kaylea is also an avid gardener, artist, Civil War buff, Special Ops aficionado, belly dance enthusiast and former nationally-carded softball pitcher. She lives in Vancouver, BC with her husband and family.

You can visit Kaylea at www.kayleacross.com. If you would like to be notified of future releases, please join her newsletter: http://kayleacross.com/v2/newsletter/

Complete Booklist

ROMANTIC SUSPENSE

Crimson Point Series
Fractured Honor

DEA FAST Series
Falling Fast
Fast Kill
Stand Fast
Strike Fast
Fast Fury
Fast Justice
Fast Vengeance

Colebrook Siblings Trilogy
Brody's Vow
Wyatt's Stand
Easton's Claim

Hostage Rescue Team Series
Marked
Targeted
Hunted
Disavowed
Avenged
Exposed
Seized
Wanted
Betrayed
Reclaimed
Shattered
Guarded

Titanium Security Series

Ignited
Singed
Burned
Extinguished
Rekindled
Blindsided: A Titanium Christmas novella

Bagram Special Ops Series
Deadly Descent
Tactical Strike
Lethal Pursuit
Danger Close
Collateral Damage
Never Surrender (a MacKenzie Family novella)

Suspense Series
Out of Her League
Cover of Darkness
No Turning Back
Relentless
Absolution

PARANORMAL ROMANCE
Empowered Series
Darkest Caress

HISTORICAL ROMANCE
The Vacant Chair

EROTIC ROMANCE (writing as *Callie Croix*)
Deacon's Touch
Dillon's Claim
No Holds Barred
Touch Me
Let Me In
Covert Seduction

Made in the USA
Monee, IL
06 August 2024

63377887R00166